Color Me Crazy

LOUISE TURNER & WANDA JENNINGS

BOOK THREE OF THE
MAGNOLIA
MANOR SERIES

Printed in the United States of America
First Printed October 2020
Cover Art by Victoria L. Hawkins

Published by:

Southern Willow Publishing, LLC
1114 Highway 96,
Suite C-1, #340
Kathleen, Georgia 31047

ISBN: 978-1-7347354-4-4

This book is dedicated to family, the one you're born with, the one you choose, and the one that chooses you.

⁓Chapter One⁓

Opal Tyler brushed through Ruby Montgomery's shoulder length hair. "You've gotten grayer since last time, Rubes. You know I can take care of that," she whispered to her best friend.

"I know. I know I need to. I just haven't had the time to devote to my hair lately. Now that Mavis is in school, I thought I'd have more time, but there's always something that needs my attention more," Ruby sighed.

"I understand that. You know I still can't believe that sweet little thing is six years old now!" Opal said.

"Time flies. It's already mid September. This whole year has just flown by," Ruby said.

"You need a vacation," Maude interjected. "We all need one!"

Opal and Ruby's other best friend, Maude Ward, was under the dryer a few feet away and rolled a cigarette between her fingers.

"I don't have the time to go jet settin' off into the unknown with you two. I've had to put that behind me," Opal said. She rolled her eyes and continued to comb through Ruby's hair.

Maude rolled her eyes and lit her cigarette.

"Put that out Maude, you know you can't smoke in here!" Opal yelled. "One of these days that thing is going to kill you."

Maude muttered something under her breath, but she did as she was told. She crossed her arms in a huff and sighed loudly. "How much longer I gotta be under this thing?" she asked.

Opal looked at her watch and sighed, "Um, my watch quit on me last week. So I'd say about five to ten more minutes." Before Maude could object, Opal launched into a new conversation about her date last night.

"Oh, I didn't tell y'all! I went dancing last night! We had the sweetest time. Such a gentleman!" Opal smiled cheerfully.

"Eddie's always been a real nice guy," Maude agreed. "Never saw him as a dancer though."

"Eddie?" Opal asked. "No, no, I went out with Ricky last night."

"Ricky?" exclaimed Maude.

Ruby leaned forward and said, "I thought you were seeing Eddie? He sent you all those flowers over yonder." She pointed to the windowsill that was full of colorful vases of eccentric flowers.

"Wait a minute! Ricky?" Maude asked again. "Ricky from over there at the alteration place? Opal! You know that ain't right!"

Opal looked rigid and pulled Ruby back in the seat. "And just what are you trying to say, Maude?" she asked sharply.

"Well, just that he's, well, you know. It's Ricky!" Maude explained. She looked pointedly at Ruby for help. Ruby shook her head and tried to hide a smile.

"He was ever the gentleman," Opal said between her gritted teeth. "That's all I'm gonna say about that."

"Ow! Opal, I'd like to keep the hair that I have," Ruby yelped. She cut Maude a look and Maude rolled her eyes.

"Sorry Ruby!" Opal squealed. Her shoulders relaxed and she sprayed more hair spray onto Ruby's head. "I hate this spray. As soon as it's empty, I'm throwing it out and never buying this brand again."

"Fine, I'll leave that one alone for now," Maude wheezed. "Whatever happened to Eddie then?"

"Nothing I hope!" answered Opal. "We had dinner Wednesday night and those arrived the next morning." Opal gestured to the windowsill full of beautiful yellow flowers.

"Geez Opal! Your day planner must be crowded. Don't you think you're getting a little too old to be dating all these men at the same time?" Maude exclaimed.

"Well, there's seven days in each week, Maude," Opal explained.

"Seven?" Ruby asked. "Opal Tyler! I do declare! Seven different men?"

"Oh, don't be silly Ruby! I was only explaining how many days per week there was for Maude. She doesn't know about those things. But Lord, I don't have the time nor the energy for seven men," she laughed.

"I was about to say!" Ruby exclaimed. "Two is enough, Lordy!"

"Well, I have room for more than two. Ricky, Eddie, and Mortie are perfectly content with the time I share with them," Opal smiled.

"There's three of them?" Ruby gasped.

"Mortie? Who the hell is Mortie?" Maude asked. She had escaped the dryer and had pulled up a folding chair next to Ruby.

"You know Mortie, from over there at Raven's," Opal explained.

"You have got to be kidding me!" Maude yelled. The group of women in the waiting area turned their heads towards the ensuing drama. Suddenly their magazines weren't as interesting as they had been pretending.

"Raven's Funeral Parlor? Mortimer Raven?" Maude gasped again.

"The undertaker?" Ruby asked.

"Well, if you must use his government name, then yes," Opal replied. She rolled her eyes at the sheer audacity of her two friends.

"Opal! Oh dear Lord! You're seeing the flower man, the flamboyant dressmaker, and a mortician? You are crazier than I ever thought!" Maude had already doubled over in laughter. "Mortimer

Raven? Oh my God Opal, I knew you were crazy, but this is a whole new level, even for you!

"Eddie is a renowned florist, Ricky is the most in demand tailor in three surrounding counties, and Mortie happens to be the most sensitive man I've ever met! He's not only a mortician; he's the county coroner, too. He has a lot of responsibility!" Opal yelled back.

Maude was too busy laughing to pay her explanation any attention.

"Laugh away Maude! I know you aren't talking about my taste in men! What husband are you on now?" Opal hissed.

Maude ignored her and kept on laughing. She had already fallen out of her chair and was bent over on the floor. The women in the waiting area were on pins and needles watching the fiasco. Ruby ignored their whispers and tried to quiet her two friends down.

"Shh! Opal! Maude! Y'all are making a scene!" Ruby whispered.

Opal ignored Ruby and leaned over Maude. "It's my shop, ruby. People expect a scene when they're here. It's part of the atmosphere."

"What a cast of characters in your life, Opal," Maude howled.

"In between two and three, huh?" Opal chided. "How's Deputy Butler these days? He about to be number three or are you still entertaining your two ex husbands over lunch?"

Maude stopped laughing and looked up at Opal in a state of shock. Ruby looked between the two women like she was caught in a tennis match.

"Oh yes, Maude Winifred! Women talk! I heard that Larry Ward took you to lunch yesterday and then Teddy Butler brought you a tub of ice cream yesterday morning! They didn't mention Allan, but did you make time for him, too?" Opal sneered.

"Ooooh, Opal! I swear if you weren't my best friend I'd knock you into the middle of next week! Larry and I had a nice lunch to celebrate our divorce being final and I ain't talked to Allan in six months. But how in the heck did you know Teddy brought me ice cream? You spying on me?" Maude asked.

"I've got better things to do than spy on an old prune like you! Nadine over there told me she checked out behind him at the Pig this morning and he was cooing about how great you are! She also may have mentioned that she saw you and Larry over at Chubby's sharing a bucket of chicken the other day," Opal laughed.

Maude looked around the beauty parlor and saw the culprit across the room reading a magazine. Nadine Waters was the operator for the town. She was also the town's busybody. Maude shot Nadine a dirty look. Nadine hid behind her magazine and looked sheepish.

Ruby rolled her eyes at the two of them carrying on. She stood up and shook the hair out of her eyes. "Y'all two done?" she asked.

"Yes. If you're sure I can't touch up some of these spots near the front," Opal frowned.

"Not right now. I've got to go get Mavis from Jameson's mother and bring her back up here. Maybe I can scoot in next week and get you to do something crazy with it," Ruby laughed.

"How'd you know? I coulda sworn I ain't told y'all that was the name of it! Ruby! Maybe you're clairvoyant, too!" Opal exclaimed.

"Huh?" Ruby asked perplexed.

"Color Me Crazy! That's the name of my new all natural hair dye line. It just came to me last night! You sure I didn't phone you about it? Oh Lordy, I just know it's gonna be a hit around here!" Opal explained.

Ruby wasn't so sure. Most of Opal's clients were well to do women who liked to keep things traditional and went with hair styles that Opal referred to as boring, but she couldn't help but share in her friend's excitement.

"Of course it will!" Ruby agreed.

"When you say all natural, what do you mean?" Maude asked.

"All natural, Maude! Like from nature," Opal said slowly. She rolled her eyes and couldn't believe how long it took Maude to catch onto things.

"Opal, I swear. One of these days!" Maude retorted.

"What kind of things from nature?" Ruby asked. She was genuinely curious by now, because knowing Opal, it could literally be anything.

"Thanks for asking Ruby! I knew it would pique your interest. I'm thinking mushrooms, some of that clay down by your creek, onions, sage, black tea, ginger, coffee grounds, and some other stuff that I haven't fully played with yet. The woods are a treasure trove!" Opal said cheerfully.

"Well, that sure is interesting," Ruby smiled.

"It sure is! So, can I go down to your creek and dig around? Your woods out there are sure to have some of the best ingredients!" Opal asked.

"Of course! Why don't y'all both come over for lunch tomorrow and then you can go digging up the creek bed for whatever it is you need," Ruby offered. "I'll fry some chicken."

"Sounds good to me. I'll come over around eleven and bring you some field peas I put up last week," Maude said. "Opal, want me to pick you up on the way?"

"I'm afraid I can't wait that long. The best time to explore is in the early morning before the heat sets in," Opal said sagely. "All the good things will be picked over if I wait 'til after noon. You know the best time to be out foraging is right after dawn."

"Of course it is," Maude grumbled.

"It's gonna take me a few hours," Opal said. "I would invite you to come with me, but your negative energy might be more of a hindrance than a help."

Maude crossed her arms again and looked like she wanted to say something, but to Ruby's surprise, she held her tongue.

"Well, you come on over anytime and I'll cook lunch and it'll be ready when you're done," Ruby smiled. "I'm going to go get Mavis and bring her back up here real quick. Thanks for fitting her in!"

"Anytime! See you in a few minutes," Opal smiled.

Ruby left and Opal helped Maude up off the floor.

"I don't know why you had to throw yourself in the floor like a child," Opal admonished. "Now you got hair all over your pants and I ain't about to help you get it off."

She settled Maude in the chair and began to take the curlers out of her hair. She leaned over Maude and yelled towards the waiting room, "I'll be with you next Nadine!"

"And I'll be with you after that," Maude hollered.

Nadine cowered behind the magazine.

"Oh hush, Maude. You'll do no such thing. Now sit still!" Opal told her. "I don't need y'all making a scene in here."

"You're pulling my hair out!" Maude yelled.

"Well if you'd sit still I wouldn't have to yank so hard! I swear Maude, the older you get, the worse you get!" Opal yelled back.

"I thought making a scene was part of the atmosphere. Ow!" Maude yelled.

It took Opal twice the amount of time it usually did to get the curlers out of Maude's hair. By the time she was finished and Maude traded places with a nervous looking Nadine, Ruby had returned with Mavis.

"Hey my precious girl!" Opal crooned. She scooped up a giggling Mavis and swung her around the shop, knocking Maude's glasses off in the process. "Maude, get up off the floor again! I swear Ruby, we're gonna have to get her looked at. She ain't been right all day!"

Ruby swallowed a laugh once she caught one look at Maude's grumpy face. She turned back towards Mavis and said, "Ok, sugar, hop up in the chair like a big girl next to Mrs. Nadine here and let's get your hair trimmed."

Mavis climbed into the chair and sat up straight. Opal began to brush Mavis' long dark hair and marveled at how beautiful it looked.

"She sure is a cute one," Nadine said from a few feet away. "Reminds me of Melanie when she was that age."

As soon as she said that, the shop went quiet. Opal immediately stopped brushing Mavis' hair and Maude dropped the magazine she was holding. Ruby smiled gently and patted Mavis on the leg and said, "thank you."

Nadine quickly realized what she had said and looked sheepish once again. "I'm sorry, Ruby. I didn't mean to upset you," Nadine whimpered.

"It's fine," Ruby smiled. She smiled again and kissed Mavis on the top of her head. "I'm not upset. I'm just so thankful for this little darling."

Thankfully Opal changed subject quickly and did an Irish jig around the salon chair to entertain Mavis. She rambled through her latest accents she had been practicing down at the Rhinestone

Community Theatre which had them all laughing hysterically.

"Your Cajun needs some work," Maude interrupted.

"I don't know how to do that one right. Ricky's been teaching me," Opal shrugged.

Ruby silenced Maude with one look. Opal finished Mavis' trim and the little girl ran off to play with her toys that she had gotten from her great-grandmother earlier that morning.

Opal went to Nadine and made sure her hair had set perfectly. She sprayed her entire head with a large bottle. "Okay, Nadine, you're done for the day. Molly will ring you out," Opal said.

Nadine thanked Opal and walked quickly past Maude who waited until she was in the parking lot before she spoke her mind.

"I can't stand that woman. And before you start, I know Ruby, it ain't Christian. But dadgum, she is such a busybody!" Maude ranted. "We weren't even talking to her and she had to go and upset you."

"I'm not upset," Ruby replied. "Mavis does look so much like Melanie. There wasn't anything wrong with her saying it."

"Well, she still didn't have to but in. Y'all know she has it out for me," Maude said.

"She doesn't have it out for you," Opal laughed. "Y'all both need to stop whatever drama it is between you and just move on."

"You know she can't let anything go," Maude retorted.

Opal raised her eyebrows at Maude.

"Well, she's still a busy body. She needs to mind her own business while folks are ringing out their items. Shouldn't matter how many tubs of ice cream a man brings a woman for her birthday!" Maude retorted.

"How many did he bring you?" Opal questioned. "She only said ice cream, she didn't say how many!"

"Never you mind!" Maude said. "I had a nice birthday breakfast of ice cream before lunch with you two."

"No wonder you were in such a good mood," Opal laughed.

"Are we done here? I'm starving!" Maude retorted.

"You were done thirty minutes ago," Opal laughed.

"I meant are we all done? Can't we go eat lunch somewhere?" Maude clarified.

"I've got two more this afternoon before I can close down," Opal said.

"Can't Molly do them?" Maude asked.

"Heavens no! She doesn't know how to do Mrs. Walker's hair. How dare you?" Opal scoffed.

Maude scowled and turned towards Ruby.

"Mavis ate with Mrs. Montgomery. She was up early this morning, so I best get her home so she can take a nap. She's had a busy morning. Plus, Jameson is home today working on some birdhouses for my front flower bed," Ruby said.

"Why don't you see if Larry wants to celebrate some more and have another lunch," Opal laughed.

Maude threw the magazine at Opal as she gathered up her purse. "Well, I can't waste away here. I'm going to get something to eat and I'll see y'all tomorrow at Ruby's."

She waved goodbye to Mavis who watched her fly out of the parking lot on her motorcycle.

❧ Chapter Two ❧

That night when Ruby tucked Mavis into bed, she allowed herself to take an extra look at the framed picture of Melanie on Mavis' nightstand.

Nadine had not been wrong when she said Mavis favored her mother. Mavis was the spitting image of Melanie. Melanie had long dark hair and big blue eyes that the photograph captured perfectly. In this particular photograph, the drugs and alcohol had not yet robbed Melanie of her natural good looks. Her skin was smooth, her face was full, and her teeth were perfectly straight. She looked happy.

This senior picture really didn't do her justice. Ruby looked down at her daughter sitting in front of the cream colored backdrop. The traditional off the shoulders drape showed off her perfect tan. She had a smile that could melt the hardest hearts. No wonder she thought she could make it out in Hollywood. She certainly had the looks to be a famous actress.

No sooner had she walked across the stage to receive her diploma had she packed up her brand new Toyota Corolla and headed out west in pursuit of fame and fortune, against Ruby's better judgment of course. She thought that Melanie should stay closer to home and settle down. Jameson, on the other hand, understood that their daughter was a free spirit. She could never be happy in Rhinestone. She had told him as much many times before. He understood that the more they tried to keep her, the faster they would lose her forever. In the end, Melanie promised to stay in touch as she waved goodbye from her car.

The letters were plentiful at first. Melanie was excited to be living what she called her lifelong dream. She was waitressing at an all night diner close to the desert and told Ruby that their frozen pies were nothing to write home about. As time went on, the communication started to break down and Ruby began to worry more than she ever had before. When they hadn't heard from her in three months, Jameson offered to fly to Los Angeles and search for his daughter, but before he could make the arrangements with his office, a car that resembled Melanie's car turned down the gravel driveway in front of the signature magnolia tree late one night. The headlights were cracked and the back windshield was all but missing, but Ruby didn't waste any time. She threw herself into her daughter's arms and immediately pulled back. This stranger driving Melanie's car couldn't possibly be her daughter.

This figure had short hair and you could see the bones in her face. She was rail thin, except for the bump on her abdomen that signified she was heavy with child. From the look of things, she wouldn't be heavy much longer.

"Mel?" Jameson asked. He enveloped her in his arms and led her up the front porch steps to the kitchen.

Ruby hurried behind them and watched as Jameson laid their daughter on the sofa lounge.

"I don't feel so good," Melanie whimpered. She moaned loudly and clutched her stomach. "I think it's coming. I swear my water broke a little bit ago."

"How long have you known, honey? You never said anything about a baby!" Ruby cried.

Jameson rang for the ambulance. By the time they all arrived at the hospital, Doctor Barnes was waiting on them. A baby girl was born less than an hour later. Melanie fell asleep without a second glance at her newborn child.

Doctor Barnes motioned for Jameson and Ruby to join him out in the hallway not long after. "When did Melanie get home?" he asked.

"Right before we called you," Jameson took out his monogrammed cloth handkerchief and wiped his glasses.

"Melanie was real lucky to get back here when she did. That baby wasn't going to wait much longer," he said stoically.

Jameson nodded and Ruby started to bite her nails.

"You know Melanie is real sick," Tim Barnes continued. He continued to stare hard at Jameson who was sweating slightly.

"I can't believe she's been out there all alone with no one to help her through all this," Ruby clutched her chest.

Tim looked over at her. "Ruby, it isn't just the baby. Melanie is in bad shape. We're going to need to move her and the baby over to Junction where they can take better care of them."

Ruby looked horrorstruck at Jameson who continued to wipe his glasses. His white t-shirt was stuck to his chest and his hair was a mess. Ruby was still in her night clothes.

"Will she be alright?" Ruby asked Tim.

"The baby'll be fine with some extra attention and time. She looks to be a bit early and pretty underweight. Probably be a little thing all her life. But Melanie has a rough road ahead."

Jameson nodded.

"This is serious, Jameson."

"She's been out there starving to death this whole time. We'll take good care of her now. We'll get fed back up. She'll be fine once we get her home," Ruby told them.

"Food ain't all she needs, Ruby," Tim told her.

"What are you trying to say, Tim?" Jameson asked his friend.

"Melanie's got a problem, Jameson. If I'm not mistaken, she's been an addict for awhile now. She needs more help than we can get her here in Rhinestone. I think it's serious," he responded.

Ruby glared at him in disbelief. "What do you mean?"

Tim ignored Ruby and continued to press on with Jameson. "Jameson, you know I'd do anything for you and your family. It's late and we can get them moved over without anyone knowing just yet. I need you to sign some things before we can load them up."

Jameson turned towards Ruby. "I need to call Mother and let her know what's going on. She's going to be beside herself if she hears it from anyone but me. You need to call your parents, too," Jameson said softly.

"I don't know what to tell them!" Ruby replied. She was already dabbing her eyes on the hem of her night gown. "We're all going to need clothes and someone will have to feed Dixie and Bobo. I'll call Maude and see if she can feed the dogs in the morning and maybe meet one of us halfway to get some clothes."

Jameson followed Tim down the hallway to call his mother and get started on the necessary paperwork. Ruby looked around for the nearest payphone. There was one at the end of the corridor by the main entrance to the emergency room. Somehow she made her way down there and picked up the receiver. Then she realized she had no money in her gown. She dialed for the operator and informed her that she needed to call her best friend collect. Maude answered the phone a few minutes later.

"Ruby, what's wrong?" Maude demanded.

"Melanie came back home tonight. She wasn't well, so we've had to take her to the hospital. They're about to transfer her to Junction and I was wondering if you could feed the dogs in the morning because I'm not sure what time we'll be home," Ruby stammered.

"Feed the dogs?" Maude yelled. "Melanie came home and is in the hospital and you're worried about a dang dog?!"

"I can't think straight right now. I just need to make sure everything at the house is taken care of," Ruby sniffed. "And maybe if you get a chance, can you bring me some fresh clothes? I rushed out of the house in a hurry."

"I'll be right there," Maude said.

"There's no need to rush. Jameson has some things to take care of. It's going to be a long night," Ruby sniffed.

"What else is going on, Ruby? Is she okay?" Maude asked.

"I've got to go. Can you just do that for me?" Ruby replied curtly.

"I'll take care of everything," Maude said. The line was dead before Maude had finished her sentence.

"I know she ain't off gallivanting with another one of those tomcats!" Maude huffed. She pulled on her housecoat and walked the short distance over to Opal's. She banged on the door for ten minutes until Opal opened the door with a baseball bat.

"Jesus Opal!" Maude cried. "It's only me! Put that dadgum thing down and let me in. It's getting chilly out here."

"What are you doing at this hour? Maude! Where's Allan? Did he put you out? Do I need to take this bat over yonder to your house?" Opal yelled.

"No, no! Calm down Babe Ruth! Allan is fine. It's Ruby, she just called. Melanie is at the hospital. She's pretty sick, Ruby said. She got back into town and she wasn't feeling well. Ruby needs us to go feed the dogs and lock up their house and pack them some clothes, so come on," Maude instructed.

"Ok," said Opal. She was suddenly alert. "Let me put on some clothes. Come on in."

Maude suddenly realized that Opal was as naked as a jaybird. She quickly averted her eyes and tried not to trip over the aging black cat in the doorway that hissed and scratched at Maude's fuzzy slippers.

"Geez Opal! Get that cat away from me and put on some clothes. You can't be answering the door looking like that!" Maude squealed.

"You startled me!" Opal replied. "And leave Leo alone. He's old and cranky and he never has liked you. I think deep down he knows you never wanted him to come back from Italy with us."

"I'm kinda surprised he's still alive," Maude said under her breath.

"What was that?" Opal called from her bedroom.

"I asked what you're feeding him?" Maude replied. "He looks so, um, timeless."

"Eggplant parmagiana. He's Italian, Maude," Opal answered.

When they arrived at Magnolia Manor, they hurried up the porch steps. They quickly packed the essentials for Ruby and Jameson, but weren't sure what to pack for Melanie.

"I bet she has her clothes in her car," Maude said.

They didn't find any clothes, but they did find burn marks on the seats, trash an inch deep, and beer bottles scattered about. If Maude didn't know any better, she would have sworn there were some needles on the floorboard. That couldn't be. What in the world would Melanie be doing with needles?

"Melanie's always been about my size. My house is on the way out of town. Stop there and I'll grab some things for her to wear," Opal said.

By the time they made it to the hospital in Junction, the sun was coming up. Opal found Ruby in the upstairs waiting room. Maude was stuck in the elevator with the bags.

"What are you doing here?" Ruby gasped.

"We came to see you, of course! I packed your clothes. Maude's taking her time, as usual, so bear with her. She hasn't had anything to eat yet and you know how she gets. Where are Jameson and Melanie? I can't wait to hug her neck!" Opal cheered.

Maude came around the corner and dropped the bags down beside Ruby. "Where's Melly?" she asked.

Jameson walked into the room. He nodded at the two newcomers, but then focused his attention on Ruby. "Sweetheart, they're going to need a name," he told her.

Opal rolled her eyes dramatically. "Good Lord, Jameson! You ought to know your daughter's name! You were there when we named her." She pushed past him and stormed down the hallway, determined to fix whatever fiasco Jameson had made worse.

"Opal wait!" Ruby called after her.

Opal could hear Maude shuffling behind her muttering under her breath. She felt Jameson rush past her and could hear Ruby calling her name. She met Jameson near a doorway with a glass window.

"Where's Melanie?" Opal demanded.

"She's resting in there," Jameson cautioned.

Maude peered in through the glass window and said, "I don't know who that is, but that ain't Melly. What in tarnation is going on here?"

Ruby finally caught up with them and sighed deeply. She looked at Jameson who took it upon himself to explain the situation to their dearest friends.

"Melanie's pretty sick. We're still processing everything. She got home after supper last night and we ended up at the hospital in Rhinestone. They ended up transferring them here to Junction and," he stopped.

"What do you mean they?" Maude asked suspiciously. "The man who did that to Melly's in there, too?"

"Ooh! Let me at him! I forgot my bat!" Opal lamented.

"Mr. Montgomery, we need a name before we can proceed with the birth certificate," the orderly squeaked.

This time Ruby spoke up. "She wants to go with Mavis Elaine. Last name will be Montgomery."

"Will somebody please explain to Maude what is going on?" Opal interrupted.

"Melanie had a baby last night. A little baby girl," Ruby explained. "She got home just in time to make us grandparents."

Maude looked flabbergasted from Ruby to Jameson. Opal looked at her shoes.

"Why didn't you tell us she was pregnant?" Opal asked after a few moments of silence.

"We didn't know," Jameson answered. He cleared his throat and continued, "Melanie isn't able to take care of Mavis right now, so she's going to come home with us and get her strength back. I think right now the best course of action is to let Mel get some rest and we can continue this conversation back at the Manor in a few days."

Maude and Opal took their cue and hugged Ruby tightly before leaving. Ruby tearfully thanked them for driving all the way to Junction and for keeping an eye on the Manor. Opal and Maude drove home mostly in silence.

The next few days flew by in a blur. Ruby fed Melanie at every opportunity once she was released from the hospital. For the most part, Melanie refused the constant attention. She was angry and hostile toward both of her parents and all but negligent with her new baby. No matter what they tried to do, she was determined to get back to her life in Los Angeles. Melanie was no longer the sweet girl they knew. She was like a feral animal left too long to the untamed world. After a week, the yelling became unbearable. Melanie could not stand the sound of Mavis crying. Ruby was certain that that meant that her maternal instincts must be kicking in because no mother wants to hear their baby cry, but Jameson understood it to be yet another symptom of withdrawals. Any sound above a whisper would send Melanie over the edge.

Ruby was ready to burst into tears at every turn. And yet, after another few days, her efforts began to show results. Melanie was a long way from regaining the weight she had lost, but at least she was beginning to regain her color. She no longer looked like a concentration camp victim. Tim had told them this was all to be expected. He said that withdrawals could be unfathomably violent and difficult. Ruby was sure that they had turned a corner for the better. Jameson, on the other hand, remained cautious. When he found his McCallan Single Malt Whiskey half gone, he knew his worst fears were true. Melanie was a long way from a cure.

"I took the rest of that bottle of whiskey to the office. You aren't getting any more of that mess in this house," Jameson announced that evening.

"Melanie's gone again," Ruby whispered into the phone the next morning.

"Where's Mavis?" Maude demanded.

"Right here with me. Melanie left her behind, too," Ruby said.

That was how Mavis came to live with her grandparents.

Ruby thought back to the last time she had seen her daughter alive. It was almost four years ago this November. Melanie had come home to the Manor for Thanksgiving. She had not seen her daughter Mavis since she was a small baby. Ruby often wrote her letters and sent pictures. She called as often as Melanie would take her phone calls, which wasn't often enough. Mavis was too young to understand who this strange woman was. She hid behind Jameson's rocking chair when Melanie tried to pick her up.

"She doesn't know her own mother!" Melanie howled. "And here I was thinking I could maybe take her back home."

"She's already home, Mel," Jameson explained. "Maybe if you could stay here awhile and get to know her. Or better yet, why don't you just come back home? Let us help you, baby."

Melanie said she did not need any help and shrugged off her father's concern. Melanie looked like a wild woman who had been living on the street for some time. She very well could have been for all Ruby and Jameson knew. They sent her money every month and tried to get her any help that she would accept, but she always refused anything besides the money.

During the holiday meal, Mavis didn't want to eat any sweet potatoes. Ruby smiled and said that Mavis always turned her nose up to those little orange devils ever since she was a baby. Melanie tried to spoon feed Mavis some across the table, but the little girl refused.

"Mommy says eat it!" Melanie yelled. Her hands shook and the sweet potatoes fell onto the formal dining table cloth and in Mavis' lap.

"It's ok baby, let's get you cleaned up," Jameson soothed Mavis. He scooped her up and took her to the sink to wipe her dress clean.

Once they returned to the table, Melanie was back in her seat. She brushed away tears before they fell from her eyes and they all finished the meal in silence. After everything was cleaned up and the guests filed out of the front door, Melanie hung back in the kitchen to talk to her mother alone.

"It's time you showed some discipline to Mavis. If she's gonna make it in LA, she's gonna have to toughen up. I think we'll have to come back for stuff another time, but I can fit her in the front with me when I leave in the morning," she explained.

"Honey, we've been through this. You can't just take her right now. Please stay with us here. This is your home, too. Let us help you. Get to know your daughter. It doesn't have to be this way," Ruby pleaded.

When Melanie yelled, her loud voice scared Mavis and she crawled up into Jameson's arms in the next room over.

Jameson walked into the room to see Ruby crying and Melanie looking angry.

"Mel, you aren't going to talk to your mama like that. Not in this house. Not after all that she's done for you," he scolded.

Melanie stomped out of the kitchen and came down the stairs in a flash with her battered suitcase. She announced that she was not able to stay after all and needed to get back to her apartment and her boyfriend in Los Angeles. Without a second look behind her, she was out the front door and revved the engine. She flew down the driveway and out of their lives for the last time.

They received a call from said boyfriend a few weeks later that Melanie had overdosed alone in their apartment. Jameson flew out there two days later to bring her home. She was buried in the family plot in Deerlane Cemetery.

~Chapter Three~

The sun had been up for four hours by the time Opal had filled three five-gallon buckets with wild herbs and wildflowers. She had two buckets left to fill before she would consider the outing a true success.

She stopped for a minute to oversee her progress. She was already sweating in the mid morning heat. It was surprisingly warm for a September morning, but the birds were chirping and Opal saw a few turtles in the creek slide down the bank. She loved being in the woods and watching nature. The woods were her element. She had always been a free spirit and a wild woman at heart, just like her great- aunt Wilhelmina. Aunt Willie was considered the town voodoo woman or witch doctor by some, but Opal knew she was just one with nature. Aunt Willie is where she learned all about medicinal herbs and natural supplements. Aunt Willie was pleased as could be about Opal's latest idea for natural hair dye. She shared Opal's excitement and said she would be on the lookout for ingredients on her travels. At age ninety-five, Aunt Willie still had an insatiable zest for life. Maude said it was her love of herbs that kept her so well preserved, but Opal knew it ran in their blood.

As Opal started to dig near the creek bed, she heard a twig snap in front of her. She shrugged and kept digging. The Montgomery's woods were full of creatures. She had never been run out of them before by a wild animal, so she was not too worried about it.

Soon she heard more rustling in the bush nearest the creek and she stood up to get a better view. Through the bushes in the morning light, she thought she saw a small pair of eyes staring back at her.

"Who's there?" she asked confidently. It wouldn't be the first time she encountered a critter in the wild. There was no response. Opal wiped her hands off on her shawl and walked towards the bush. It started to rattle and she was certain that there was a large creature hiding in it.

"I ain't gonna hurt you," Opal crooned. She reached in front of her to push back some branches and saw the dirty face of a child looking up at her.

"Oh! What are you doing in there?" Opal asked. "Come on out of there."

She helped the boy off of the ground and looked him up and down.

"What's your name?" she asked kindly.

"Wilbur," the small voice replied.

The wide-eyed boy was wearing dirty overalls and his big toe poked out of one of his shoes. His hair was matted and he looked like he was in dire need of a bath.

"Hello Wilbur! I'm Opal," she smiled. "What are you doing out here so early?"

"I'm sorry," he stuttered. "I didn't mean to cause any trouble. I better be getting back home."

"Wait a minute, son. What's your hurry?" Opal asked. She smiled warmly at the boy and then looked around to see if anyone else was around. "Anyone else hiding around here?"

"No ma'am, it's just me," he answered.

"You come out here often?" she asked.

He nodded and hid his face. "I just come out here to watch the birds and deer. I didn't mean to cause any trouble," he said meekly.

"These are great woods for animal watching," Opal agreed. "Good for hiding out, too."

Wilbur nodded again and wiped his nose. "It is good for hiding," he agreed.

Opal watched him for a few moments. She knew she had seen him around before, but she could not quite place him.

"Your mama know you're out here?" she asked.

Wilbur shook his head and looked down at his feet.

"Think she might be worried when she notices you're gone?" Opal asked.

"My mama died when I was little. My daddy doesn't know I'm out here though, so I better get on," he muttered.

"What's your daddy's name?" Opal asked. Her interest was piqued by this strange boy.

"Pete," he whispered. "Pete Reynolds."

Opal caught her breath quickly. Pete Reynolds was nothing but a layabout drunk that was in and out of jail. He lived in a rundown shack near the river with his son who had to be about twelve years old by now. His wife Catherine had passed away a decade ago from a short battle with cancer.

Opal remembered that Catherine has always been a sweet girl when she would come to The Comb Over for Ms. Belva Sinclair, the original owner of the beauty parlor, to do her hair. The town was shocked when she married Peter Reynolds, a lazy and arrogant man a few years her senior. Pete was always in and out of a job and spent more time drunk and passed out than he did sober and awake.

Catherine worked hard to support their growing family. She was frequently seen at the office of The Rhinestone Reaper late at night with the baby in tow. When she was diagnosed with end stage breast cancer, she continued to work late and tried her hardest to be a good mother. Even after her hair fell out, she would stop by the beauty parlor to see Ms. Belva and show her how fast her son was growing. After she died, Pete and the toddler son disappeared from Rhinestone for a few years. When they returned, everyone left them pretty much alone per Pete's constant requests and brawls.

Never did she imagine seeing Pete Reynold's son in the bushes, but here he was standing clear as day in front of her. She could see the dirt and grime beneath his nails and the bones in his hollow cheeks.

"Well Wilbur, if you don't mind, I've got these buckets I need to get back up to the house. Think you can help me?" she asked.

Wilbur nodded and grabbed two buckets full of herbs and flowers. Opal grabbed the third bucket that was full of herbs and wild mushrooms and placed the bucket half full of clay into the empty bucket to make them easier to carry. Wilbur followed Opal through the woods back towards the looming Manor.

"Is this where you live?" he asked.

Before Opal could respond, Maude strode down the porch steps.

"About time you got here! I'm starving!" she moaned. "Wait a minute, who's this?"

"Welcome to Magnolia Manor, Wilbur. This is Maude. Maude, this here is Wilbur. He's going to be joining us for lunch today," Opal smiled.

Maude took the buckets from Wilbur and carried them up the porch. She set them behind the porch swing and turned to see Opal behind her.

"Should I even ask?" she whispered.

Opal motioned for Wilbur to follow them up the steps to the front door. Maude held the door for them and entered the kitchen behind them.

"Hey Ruby! I hope you don't mind, but I invited my new friend for lunch with us," Opal called out.

Ruby turned around from the stove in a state of surprise. She expected to see a grown man, one of Opal's latest boyfriends, standing in between Maude and Opal, but she was surprised to see a young ragtag looking boy instead.

"Of course," Ruby smiled. "Y'all go wash up and we'll eat in a few minutes."

Maude directed Wilbur to the small bathroom near the kitchen and rounded on Opal. "Who, what, when, where, how? Did you kidnap a child Opal?"

"Of course not! I just found him," Opal explained. "He was hiding in the woods. You know who he is. It took me a minute, but when he said his name, I knew him. It's Pete Reynolds' boy."

Maude gasped and moved closer to Opal. "Pete Reynolds? Does he know he's here?"

"I don't think so. He didn't seem to want to talk about it. Look, he's filthy and looks like he ain't had a good meal in ages. It's the least we can do for helping me carry those buckets back here," Opal said.

Ruby nodded and set out an extra plate and glass at the table. "Opal's right. We can't turn away a hungry baby. Run go check on him and I'll get Jameson and Mavis."

Maude and Opal went to check on Wilbur while Ruby went upstairs to update Jameson on their guest.

When they all met downstairs at the table a few minutes later, Ruby directed Wilbur to the empty seat next to Opal who helped him pile his plate high with fried chicken, peas, mustard greens, mashed potatoes, gravy, and homemade biscuits. He drained his glass of ice cold sweet tea and Ruby quickly poured him more from the glass pitcher on the corner of the table.

"Make sure you save room for Ruby's famous pecan pie over there," Opal said. She pointed to the pie that had just come out of the oven.

Wilbur ate ravenously. The adults made small talk, but their main focus was on the underfed child who stayed quiet and continued to eat. When Jameson cut the warm pie, he asked if anyone wanted vanilla ice cream on their pie. Everyone readily agreed and Jameson made sure Wilbur's scoop of ice cream was the biggest. He made eye contact with Ruby and winked.

After the meal was over, the women began to clean the kitchen. Jameson took Mavis outside to play and asked Wilbur if he would like to come, too. Wilbur followed Jameson and Mavis outside to the porch where Mavis ran off after the cat who had been curled up on the porch swing asleep. Mavis' legs couldn't quite carry her fast enough to catch up to the hissing orange cat. Wilbur watched the cat reach the open door of the barn and disappear. Jameson swore he caught a glimpse of a small smile on the boy's face. Mavis wandered over to the magnolia tree in the middle of the yard and began to play on its lower branches.

Jameson pulled out a small knife from his pocket and picked up a thick chunk of smoothed wood from under his rocking chair. Wilbur watched him quietly.

"You like to wood carve?" Jameson asked him.

Wilbur shook his head and answered, "No sir."

"It's one of my hobbies," Jameson continued. "Do you have anything you like to do for fun?"

Wilbur shook his head.

"Why not?" Jameson smiled.

Wilbur didn't answer other than a shrug from his thin shoulders.

"Woodworking relaxes me. I love to come out here in the afternoons when I can find the time and create something beautiful. It doesn't look like it now, but this block of wood is going to be another birdhouse for Mrs. Ruby in there. See that one hanging in the garden over there? Finished that one last week," Jameson smiled.

Wilbur stood up to look over the porch rail and saw a simple, yet beautiful birdhouse near the tall sunflowers. "You know, if you ever want to come down here in the evenings or weekends, come on over. I can show you how to make one of those if you'd like," Jameson offered.

Wilbur considered the offer before turning back around. "I don't know if I can," he replied. He put his hands back in his pockets and sat back down in the swing.

"I understand," Jameson nodded. "It's hard to find the time sometimes, but it's important to have a hobby. Find something that you love that relaxes you. After all day in the office or courtroom, nothing beats sitting out here in the cool air."

Something he said must have caught Wilbur's attention because he suddenly looked up at Jameson.

"Are you a policeman?" Wilbur asked nervously.

Jameson shook his head and explained that he was a lawyer, not a police officer.

"I best be getting home, sir," Wilbur said quietly.

"I'll drive you over myself," Jameson offered.

"No sir, I better walk," Wilbur responded.

Jameson set the knife and block of wood on the porch. He took off his glasses and cleaned them on his handkerchief. Wilbur shoved his hands in the pockets of his overalls and started to walk down the steps back towards the creek in the woods.

"It's a long walk. I don't mind taking you," Jameson called out after him.

Wilbur shook his head and trudged on. Jameson watched him until he was lost in the trees.

Later that night, Ruby sat on the edge of the bed and asked Jameson what he thought about Wilbur. "He's such a sweet boy," she said. "But there's something strange about him."

Jameson nodded and pulled off his house shoes. "I don't imagine Pete's taking real good care of him," he sighed. "He's pretty small for a boy his age. He's what, twelve years old?"

"That's what Opal reckons. She knew Catherine better than I did because of Ms. Belva. I remember Pete though. He was a few years behind me in school and he was always into some kind of trouble. Opal says Catherine kept to herself after she married Pete and I don't think I ever saw her son until now. He looks so much like Pete. Well, like Pete did when I knew him. I haven't seen him in ages," Ruby said.

"I saw him about a month ago when they brought him in," Jameson sighed. "He looks worse every time I see him. I've never seen a man so angry. I would have understood how a man can descend to that level after he loses his wife like he did, but I've heard Pete was this way before Catherine. Mitch has tried to get him help, but you've heard how he is. You and I probably know better than most how that goes. You can bring a horse to water, but you can't make them drink."

Ruby knew he was also thinking of Melanie. They would have continued doing everything possible to save their daughter, but Melanie never made it to the point of accepting that she had a problem. She never wanted help and she rebuffed any semblance of help or love for years. Her spiral downhill was quick. Mavis was too young to remember her, but they tried to talk about her in a good light for her daughter to one day hopefully want to learn more about the wonderful girl Melanie was before she became an addict.

"What happens to Wilbur while Pete's in jail?" Ruby asked.

"I don't know really. Pete says his mother looks in on him. Pete doesn't ever stay in jail for long. The school says Wilbur doesn't miss many days, so there's never been a wellness check called in on him, according to Teddy. I know Pete's not a standup guy, but I don't think Wilbur's in any danger with him. He's just a drunk who likes to fight with the bartenders when they take his keys," Jameson acknowledged.

"That boy needs some good southern home cooking," Ruby said.

"He needs more than a good meal," Jameson replied.

Ruby agreed and asked what they could do about that.

Jameson shook his head and shrugged. "I don't really know what we can do, if anything. I don't know if he's outright hurting the boy. He's clearly underfed and pretty neglected, I'd say. But if he ain't tossing him around and putting his hands on him, I don't reckon there's much to be done."

"Who's to say he ain't?" Ruby asked.

"I guess at the end of the day, we don't know," he lamented. "I'll be sure to keep an eye on him, but I doubt we ever see him again."

Ruby hoped he was wrong.

✑Chapter Four✑

The following Sunday morning, Opal found herself back in the woods looking for more ingredients for her up and coming natural hair dye line. She had been busy all week brewing different mixes and concoctions.

There wasn't much of a breeze unfortunately, so she was already starting to sweat. Her arms were already aching from carrying two large buckets full of clay back to the Manor an hour ago. Once she finished collecting clay in these last two buckets, she was going to take a nap on Ruby's couch and rest her tired body.

She was covered head to toe in red clay. Anyone who knew anything knew that in order to get the best river clay, you had to dig deep. Opal was never one to shy away from a mess either, so she was once again in her element. As she stood up and stretched, Wilbur appeared silently from behind a tree about twenty yards away.

"Hey!" Opal called over to him. She waved and motioned for him to come over.

Wilbur walked slowly towards her with his hands shoved in his pockets.

"Good morning Wilbur! How long you been here?" Opal asked. She was almost out of breath from her work.

"I just walked over," he said quietly. He gestured towards the buckets and asked, "Do you need any help with those?"

"Won't say no!" she smiled. "You ever dig for clay?"

Wilbur shook his head and kneeled down on the creek's edge. "What are you looking for?" he asked.

"Different minerals and clay bits," she shrugged. She told him all about her new hair dye line and how it would be sure to revolutionize the fields of both women's and men's hair care products.

Wilbur listened to her talk all about her job, clients, and her passion for nature. It wasn't until she mentioned her menagerie of cats at home did Wilbur begin to speak.

"I had a cat once," Wilbur said quietly.

He was not much of a talker, so any time he added to the conversation, Opal made sure to encourage it.

"That's nice! What was his name?" she asked.

"I don't reckon he had a name. I found him on the way home from school one day. He was just a tiny baby, but my daddy said I couldn't keep him. But I kept him in my room in a box under my bed for a few days. When I came home from school one day, he was gone," he replied.

"Maybe he got out for an adventure," Opal smiled.

Wilbur shook his head. "My daddy said he took care of him," he whispered. "He said we didn't need any more mouths to feed and that I better listen the next time he said something." He didn't mention the beating he got that evening for his deception.

Opal tried to make sure that her face did not reveal what was running through her mind.

"Well, I know I'd sure love for you to come by one day and see my cats. I have nine of them right now. You would love Leo! He's my favorite. He's an immigrant all the way from Italy. He only speaks Italian, although Maude is constantly fussing at him in English. She gets so upset because all he does is hiss at her, but he doesn't understand anything she says to him," Opal smiled. "She was there when I got him, so you think she'd remember."

"Italy?" Wilbur asked.

"Oh yes. Maude, Ruby, and I went to Italy back when we were youngins," Opal explained. "I saw Leo in one of the bushes at the airport and snatched him up. He was alone and looked so sad. He's been the best little baby there ever was."

Wilbur smiled softly. He scooped more clay into the bucket nearest him and Opal pronounced it perfect. Together they carried the full buckets back towards the Manor.

"Right here will do," Opal said. She set her bucket on the lowest step and Wilbur set his bucket next to it.

Ruby walked out of the door and smiled down at them. "I thought I heard voices. Hi again Wilbur. Jameson is cutting up some watermelon in the kitchen. Y'all want some?" she asked.

"I won't say no!" Opal laughed. She motioned for Wilbur to follow her up the porch stairs to the front door. He slowly followed with his hands in the pockets of what looked to be the same overalls from last weekend.

They sat down in the rocking chairs on the porch so they wouldn't track mud and water all over Ruby's clean floors.

"Morning Opal. Well, hello Wilbur! Good to see you again," Jameson called through the screen door. He had a kitchen towel over his shoulder and was almost done cutting up the large watermelon on the counter in front of him.

"Here you go honey," Ruby said. She handed Wilbur a glass of iced tea and sat in the empty porch swing near him.

"Big Mama?" a small voice called from inside the kitchen. "Where are you?"

"Right here, sugar!" Ruby called.

Mavis ran outside and jumped into Ruby's arms.

"Mavis, you remember Wilbur from the other day?" Ruby asked.

"Yes ma'am," she said shyly.

Wilbur smiled softly and gave a small wave before Mavis bounded down the stairs towards the barn.

"She keeps you busy, don't she?" Opal laughed.

"She goes a mile a minute," Jameson agreed. He had come through the door with the platter of cut up watermelon pieces.

After they worked their way through the watermelon, Jameson stood up and returned the empty platter to the kitchen. He came back outside a few minutes later and said he needed to finish cutting down the tree that had split near the driveway.

"I sure am glad you stopped by today. Why don't you come with me Wilbur?" he asked.

Wilbur looked at Opal who nodded and motioned him on.

"Yes sir," Wilbur whispered. He followed Jameson to the barn where they passed Mavis swinging on an old tire swing.

"I've been meaning to chop this old tree up, but it's a pretty big job for just one person. I sure could use the help. Mind lending me a hand?" Jameson smiled down at the ragamuffin lad before him. "Good way to earn some pocket money."

Wilbur stood up a little bit straighter. "Yes, sir," he nodded.

The two set out to work. Jameson soon learned that Wilbur was well versed in swinging an axe. He split the logs as though he'd been doing it for years, which Jameson feared he probably had. While Jameson cut the trunk of the felled tree into sections with the chainsaw, Wilbur took the wedge and tapped it into place with the sledgehammer. Then, with a few well aimed swings, he drove the wedge through. Silently, he picked up the wedge and began again.

"This is almost like work," Jameson said, taking his handkerchief out of his pocket and wiping his forehead. The afternoon sun had already begun to burn through his thin shirt.

Wilbur nodded. The boy was not one to waste words in idle chit chat. Jameson looked around. The tree was now piled up neatly, waiting on the cool nights of winter.

"You thirsty? I sure could use another big glass of sweet tea," Jameson nodded toward the house.

About that time, Opal appeared and said, "Time to eat, y'all. Maude's already at the table, but hopefully she's left us some. Lord knows how that woman likes to eat. Come on Mavis, time to wash up!"

"You don't have to tell me twice," Jameson laughed. He wiped the sweat off his brow with his handkerchief. "Come on and have some dinner."

"I should probably be getting home." Wilbur stared down at his feet.

"Aren't you hungry?" Jameson asked him. "I know I am."

Wilbur wanted to say something, but was clearly struggling to get the words out. He didn't know how to tell them how mad his dad would be if he ever found out Wilbur was taking charity from the rich family in the big house. Wilbur still remembered how angry his dad had gotten when the church ladies brought the basket of food around the house a few weeks back. His daddy had cussed up a storm. "No Reynolds ever needed any help from a bunch of busy body do-gooders! Who did they think they were anyway? Coming around his house like we was a pauper!"

Pete Reynolds practically threw the basket back in their faces. Wilbur wished he hadn't. He, for one, would have liked to have had a home cooked meal, but his dad wouldn't hear of anyone helping his family no matter how badly it was needed.

"What's wrong, son? Why don't you have dinner with us? It's the least we can do since you helped out so much today. Here's some money, but even still, you did a man's job today. You need a good meal to keep up your strength," Jameson said, putting his hand on the boy's shoulder.

Wilbur looked up at Jameson and smiled. He nodded and hurriedly followed behind Jameson and washed up quickly. Truth be told, he was starving, and strictly speaking, this wasn't a charity meal if he earned it.

"Wilbur was a big help today," Jameson smiled as he took a seat. He patted Wilbur on the back and said, "You know I was thinking, there's quite a bit of stuff that needs fixing up around here. I could definitely use some help, if you'd like to come over on Saturdays and even Sunday afternoons and help me. I sure would like to clear up some of that mess over by the barn and I need someone I can count on. How about it, Wilbur?"

Wilbur almost choked on the chicken leg he was gnawing on. When he finally swallowed, he looked at Jameson. "Every weekend?" There was eagerness in his voice that hadn't been there before.

"Every Saturday or Sunday that you can come over. Of course, I understand if you have other things that you need to do once in awhile, but the job is yours if you want it," Jameson sipped his tea.

"Yes, sir. I'd like that." For the first time since they'd met the boy, he smiled.

"We got to church over at Beaver Crossing most Sunday mornings if you'd like to come. Then Ruby cooks us a fine meal and we get some work done," Jameson said.

"I have some things around the yard I need to get looked at. Think you'd like to come over one weekend and help me out some, too?" Opal asked.

"Me too!" Maude agreed.

"Yea, she ain't as young as she used to be," Opal explained.

"Neither are you!" Maude snapped at her.

"Some of us were born younger," Opal sneered. She patted her hair gracefully.

"I swear to God Opal, one of these days I'm gonna send you back to wherever you came from!" Maude growled under her breath.

"No returns," Opal shrugged. She winked at Wilbur who couldn't help but smile. Opal was a strange woman, but there was something about her that made him chuckle and relax.

While Wilbur was listening to Maude and Opal carry on, Jameson looked over at Ruby. He gave her a quick wink, and then turned his attention to the antics of her two best friends.

"Besides, what in the world kind jobs are you trying to get Wilbur to do? He doesn't need to be dyed fourteen different colors while you're trying to perfect your hair dye concoction. You ain't turning that boy into a giant Easter egg!" Maude fumed.

"Never you mind that! I had the best idea this morning down by the creek. Picture it: a cat playground. I'm telling you, won't be a cat in a hundred miles that won't want to come play at my feline paradise!" Opal squealed.

"There ain't no way Opal!" Maude declared. "Don't you build some crazy mess as that! You got forty cats over there now!"

"It's my house and I'll do as I please," Opal grinned.

"Your land butts up against mine. I know exactly what will happen. Every critter in Rhinestone will be at your door and they'll end up in my yard, I just know it," Maude huffed.

"And what's wrong with that? Animals are calming," Opal explained.

"That's what you think! You're gonna wake up one day and one of those cats will have done ate your nose off," Maude said.

"You just aren't one with nature like I am," Opal replied. "I'm not surprised a bit. Animals have a sense about them. They know things."

"They know you're crazy and you ain't got no better sense than to go and build a dang cat amusement park!" Maude countered.

"Stop it, you two! Cut that out. You're scaring Wilbur and Mavis," Ruby scolded.

Mavis was clapping her chubby little hands at the two of them while Wilbur sat back in his chair and held his stomach from laughing so hard. Ruby had to admit to herself that it was a pleasant surprise to see him enjoying himself.

"The truth is a scary thing sometimes, Ruby," Opal said sagely. Maude glared at her.

"You got any of that cake left, Ruby?" Jameson said with a big grin.

"We have just enough to go around," Ruby said. She stood up and walked over to the kitchen counter. Maude helped gather up the plates and joined Ruby at the counter. Standing beside her best friend, she gave Ruby a silent smile before returning to the others.

Two hours later, Wilbur made his way back through the woods toward his house. His belly hurt, but he wasn't sure if that was from the feast he'd eaten or from laughing so hard. He honestly didn't know which part of dinner he enjoyed more. Jameson had offered to drive him home, but he had again refused. Wilbur loved spending time alone in the woods. It was safe here. It was peaceful. Usually it was his safe haven to escape, but today it was a sanctuary to reflect on all that had happened. He was still laughing at Maude and Opal when he stepped out into the yard of his house. Part of him had thought and even hoped that his dad would be down at the bar already when he got home. The smile evaporated from Wilbur's face when he saw his father's beat up pickup truck in front of the small cabin. He quietly tipped toed up the rickety porch steps and looked around. He slipped out of his muddy boots and left them behind the rusted pot that collected rain water from the leak in the roof.

"Where you been, boy?" Pete demanded as Wilbur opened up the screen door.

"Down by the creek mostly," Wilbur muttered. It wasn't a lie exactly. He had started off by the creek after all.

Pete looked at the mud and clay on Wilbur's pants. "What're you doin' down there, boy? Huh? You all covered in dirt and God knows what else. What was you digging for? Lookin' for gold or somethin'?" Pete laughed.

Wilbur shrugged. "I was just digging." He knew better than to try and explain where he had been or what he had been doing.

Pete gave another menacing laugh. "You let me know when you find that gold, boy. We sure could use a little gold around here, huh?" Pete tousled his hair roughly. He swung the screen door wildly and headed to his truck. His hands were feeling lucky tonight and he was itching to get in the game. Without a backward glance at his only son, he drove down the dusty drive headed toward town leaving Wilbur once again. Pete had been disappearing for days at a time lately. That didn't bother Wilbur. In fact, he preferred the quiet times when his father was absent.

Wilbur waited until his dad was out of sight before he closed the front door and headed toward his bedroom. He opened up the top drawer of his chest of drawers and pulled out his favorite T-shirt. It was well worn as all his clothes were, but it was larger than the rest and wasn't tight around the middle. He found a clean pair of underwear and dropped both of them on his bed. Once he had changed out of his dirty clothes and into clean ones, he carried the bundle of laundry down the hallway to the old washing machine beside the kitchen. He dumped the clothes into the machine and added what was left of the powdered soap. With the dryer still broken, he had to go ahead and get his clothes washed if he wanted them to be half way dry by tomorrow morning.

~Chapter Five~

Wilbur was faithful in his weekend duties with Jameson at Magnolia Manor. The boy arrived around eight o'clock every Saturday and worked without question until after Ruby had fed them all dinner. This was the fourth weekend in a row that he had stayed all day to help with odd jobs around the property. Wilbur looked forward to it all weekend long. If his dad was still too hungover from his outings on Friday and Saturday night, Wilbur could escape Sunday mornings as well. If he could manage it, he would be waiting for the family on the Manor's porch when they arrived home from Sunday morning church.

Truth be told, Jameson was enjoying having a young man to teach woodworking and carpentry to. He had tried to teach Melanie years ago when she was younger, but she took no interest in which side of a hammer to use. Neither had Mavis, although Mavis did attempt to help him on rare occasions. Unfortunately, the little thing was more of a destructive force than a help. She felt that beating a board into submission was the best way to build anything, regardless of whether the nails cooperated or not. Jameson tried to give her safe little projects whenever she wanted to help him, but even they posed unspoken dangers. She was apt to use half his supplies with no tangible results before getting bored and setting out on another adventure.

On the other hand, Wilbur had the patience of Job. He would listen intently as Jameson explained the details of the projects they were about to work on. Then Jameson would sit back and watch the boy work for a little while. Jameson swore on several occasions he could actually see the gears in Wilbur's mind turning as he contemplated the best way to go about things. Jameson soon learned that Wilbur and Mavis were as different as night and day. Where Mavis jumped head first into the next adventure, Wilbur was slow and calculating. He never got in a hurry. Mavis, it seemed, never slowed down. She was wide open all the time. Even though they were six years apart in age and practically strangers, Mavis and Wilbur got along splendidly.

When they finished cleaning out the barn's loft after lunch, Jameson loaded Mavis, Ruby, and Wilbur in the truck to head over to Opal's house. Mavis made a beeline for the nearest cat that was trying its darndest to make it under the porch before being snatched by the young girl. Ruby laughed and called out to Mavis to be careful.

"That's Mr. Jingles," Opal said. "She'll never catch him!"

Sure enough, the bright white cat disappeared underneath the porch before Mavis could close the gap.

"I'm going to walk over and let Maude know we're here," Ruby said. "Keep an eye on Mavis and those poor cats."

"Howdy Wilbur!" Opal smiled. "I want you to meet Leo." She handed Wilbur a rather large midnight black cat that eyed him cautiously. "Remember, he only speaks Italian."

Wilbur looked at Jameson who shrugged. "I don't know any Italian," Wilbur whispered.

"Sure you do!" Opal encouraged. "Ciao Leo!"

The cat's ears perked up when he heard Opal's high pitched voice. "See? What'd I tell you?" Opal crooned.

Wilbur cradled the cat and followed Opal and Jameson to her backyard that was full of different flowers, plants, and trees.

"You've got quite the assortment here, Opal," Jameson said. "What exactly can we help you with today?"

"Well, my black locust over by the fence needs somewhere to go. I'm thinking a trellis like you have behind the Manor," she mused. "Ooh, don't touch it Wilbur!"

Wilbur pulled his hand back like a whipped puppy.

"It's poisonous," Opal explained.

Jameson turned to Opal in shock. "Why in the world do you have it in your backyard?"

"Because it's beautiful," she smiled. "Honestly, most everything back here can kill you."

She looked as unbothered as could be at the fact that her backyard was an apothecary's worst nightmare.

"The crocus in the corner, the nightbane under the window, the oleander to your left. All of them are beautiful, but deadly. You can't tell by just looking at them, but they'll kill you fast if you taste them. Some of them if you touch them, but they won't mess with you unless you destroy them. They're such poetic metaphors," Opal shrugged.

Jameson nodded and crouched down to look at the pale pink oleander. He motioned for Wilbur to take a closer look, too.

"Here comes Maude and Ruby. Oh Lordy, looks like Maude is bringing half her kitchen with her. That woman eats more than a passel of men after a barn raising," Opal laughed.

Jameson and Wilbur stood up just in time to see Maude, Ruby, and Mavis, who was holding a squalling calico kitten, enter the backyard.

"Y'all be careful!" Maude warned. "Opal's got her voodoo stuff back here. I swear I saw a snake here last week."

"John wouldn't hurt anyone," Opal scoffed.

"Who the hell is John?" Maude asked. She looked around at Ruby who shrugged.

Opal rolled her eyes and ignored Maude. She turned her attention back to Jameson and Wilbur. "Anyway, I'd love a trellis or two and a big stand in the corner. I'm ordering a large bee hive to get in place for next year," Opal said.

"Bees? Are you deranged?" Maude gasped.

Opal continued to ignore Maude. "I still want to do that playground for the cats we talked about, but winter is coming and I need those trellises and the stand for the hive boxes first."

Jameson nodded and patted Wilbur on the back. "Ready to spruce up Ms. Opal's garden?"

"Yes sir," Wilbur smiled. He handed Leo back to Opal and followed Jameson to the truck to grab their tools and piles of wood.

"Now Opal, you can't be serious? Cats, snakes, and now bees?" Maude declared.

"I don't know what the big fuss is about?" Opal shrugged.

"Snakes are evil! They'd sooner bite your leg off if they could!" Maude responded.

"There's a snake been sitting by your foot for the last two minutes and you ain't even noticed," Opal laughed. She and Ruby laughed hysterically as Maude jumped and ran quickly back towards her house.

"I didn't know she could move that fast," Ruby laughed, but she checked the ground around her feet all the same. Nothing Opal did surprised her and as much as she liked to believe Opal was only pulling Maude's leg, it never hurt to be sure.

"She surprises me every now and then," Opal agreed. "I'll go get her."

Opal ran off towards Maude's house to calm her down while Ruby took Mavis by the hand and led her to Opal's porch where the cats who had been lounging in the sun quickly scattered. It seemed much safer here away from the poisonous garden and wild beasts that Opal was so fond of.

She was resting in the rocking chair when Opal reappeared a few minutes later without Maude.

"I tell you, she gets worse and worse with each year. Can't take a little ol' joke. She knows good and well I wouldn't let her get within ten feet of John. Big ol' clodhopper feet like she has, he wouldn't stand a chance," Opal flopped down on the swing across from Ruby.

Ruby eyed her friend suspiciously. "Opal, you don't really have a pet snake, do you?"

"Oh Ruby, of course not. John's not a pet. He's free to roam wherever he wants to. Keeps all the vermin down in the area. Maude for all her fussing hasn't had a mouse anywhere near her place in ages thanks to John. He's a real sweet thing. Always knows where he can get a snack if he wants one. He wouldn't hurt a fly. Snakes get a bad reputation, you know," Opal said sagely.

"It's not back there now, is it? You know there's only one thing in the world that Jameson is afraid of and that's a snake," Ruby reminded Opal.

"Oh no. John won't bother a soul," Opal assured her.

Ruby merely nodded, but she made a mental note to keep a much closer eye on Mavis when they visited. They chatted for several minutes before Maude eventually returned with a cigarette firmly in her hand.

"Those things are going to kill you," Opal told her.

"They're not going to have a chance to kill me between the damn snakes and toxic garden you've got around here. I swear Opal, one of these days,"

Maude shook her head and lit another cigarette with her free hand. Having one in each hand seemed to calm her down a bit or at least it diverted her attention away from Opal and her unique gardening preferences.

Ruby cleared her throat. "So Opal, when is opening night for your play?" she asked to change the subject.

"We open next Friday. Y'all're coming, aren't you?" Opal demanded.

"Of course we are. We wouldn't miss it for the world," Ruby assured her.

"Which play are you doing again?" Maude asked, taking a particularly long drag on the cigarette in her left hand.

"The Muse," Opal said dramatically.

"Right. I knew it was something funny like that," Maude said.

"It's not a comedy. It's very serious, Maude," Opal said. She looked very affronted.

"I just meant the name was funny. Anyway, what's the muse?" Maude asked.

"Not a what," Opal smiled. "A who."

"Who's the muse then?" Maude asked.

"Who do you think?" Opal said through pursed lips. "Why, me of course!"

Maude and Ruby locked eyes. "Well, we can't wait to come see you shine," Ruby smiled.

"It's a grand role. Ricky wrote it with me in mind. He said I was the only one within a hundred miles of this ol' town with enough je ne sais quoi to bring the character to life. I was born to play her," Opal said dramatically. She wrapped her colorful scarf around her shoulders as she waved her arms through the air.

"Ricky wrote the play? Well, I guess you were born for that part if your boyfriend wrote the damn thing for you," Maude had finally finished both cigarettes and was snuffing out the butt in the ashtray on the table.

Opal rolled her eyes. "You are so uncouth, Maude. Ricky is the only one who truly understands what brings my passions to life."

"Ricky McNeal, the tailor?" Maude demanded clarification.

Before Opal could answer, there was a commotion from the backyard. Jameson came scurrying out dragging Wilbur with him.

"Dadgummit, Opal! You really do have a snake back there!" Jameson was clutching his chest trying to breathe.

"I told you I did. You didn't hurt him, did you?" Opal asked.

"Hurt him? Hurt HIM?!" Jameson was still trying to catch his breath. "That thing is ten feet long. Biggest snake I ever saw."

"He ain't done it," Opal scoffed. "John's probably six or seven feet at most. He's still a baby."

"Are you okay? You two didn't get bit, did you?" Maude asked. She grabbed Wilbur and began checking him for any visible signs of a snake attack.

"No ma'am. He didn't bite me," Wilbur told her. "He was in the tree we were under."

"Biggest snake I ever saw," Jameson continued to mumble to himself. He took out his handkerchief and wiped off his brow. "I thought she was just teasing Maude. It's curled up there in that tree by the back door. I'll say Opal, near about gave me a heart attack. He's a big old monster," Jameson gasped.

"Did he strike at you?" Maude asked.

"No ma'am," Wilbur said. "He's just sitting up there watching."

"Opal! You've got to get rid of it," Ruby gasped. She hugged Wilbur close to her side.

Opal rolled her eyes and looked at Ruby. "He's a wild animal, Rubes. I can't tell him to pack his bags and evict him." Nothing they were saying made any sense to her. "He doesn't bother a soul up there. He's just watching y'all to see what you're doing."

Jameson was still clutching his chest trying to catch his breath. "I swear Opal, I can't do snakes, I'd rather a bobcat tear my arm off than come across a snake," he said.

"Oh good heavens, if y'all are gonna make a scene about it, I'll just move him over to Maude's while y'all work," Opal sighed.

"The hell you will! Opal! I've made threats your whole life, but if you put that snake in my yard, I will personally end your life!" Maude screeched.

"Can't you get one of your beaus to come get him?" Ruby asked.

Opal sighed deeply and thought about it for a minute. "I guess I can call Mortie," she said. "He's got a big enough yard for him and some fig trees out front John would love."

"I don't care who you call!" Maude huffed. "Mortimer, Ricky, Eddie, the preacher, whoever!"

Opal shook her head and hushed Maude. "I can't call Ricky or Eddie. What are they gonna do with a snake? Sometimes I worry about you, Maude," Opal vented. She walked up her porch steps and disappeared through her front door. She returned a few minutes later with a basket of eggs.

"What are those for?" Maude asked.

"For John," Opal said. "Mortie's coming to get him in a few minutes."

Opal sat down in her rocking chair and looked upset. Ruby sat down in the chair next to her and patted her arm. "Thank you, Opal. I'm sure Mortie will take great care of him," she whispered.

When Mortimer Raven pulled up in the driveway fifteen minutes later, Opal met him at the hearse's passenger door. She laid the basket full of eggs in the seat and followed him to the backyard. They returned a few minutes later with a large solid black snake that was indeed the biggest snake any of them had ever seen. Mortimer placed John in the large body bag that he had in the back of the hearse.

"Why does she look like she's going to a funeral?" Maude asked Ruby.

"Shh, she's doing this for you. Well, for all of us," Ruby smiled weakly. Ruby hated snakes just as much as the next person, but she hated to see her friend so upset.

"I hope he throws the whole damn thing in the crematorium," Maude muttered.

"Maude! Hush up!" Ruby scolded her.

"Well, I do," Maude whispered under her breath.

"That should work fine for transport," Mortimer said morosely. "I will call you tonight for our evening phone call." He nodded to Jameson and then to the women. Opal thanked him and he drove off just as quickly as he had arrived. Opal returned to the porch and sulked.

"Alright, well, I guess we better get on back to work, Wilbur," Jameson said. Ruby swore she saw the boy smile as he traipsed off after Jameson.

~ Chapter Six ~

"Dress rehearsal went perfect last night," Opal moaned.

"Well, that's great!" Ruby said.

"No, that's bad. You want a terrible dress rehearsal so opening night goes good," she sighed.

"Huh? That don't make no sense," Maude replied. "You've been practicing for weeks."

"It's called rehearsing," Opal said. "Practicing is for sports, not theatre."

"Whatever. Y'all run around up there and yell, so close enough. There's even a half time for some of them," Maude mumbled.

"It's called intermission. I don't expect you to understand the inner workings of theatre," Opal retorted.

Maude looked at Ruby and rolled her eyes. She was more than ready for this show to be over. Opal got kookier each time the theatre unveiled a new play.

"Well, we have our seats reserved. We got third row!" Ruby exclaimed.

"Good, good," Opal said. "Please try to behave this time Maude. Last time everyone could hear you opening up your snack bags and crunching on those chips."

Opal walked to the kitchen and poured herself another glass of water.

"What does she expect me to do?" Maude asked Ruby. "I get a little hungry sometimes."

Ruby shrugged and tried to change the subject. "So, Opal, how many um, costume changes do you have?"

Opal sat back on the couch with Maude and answered, "Eleven."

"Eleven? Geez Opal! I don't even own eleven outfits myself," Maude gasped.

"I know," Opal muttered.

"What's that supposed to mean?" Maude asked.

"I've seen your closet," Opal replied.

"Well we can't wait to see them all," Ruby interrupted. "We'll be there as soon as the doors open. Wilbur said his dad will be out of town tonight, so we're going to bring him along, too. I laid one of Jameson's ties out for him to wear and Mavis has a new pink dress she's been wanting to wear."

"We gotta get dressed up for this?" Maude asked.

"This is the event of the year!" Opal looked affronted. "You can't show up looking like you do now, that's for sure."

Ruby stood up to refill their glasses before Maude could offer her retort.

"I guess I better get on home so I can get ready," Opal said. "Ricky's picking me up in a few hours so we can rehearse the last number one more time."

"See you there! Good luck!" Ruby called after her.

"No, no, Ruby. It's break a leg," Opal said.

"I'll break her leg," Maude grumbled.

"Break a leg then dear," Ruby smiled.

They watched Opal peel out of the driveway in her red sports car.

"This is a one night only thing, right?" Maude asked.

"This particular one is, but she's already talking about doing the Christmas pageant in a few months. You know that runs all weekend long," Ruby answered.

"Show business is gonna kill me," Maude mumbled.

"I'm excited for tonight," Ruby said. "It'll do us all good to go out and have a nice time. Opal always does a real nice job in these kinds of things."

"Oh, she's dramatic alright," Maude replied. "I reckon I better get on too so I can figure out what I'm supposed to wear."

"We'll meet you at The Big Steer around five thirty. The show starts at seven so that should give us plenty of time to eat and walk over to the theatre," Ruby reminded her.

Maude waved and jumped on her motorcycle. She sped out of the gravel driveway and zipped down the road before Ruby could tell her what she had planned to wear.

Being a regular at the only steak house in town had its benefits. Jameson was able to get a table for six within minutes of arriving. He motioned for the ladies to go ahead as the maitre d led them to the table in the back corner of the restaurant. He waited until Maude, who had decided to bathe in her favorite perfume, sat down so that he could choose a seat downwind. Ruby wasn't so lucky. She was sitting right beside her best friend. On several occasions, Jameson looked up in time to see her wiping a tear away. Maude thought that Ruby had a cold, but Jameson knew that the fog of cheap perfume was getting to her.

"Ruby, you need something for your nose?" Maude asked.

"I'm good, thanks," Ruby answered.

"Here's some tissue," Maude said. She reached into her purse and pulled out a wad of tissues.

"That's sure something you got going on there Maude," Teddy Butler said. The smell was getting to him, too. Maude didn't seem to understand what he meant, but she smiled coyly. He returned Maude's smile and quickly finished his mashed potatoes.

"About ready to head over?" Jameson asked.

Ruby and Teddy nodded quickly and stood up from the table.

"I ain't had dessert yet," Maude complained.

"We don't want to be late," Teddy smiled.

Jameson and Teddy paid the bill and they all walked outside in the chilly evening air to make their way to the nearby theatre.

The community theatre was packed. It was standing room only for those who hadn't made a reservation ahead of time. Jameson carried Mavis, who had already fallen asleep, into the third aisle from the front. Wilbur followed and sat in between him and Ruby. Maude took the seat next to Ruby and Teddy sat on her right near the aisle.

Maude took off her coat and opened her purse that was full of snacks.

"Maude! You can't eat those in here!" Ruby chided. "Remember what Opal said."

"Why the hell not? I was gonna share," Maude said grumpily.

"We just had supper," Ruby reminded her.

"Then we had to walk over from the restaurant. My feet hurt in this getup and I didn't get to order dessert. Here, have a chip," Maude offered.

"Shh," a voice behind them whispered.

Maude looked at Ruby with her eyes wide. Who in the world had the gall to shush her? She whipped around in her seat and stared straight into the eyes of Nadine Waters.

"You shushing me?" Maude asked.

"There's a sign that says no food or drink in the theatre. And it's about to start," Nadine said in her high pitch voice.

"You start it and I'll finish it!" Maude howled.

"Maude! Turn around. You're embarrassing me!" Ruby whispered. She pulled Maude back into her seat and gave her the side eye. The theatre lights dimmed twice to signal the start of the show.

"I'll see you afterwards," Maude whispered loudly over her shoulder to Nadine.

Ricky McNeal walked onto center stage to a thunderous round of applause. "Welcome ladies and gentlemen, tonight's gala is one for the ages. I wrote this play this summer. I was inspired, of course, by Rhinestone's own Opal Tyler, the muse to my creativity. You will laugh, you will cry, you will be inspired! Please remain in your seats and try to not be too overcome with emotion. We will have a brief intermission between acts one and two, so please hold off on exiting the theatre until then. The restrooms are just off the lobby and, one moment please," Ricky smiled. He poked his head between the heavy curtains and backstage. "I have a special announcement from the star of the show. Opal requests that there be no flash photography as it hurts her eyes. And she said, um, please no eating or drinking in the theatre. Sounds tend to carry. Now, everyone, if you're ready, I present, The Muse."

Maude could hear Nadine laugh behind her, but she silenced her with one look. She was going to have to get backstage somehow and strangle Opal during intermission when the lights came back on. It was too dark to see where she was going if she got up now.

The curtain rose and the bright lights lit up the bare stage. A man dressed in black quickly pushed a heavy staircase on wheels across the stage. A few seconds later, Opal appeared atop the staircase in a tight red dress that sparkled in the spotlight. She stayed rooted in the spotlight while she sang the opening number. As act one continued, Maude had to admit that Opal was doing a great job. She was a very accomplished dancer and singer, but the plot play made no sense at all.

Opal's character was a recluse who kept to herself on a remote island. She wore numerous beautiful gowns and sang to herself in solitude. Ricky's character, the leading man, was a down and out artist who watched her from afar and painted the lonely woman who had stolen his heart. Maude hoped something exciting would happen in act two or she was going to end up asleep like Mavis.

Opal changed a total of seven times before intermission. When the lights rose, Maude stretched her arms out in front of her and yawned. Nadine loudly sighed, but hurried to the lobby before Maude could retort. There was already a long line for the restroom, so Maude stayed put in her seat. With the lights fully up, she could finally see how crowded it was. Eddie Walker sat two rows in front of them. The seat next to him was piled high with flowers. She hadn't thought to bring Opal flowers. She had been too busy squeezing herself into this pantsuit before Teddy arrived to pick her up. Speaking of Teddy, he had dozed off to sleep at some point, so she elbowed him to jar him awake.

"Who shot who?" he yelped. He rubbed his eyes and looked around. "Oh, we're still here. Great show!" He stood up and stretched before taking his seat again.

"Good evening," a low voice said.

"Hey there, Mr. Raven," Teddy smiled. "Great show so far, huh?"

"Opal is indeed lovely," he replied in his monotone voice.

Teddy swallowed hard and looked at Maude for help. She merely shrugged. Mortimer Raven nodded to them both before taking his seat in front of them. Maude rummaged through her purse and found her perfume bottle and started to spray more on her, just in case some of it had rubbed off during the hour long act one.

"What is that smell?" Nadine shrieked.

Maude looked around for the source of whatever Nadine smelled, but she couldn't detect anything out of the ordinary. Ruby pulled her coat closer to her and sniffed a few more times.

"You might have to go get that cold of yours seen about," Maude declared.

Ruby smiled and was thankful that the lights dimmed twice again to usher everyone back to their seats.

Act two was more of the same. Opal opened the scene in emerald green spandex and sang an upbeat power ballad about finding oneself in the midst of a hurricane. The cast of townspeople wore neon orange and provided the backup dancing and singing. Ricky's character edged onto the scene and joined the song. As the play continued, Maude was even more confused on the actual plot of the play. After thirty minutes of back and forth between the two, Opal two stepped across the stage in a peacock blue gown and ended up in Ricky's outstretched arms. He leaned in to kiss her as the stage went dark. It was finally over.

Maude rose to her feet following Ruby and Jameson's cue. One by one the entire audience rose to their feet and clapped for the cast. Ricky and Opal received the loudest thunder of applause as they took their bows.

Opal bounded off the stage and hugged her friends tightly. She was sweating profusely and had thick layers of makeup caked on.

"Dear God, Maude! Are you wearing perfume?" Opal asked, by way of a greeting.

"Why, yes," Maude smiled. "It's the latest thing from that mail order subscription. Myra Wilcox gave me a deal on it."

"How many gallons did you buy?" Opal asked.

Maude huffed. "You don't buy fancy perfume by the gallon. Everybody knows that!"

"Well, you ain't supposed to bathe in it either, but here we are," Opal shrugged.

"Opal, I don't know what you're talking about. No one else has said a thing!" Maude turned to Ruby. "You like it, don't you?"

Ruby cleared her throat and sniffed loudly. "Well, it is a bit loud."

"A bit loud?" Opal said, much louder than was necessary. "It was screaming for mercy as soon as you walked in. I'm surprised we didn't miss our cues because it was hollering so bad."

"Opal!" Ruby chided her.

Opal looked at her. "What?"

"Be nice," Ruby told her. "Maude, I'm sure it was a great deal and I'm sure it's lovely in, um, smaller doses."

Before Opal could say another word, Mortie was by her side handing her a bouquet of white roses. "For you, my dear," Mortie said, bowing dramatically.

"Oh, these are so lovely, Mortie," Opal gushed. She kissed him on the cheek and turned to see Eddie on her other side holding enough rainbow colored flowers to cover a small float in the Rose Bowl Parade.

"You shouldn't have!" Opal squealed.

"Anything for the belle of the ball!" Eddie beamed.

Mortimer watched everything unfold without expression. When Eddie finally caught his eye, he merely nodded his head casually and said, "Edward."

"Hey Mortimer, good to see you," Eddie smiled cautiously.

Mortimer bowed before turning towards the side door. He opened it without a sound and walked out into the dark night.

"That was scary," Maude mumbled to Ruby.

"I'm sure he's harmless," Ruby offered diplomatically. Maude gave her a sideways look.

Jameson nodded. "He's always been a nice guy."

"Oh, here we go," Ruby whispered.

Nadine was making her way around to congratulate the cast. "Why Opal Tyler, who in the world knew you had so many hidden talents?"

Maude glared at Nadine. Ruby maintained a tight grip on Maude's arm. The last thing they needed was to have a murder during the grand gala.

"Opal sure was lovely!" Ruby agreed.

"Aren't you lucky to have a director who's so devoted to your, ahem, theatrical career," Nadine said with a sinister smile.

"Everyone was invited to audition, Nadine," Maude said.

"Yes," Nadine turned to her. "So I remember. But I daresay no one could compete with Ricky's little muse here it seems." She walked away before Maude could free herself from Ruby's grip.

"One of these days I'm going to clock her one good," Maude said through gritted teeth.

"But not today," Jameson laughed. "We need to get these little ones home."

"Fine, but one day," Maude grumbled.

The walk back to the steakhouse parking lot where they had left their cars was a chilly one. Jameson carried Mavis out to the backseat of the car and laid her down beside Wilbur who had climbed in behind Ruby. They waved goodbye to Maude and Teddy and backed out of the parking lot. It was a good thing they had parked at the steakhouse. They were able to get out much quicker than the crowd at the theatre.

"Your daddy won't mind us bringing you home so late, will he Wilbur?" Jameson asked.

Wilbur shrugged. "No sir. Not exactly."

"Not exactly?" Ruby asked

Wilbur was quiet for a minute.

"He knows you're out with us tonight, doesn't he?" Jameson asked pointedly.

"Not exactly," Wilbur muttered.

"You mean you didn't tell him, Wilbur? Oh, I'm sure he'll be worried sick," Ruby said.

"He's not worried. He won't even know I'm not there. He hasn't been home in a week or so now," Wilbur said.

"A week? You mean you've been staying in that house all alone for a week?" Ruby was aghast.

Jameson cleared his throat. "Has this happened before, son?"

Wilbur nodded. "Yes, sir. It happens every now and then. He travels to different places. I don't really know where all he goes. But he always comes back home after a few days, sometimes a week or so. He was gone for three weeks last year, but that only happened one time." Wilbur stared out the window into the darkness.

"Does your grandmother look in on you when he's gone?" Jameson asked.

"No sir. All of my grandparents are passed away. We don't really have any family so to speak of," Wilbur said quietly.

"Well, then I guess he won't mind if you come back to our house for some of Ruby's world famous hot cocoa. You just haven't lived until you've tried it," Jameson said with a weary smile at the lad.

"I don't want to be any trouble," Wilbur mumbled.

"Are you kidding? If you come home with us, Ruby will make an extra big batch. That's more for me!" Jameson winked at the boy.

Wilbur smiled at being part of the conspiracy. "Yes, sir."

Chapter Seven

As autumn set in, Wilbur spent every waking moment that he could with the Montgomerys. The Montgomerys were the family he never knew existed, but that he had always secretly hoped for. They were just as crazy about him as he was them. There was always something new and exciting to do at the Manor and Wilbur took to it like a pig to mud.

The Saturday before Halloween, Wilbur arrived much earlier than usual. Jameson had been working on the outboard motor for his jon boat and was eager to test it out in the water. He promised to take Wilbur over to the river on the other side of Junction to do a little fishing. Ruby had sandwiches, several snacks, and a six pack of RC Cola ready for their adventure. She waved after them as they headed down the drive in Jameson's truck.

Wilbur stared out the window as the sun began to peak above the horizon. The morning haze lay like a blanket over the fields, now empty except for a few stalks missed by the plow. Jameson fiddled with the radio for a few moments until he finally found an old country station. It faded in and out as they crested a new hill. By the time they passed Junction, he gave up and turned the thing off. The silence was fine with Wilbur. Alone with Jameson, quiet was peaceful. Jameson seemed to enjoy the tranquility as well. It wasn't always quiet at the Manor, at least not while Mavis was awake. For someone so young, she sure could get loud.

When they arrived at the river, Jameson backed the boat down the ramp and jumped out to unhitch the boat from the trailer. Wilbur was on the other side watching his every move. Together they quickly had the boat in the water. Wilbur was given the job of keeping the boat close to the ramp while Jameson parked the truck.

"Which way do we go?" Wilbur asked.

"I know the perfect little spot I'd like to show you," Jameson smiled. "The same spot my daddy showed me when I was a little younger than you. We called it our honey hole."

Wilbur returned his smile and felt the cool wind against his cheeks as the boat went up the river. Jameson settled the boat under a low hanging tree not far from the bank and pulled out the fishing poles from under the row of seats. After showing Wilbur how to bait his hook one time, Wilbur took to it like a fish to water. He was a natural fisherman.

By midmorning, they were both starving. They broke into the small cooler of wrapped BLT sandwiches that Ruby had packed for them. Want some pretzels?" Jameson asked with a wink.

"Yes sir," Wilbur grinned. Pretzels were his favorite. He loved to eat them while working outside with Jameson on the weekends. Ruby must have been paying attention, because she packed them plenty of pretzels, sliced apples, and two lemon cake bars along with their sandwiches. Ruby had long since discovered that Wilbur also loved anything lemon!

"Hey, look! You've got a good bite!" Jameson said as he was putting the trash back in the bag.

"I do?" Wilbur turned so quickly he almost knocked the cooler into the water.

"Grab the pole!" Jameson lunged for the pole and the cooler at the same time.

The boat rocked dangerously as they both struggled to grab the wayward fishing rod. Finally Wilbur had it in his hands.

"Reel him in!" Jameson yelled, trying to calm the boat which was still swaying.

"I got him! I got him!" Wilbur said.

"Give him some slack, now reel him on up!" Jameson spoke in a rush.

Wilbur leaned back in the boat and turned the handle with all his might. The tip of the rod bent over in two. A moment later, the bass broke through the water against his will. He jumped and thrashed around, churning the muddy river water for all his worth.

"He's a monster!" Jameson yelled. "Stick with him son! You got him!"

Wilbur dared not to let go of the line. He continued to turn the handle.

"You got him, you got him!" Jameson reached for the line. Once he finally had the line in his grasp, he hoisted the largemouth bass into the boat where the beast floundered about until he was left gasping for air.

"Will you look at the size of that thing! Must be at least five pounds!" Jameson thumped Wilbur on the back.

Wilbur was too excited to notice. He picked up his worn ball cap that had fallen off in the melee and returned it to the top of his head. He was smiling as broadly as Jameson had ever seen him.

"This guy sure puts the rest of the fish we caught today to shame, doesn't he?" Jameson said, beaming with pride.

"He sure is a whopper!" Wilbur finally seemed to find his voice.

"He sure is," Jameson said.

Jameson and Wilbur arrived back from their time on the river late afternoon. They had a cooler full of fresh fish waiting to be fried.

"Will you look at this monster that Wilbur brought home," he told Ruby as they unloaded the truck. He was holding the bass up with pride.

"Wilbur, you caught that?" Ruby gushed.

"Yes, ma'am," Wilbur smiled.

"We gotta get a picture! Maude, go get the camera!" Opal yelled in the house to her friend.

Maude came out on the porch a few minutes later holding up the Kodak disc camera. "What are we taking pictures of?" she asked.

"Wilbur's fish. Look at this. He caught the biggest one I've ever seen!" Opal squealed.

"Well, I'll be. Wilbur, you do that all by yourself?" Maude asked.

"Mr. Jameson helped me," Wilbur said honestly.

"I did not," Jameson corrected him. "He already had it out of the water by the time I got to him. He reeled this fella in all by his lonesome."

Maude began taking photos of the two proud fishermen and their bountiful catch. When they had finished, Jameson took the cooler around back while Wilbur put the rods and tackle box back in the barn.

"Put this big guy in the freezer for me if you don't mind. I'm going to have this one mounted for the wall," Jameson told Ruby as he handed her Wilbur's prize fish. "I'm going to try to surprise him with it," Jameson winked.

By the time Wilbur had finished putting the gear away, Jameson had started cleaning the fish for dinner. Wilbur helped him finish the last few fish and washed his hands at the hose spigot.

"We're going to eat good tonight, aren't we?" Jameson asked while he and Wilbur walked around the back of the house.

"Yes, sir," Wilbur said. The boy was still smiling.

"This is the last one and then they'll be ready to fry," Jameson told him. Wilbur nodded and watched his every move.

Opal's jalapeno cornbread and Maude's pickled okra were already wrapped up on the stove. Ruby finished stirring the creamed corn on the stove and covered the fried green tomatoes she had just fried. As soon as Jameson finished dipping the fish in batter and fried them, they'd be ready to sit down and eat.

Wilbur sat at the table watching Ruby and Jameson work.

"What's your favorite holiday dish?" Ruby asked Wilbur.

He thought long and hard and said, "I don't think I have a favorite."

"What about a Thanksgiving turkey or a Christmas ham? Surely one has to rate pretty high on your list! Holidays are the best time of the year for food," Jameson said.

"We don't usually celebrate Thanksgiving," Wilbur shrugged. "And Christmas isn't a real big deal at our house."

"Well, here in the Montgomery house we do!" Jameson shouted over all of the noise.

Mavis and Opal were running around the kitchen table and bounded out of the front door. Opal had told Mavis that Maude was a bear and they were both running away from her. Unfortunately Opal hadn't told Maude about their little game, so every time Maude came up to Mavis, the little girl would scream and run away laughing.

"What's gotten into her?" Maude asked Ruby.

Ruby hid her laughter in the dish towel and shrugged as Maude went onto the front porch after Opal and Mavis.

"Alright, let's get these in the fryer," Jameson said. Wilbur followed him outside and watched him drop the battered filets into the deep fryer. Maude was now chasing after Opal and Mavis who kept eluding her at every turn.

"Mavis outta sleep well tonight," Jameson laughed.

Wilbur nodded and continued to watch them.

"What's on your mind, son?" Jameson asked after a few minutes.

Wilbur had been mighty curious about Mavis and the Montgomery family. He knew that Mavis was their granddaughter. He knew that she was six years old. He knew that she called Ruby Big Mama and Jameson Big Daddy, but he wasn't quite sure where Mavis' mother was. He wasn't sure if the Montgomery's had other children or not. He didn't feel like he should ask, but Jameson told him that he could ask anything he wanted. He promised him that he would always be honest with him.

"Do you have other children?" Wilbur asked. "Besides Mavis."

Jameson took off his glasses and wiped them clean on his handkerchief. "Mavis is our granddaughter, but she has lived with us since the day she was born. We are the only parental figures she has ever known. Her mother, our daughter Melanie, passed away a few years back. Mavis has been our pride and joy since we first laid eyes on her. But no, Ruby and I don't have any other children," Jameson answered.

"My mother passed away too," Wilbur said. "I don't remember her really."

Jameson nodded. He had been wondering if Wilbur would bring up his mother eventually. It was as if Jameson and Ruby could see the walls slowly breaking down around the young boy. He was less rigid and readily joined Mavis when she asked him to play. He helped to set and clear the table before meals. He even laughed when Opal teased Maude, which was every time the two women joined them.

"What are we going to work on next?" Wilbur asked.

Jameson and Wilbur had already finished all of Opal's projects and even found the time to build Maude a new doghouse for her bulldog named Buford. Opal wanted them to build a fence for Maude to keep Buford away from her chickens, but Maude wouldn't hear it. She said Buford needed to be able to roam since he was a free spirit.

"I'm thinking ahead for Ruby's Christmas gift. I think you and I can handle it," Jameson winked. "I'll tell you about it later."

Ruby walked over to them and asked what they were whispering about.

"Nothing, nothing," Jameson smiled. "You about ready to eat? Wilbur and I caught some good ones that are frying up nicely."

"I'll get Mavis cleaned up and meet you at the table!" she replied. Ruby ushered Opal, Maude, and Mavis back up the porch and through the front door.

"Boy howdy, these sure look good!" Jameson said. He carried the hot pan of steaming fish up the porch steps. "Come on, Wilbur. I'll come back out and take care of the fire while you wash up."

Wilbur followed behind him and waited for Mavis to finish playing in the bathroom sink before he washed his hands.

"You stink," she said with a frown. "You smell like stinky fish."

Before he could respond, she skipped off to the dining room singing some song Wilbur had never heard of. By the time Wilbur got to the table, Jameson had taken care of the open flame outside and was washing his hands in the kitchen sink. Ruby finished pouring the drinks and everyone settled into the chairs at the table.

"These are plum good," Maude said in between mouthfuls of fish. She pulled one of the soft bones from her mouth and sucked all of the meat clean from the bone in one motion. "I know they say the hot summer months are the best time to catch them, but the catfish around here must not know that because every time I go, they practically jump in the boat! Isn't that right, Opal? We went two weeks ago late at night and we got us a whole mess of them!"

"Leo did enjoy his share," Opal mused. "I took some over to Mortie and he promised to give John the scraps. He's such a sweet man."

"What about Eddie and Ricky?" Maude asked.

"Oh goodness Maude, you know Ricky is vegan! He won't touch anything from an animal with a ten foot pole. Not even eggs from my chickens. Eddie, well, he's allergic to fish. It's the craziest thing. I can't even eat fish if I'm gonna see him that day. He'll swell up like a balloon!" Opal said seriously.

Ruby kicked Maude under the table before she could open her mouth to ask any more questions.

"I guess we need to talk about Thanksgiving while we're all here. It's coming on fast, less than five weeks away. Mother and Daddy are going to Robert's this year over in Fayette, but Jameson's mother will be here with us. It's her first big holiday without Mr. Montgomery, so we want to make it special for her. We're planning on an early supper so everyone has time to eat and spend some time together before it gets too late. I know Jameson will want to watch the football game during the day, so y'all invite Teddy and whoever you want Opal. The more the merrier," Ruby said.

"Teddy'd love to come watch the game and eat. That's all that man ever does when he ain't working. He talks about football and stuffs his face," Maude announced. "Opal, you going to invite all three of those men? I can see it now! A deputy, lawyer, mortician, florist, and tailor all huddled around the TV. That'd be a sight to see!"

Opal shrugged. "Mortie probably won't come. You know the holidays are his busiest times. He says there's nothing like the holiday spirit to inspire hostility and accidents. And Ricky will probably go up to New York to visit his family, but I'm sure Eddie would love to come. I'll see if he'll bring his butter rum pound cake. I'm telling y'all, y'all haven't lived 'til you've tasted Eddie's pound cake."

For the second time that evening, Ruby kicked Maude underneath the table.

"Ruby!" Maude yelled. "Will you stop?" Maude rubbed her leg.

"Maude what are you talking about? You know as well as I do that Ruby hasn't said a word," Opal said rolling her eyes.

"That wasn't what I was talking about," Maude mumbled.

"Like I was saying, y'all invite whoever you want. Just give us a head count closer to time so we know how big a turkey to get. We'll go over the details closer to time about who's bringing what," Ruby smiled. "Wilbur, we expect to see you here, too. Tell your daddy he's welcome to come, too. We'd all love to have you both."

Jameson watched the boy's reaction to the invitation. It was the first time since lunch that Wilbur's smile faded from his face.

"Thank you," he stuttered. "I'll let him know."

Wilbur went back to his plate and continued to eat as the conversation carried on without him. As soon as the meal was over, he scraped his plate in the trashcan and helped Mavis put hers in the sink. He waved goodbye and hurried out of the front door. Ruby watched him disappear into the darkness at the tree line.

"Should I not have mentioned his father?" Ruby asked.

"Honey, I think it's good that you laid out the invitation. I just think there's something fishy going on there. I think you may have been right weeks ago when you had that inkling of suspicion.

I'll see what I can find out down at the office. I sure do like having him around, I'll tell you that," Jameson said.

"I do, too," Ruby smiled. Her eyes were already watering.

Chapter Eight

"Did you go trick or treating last night?" Ruby asked Wilbur as she dipped some scrambled eggs onto his plate. His face was fuller now than the first time she laid eyes on him months ago. There was color in his cheeks and his eyes had a new life in them.

Wilbur shook his head and shrugged. "My daddy says Halloween is the devil's day, so he says we have to stay inside," he said quietly.

Ruby tousled his hair as she set the glass jar of jelly down on the table. "Well, I know there are quite a few people who do believe that. To each their own," she smiled.

"Do you think that?" he asked sheepishly.

"No, I don't think that. I think it's a fun time of the year for little ones to dress up and get candy. It's a time for us all to be together and stay up all night with a toothache," Maude interjected.

Wilbur smiled and took a big bite of bacon. When he swallowed he asked, "Did y'all go out last night?"

"Mavis was the sweetest little ghost you ever did see! We went downtown and she trick or treated the different shops on Main Street. Didn't take her long at all to get a whole pillowcase full of candy," Ruby smiled.

"Well, it didn't hurt that Opal emptied the rest of her candy bowl into her sack," Maude whispered to Wilbur. "She sure had a time dragging that sack down the sidewalk. I'll bet she'll be willing to share with us after breakfast!"

Wilbur smiled and spread grape jelly onto his toasted bread. He hoped Maude was right about Mavis sharing her Halloween candy.

Moments later, Opal flew in through the front door like a rabbit on steroids. "Morning y'all! The sun sure is bright this morning! I've been up since before dawn!" Opal all but shouted.

"Dear Lord in heaven, why are you shouting?" Maude asked. She held her hands up over her ears and shook her head.

"Am I? Must be all the chocolate I had earlier!" Opal chattered. Her eyes were as big as saucers.

"Want anything to eat?" Ruby asked. "We've got bacon and eggs, toast, and cinnamon apples."

"No time!" Opal laughed. "I've got to get to auditions down at the theatre. I've been practicing my monologue all morning!"

"I thought you said it was rehearsing, not practicing," Maude asked.

"Shh! No time to educate you," Opal interjected.

"Then why exactly are you here?" Maude asked.

"Just thought I'd grace you with my presence for a little bit. And to see if you'd like to come down and audition, too?" Opal smiled. "There's a part that'll fit you like a glove!"

"What play are you doing?" Ruby asked.

"A Christmas Carol," Opal mused. "It's going to be spectacular."

"And who exactly would I be?" Maude asked.

"The Spirit of Christmas Present, of course! He's the jolly fat one who eats the whole time," Opal said matter of factly.

Maude's face got so red that, for a minute, Wilbur thought she was going to have a heart attack.

"I'm only kidding," Opal said. "You could play Marley though. He's real pale on account of being a ghost. I think you'd love it. Plus, we could spend more time together!"

"We already see each other every day!" Maude huffed.

"Well fine then!" Opal pouted.

"What time are auditions?" Ruby asked.

"They start at one. Well, I guess I better run. Mortie's meeting me down there. I'll keep you posted," Opal replied.

"You just got here!" Maude said.

"Mortie?" Ruby asked.

"Oh yes. He is an avid supporter of the theatre. I finally convinced him to audition for this one. He's a little nervous though, so I told him I would show him some exercises to shake those nerves," Opal said sagely.

"This should be interesting," Maude laughed.

"If you change your mind, let me know! Otherwise I'll keep you posted!" Opal hollered behind her. They heard her peel out of the driveway just as quick as she had come.

"That woman never stops, I swear!" Maude said. "I don't know why she's always joking about me and food." She crammed another slice of toast into her mouth and shrugged her shoulders.

"I have no idea," Ruby smiled. She winked at Wilbur who tried to stifle a laugh.

"Alright sugar, why don't you and Wilbur run off and play while we clean up the kitchen," Ruby said gently. Mavis flew out of her chair and called for Wilbur to follow her up the stairs to her room.

"Come on Wilbur! Come see my new baby doll I got yesterday. She's the prettiest baby I ever did see!" Mavis squealed. She took the stairs two at a time leaving Wilbur to scramble after her.

Maude watched the kids scamper out of the room. "I meant to tell you that I saw Pete last night," Maude said. "He was slumped over the counter over at the Tipsy Toad. Saw him when I passed by on the way to The Comb Over. It couldn't have been five o'clock, but he was already three sheets to the wind."

"No," Ruby said, shaking her head.

"I'm telling you I did. Pitiful sight. No wonder Wilbur didn't get to go out last night," Maude leaned back in her chair.

"Sometimes I want to ring that man's neck! The very idea that he's out acting a fool in some bar instead of staying home and taking care of his son," Ruby said. She was scrubbing the counter with a fierceness Maude rarely saw in her.

"You okay, Rubes?" Maude asked.

"No, no I'm not. Wilbur is a wonderful boy and he deserves so much more than a drunk for a father," Ruby huffed.

"I know what you mean, but unless you're planning on kidnapping the boy, there's really nothing much you can do about it. Pete is his father after all," Maude told her.

"I know," Ruby muttered.

They heard Jameson scamper up the front porch steps and call for Wilbur to join him in the barn when he was ready. Wilbur came down the stairs a few minutes later with Mavis skipping after him. Mavis sang a song of her own making that got shriller as she walked outside. Ruby watched them from the kitchen window.

"What are you thinking so hard about, Ruby?" Maude asked after watching her friend for a few minutes.

"Nothing," Ruby replied.

"Nothing my foot. You're thinking awful hard about something," Maude corrected her.

"No, it's nothing really. I just wish I could do more for him," Ruby said.

"You're already doing more for him than anyone else ever did. He knows that," Maude reassured her.

"Yeah, maybe," Ruby said.

Maude decided to change the subject. "So what do you have planned for today? Anything exciting?"

"I'm taking Mavis over to see Mrs. Montgomery around eleven," Ruby said, stacking the dishes in the sink to wash.

"Hey, why don't we make a day of it? We'll drop Mavis off and then go out for lunch in town. Then," Maude offered a wicked little smile, "We can go over to the theatre and watch the tryouts or auditions or whatever the hell they're called. I can't wait to see Mortie and Opal on stage together."

"Oh, we can't do that!" Ruby said. "Can we?"

"Why not? She wanted me to try out for the fat ghost for crying out loud. I think turnabout is fair play with this thing," Maude said. "Auditions are open to the public."

"It's so mean, Maude. You're just going to make fun of them," Ruby said.

"I am not. I'm supporting the cultural activities of Rhinestone," Maude corrected her.

"Now who's fibbing?" Ruby laughed.

"Ooh, I wonder if Ricky and Eddie will be there, too. This day could be the best one all week!" Maude laughed. "Come on, Ruby. You know you want to."

"Oh, alright," laughed Ruby.

Ruby and Maude walked out to the barn a half hour later to round up Mavis and let Jameson know that they would be leaving for the afternoon.

"Guess us men folk will have to fend for ourselves, huh Wilbur?" Jameson winked at him.

"Yes, sir. That's what it looks like," Wilbur smiled over at Jameson.

"Behave for Grandma Montgomery, sugar," Jameson said. He hugged Mavis tightly and kissed her on the top of her head. "What are y'all two going to do while Mavis entertains her great grandmother with her wild tales?"

"We were thinking of heading down to the theatre to sit in on the auditions for the Christmas play," Maude smiled.

"Oh my! I bet that'll be a ruckus in itself," Jameson laughed. "Y'all have fun and try not to send Opal into another tizzy. She near about took out the magnolia tree on her way out of her earlier."

"Cross my heart I'll behave. Can't say the same about Ruby," Maude winked.

"Oh goodness! I'm only going so I can be a witness when the law has to come pull those two off each other. I swear y'all two make me grayer every day!" Ruby chided. "Jameson, there's leftover ham in the fridge if you want to make some sandwiches for later."

Jameson kissed Ruby goodbye and waved as her car backed out of the long driveway.

"I bet this Christmas pageant will put that one we saw a few weeks ago to shame. Every year is a different play, but it's always about Christmas. I know you're already counting down the days," Jameson said to Wilbur as they walked back to the barn. "All teasing aside, it really is a lot of fun to go see. We all get dressed up and have a nice party over at the house after the matinee on Sunday. Ruby makes these little molasses cookies that will change your life."

"Better than the lemon ones?" Wilbur asked.

"Ten times better. They're sin on a plate," Jameson told him with a wink.

Wilbur smiled, although he seriously doubted anything could be better than the lemon cookies Ruby made. They finished working on the tractor an hour later and decided it was the perfect stopping point for lunch.

"What are we going to work on this afternoon?" Wilbur asked, before taking a bite of his ham sandwich.

"I just have a couple of odd things to tidy up before I go out of town on Monday," Jameson answered. He balanced the knife on top of the mayonnaise jar to use for his next sandwich.

"You're going away?" Wilbur asked him.

"Only for two weeks. I have a business trip up to Nashville for a conference and a few classes. I'm teaching a lecture at one of the colleges there, too. Ruby used to go with me, but with Mavis, it's hard for her to get away," Jameson told him.

Wilbur shrugged, but continued to eat his sandwich. These next few weeks were going to be awfully boring without his adventures around the Manor.

Meanwhile, Ruby and Maude dropped Mavis off to Mrs. Montgomery who lived twenty minutes from the Manor and made their way back into town.

"What about Chubby's?" Maude asked.

Chubby's Chicken Coop was the best place to get fall off the bone fried chicken this side of the Mississippi. Ruby agreed and turned her car into the small parking lot near the bank. They ordered at the greasy counter, took their table numbers to the closest booth, and sat down.

"I'm so hungry, I could eat these!" Maude said. She picked up the cheap rooster shaped salt and pepper shakers and looked around. "I hope those livers are extra crispy. Ain't nothing better than crispy fried chicken livers."

Thankfully the teenager behind the counter brought over their chicken dinners before Maude had to resort to eating the plastic tableware.

"Oh yes, crispy as can be. Want to try one?" Maude asked.

Ruby politely shook her head and said she would stick with her fried chicken breast meal.

"You don't know what you're missing," Maude said with her mouth full. "These taste just like my granny used to make."

When they finished their lunch, they hurried back to the car to beat the afternoon rain shower. When they pulled into the theatre's parking lot a few minutes later, they were surprised to see so many cars already there.

"I thought Opal said auditions didn't start until one o'clock?" Maude said.

"I reckon all these people are here to audition."
Ruby replied.

"Or are like us, here to laugh at those who audition," Maude said under her breath.

Maude followed Ruby through the ornate doors and saw the first three rows of seats full of people of all ages. Ricky sat in a director's chair in the center of the stage. He wore dark sunglasses and a red beret that matched his tight red pants. Opal sat on the edge of the stage with her legs dangling off.

Maude and Ruby managed to slip into one of the last rows without attracting any attention. Opal hopped gracefully from the stage and began to collect sheets of paper from everyone in the crowd. She handed them to Ricky and sat down between Eddie and Mortimer in the audience. Ricky began to read through the stack of papers and cleared his throat a few times.

"Ok, thank you all for coming here today to audition for our fabulous Christmas play. I see we have quite a bit of talent here today. I'm going to call you up one by one and hear your prepared monologues. I will cut you off after I've heard what I think is enough, so please don't be offended if I let you do the whole thing or cut you off after a few lines. Ok, Opal darling, will you be the first?"

Eddie and Mortimer immediately jumped to attention to help Opal back onto the stage. Opal positioned herself and began her dramatic piece that she had clearly written herself. Once finished, she bowed and accepted help from Eddie and Mortimer again to reclaim her seat.

"As usual, that was perfection. Next, may I have Edward Walker followed by Marcia Walters," Ricky announced.

One by one, people began their monologues. Ricky stopped most of them after thirty to forty seconds. When Mortimer Raven's name was called, the room fell silent. He walked up the six steps to the stage and took a deep breath. Ricky stopped Mortimer after ten seconds and thanked him.

"I believe everyone has now performed their prepared piece. We will take a short ten minute break and when we return, I will call you all up to read some scenes," Ricky said.

Everyone disbanded and began to mill about. "I knew you'd show up!" Opal called across the theatre.

Before Maude or Ruby could react, Opal crossed the length of the room and pointed her finger less than an inch from Maude's nose. "I'll fill out your paper for you and make sure we read a few scenes together! Thank you for bringing her Ruby!"

"Oh no!" Maude shouted. "I ain't here for that."

"We'll see about that," Opal smiled ruefully.

Opal skipped back to the stage and began to help Ricky pair up people based on their sheets of paper. Once the ten minutes were up, Ricky began to group people accordingly.

"I have handed out different scenes for some informal readings. Now, please raise your hand if you would like to audition for a specific part and I will make sure I have you read for that character in the next round of scene work," Ricky smiled.

A few people raised their hands, including Mortimer.

Ricky shook his head quickly. He began to go down the line asking what roles the people who raised their hands preferred. "And what role do you prefer, Mortimer??"

"Fezziwig," Mortie said.

Ricky began to choke on his Coca-Cola. When he finally cleared his throat, he asked for clarification. "You want to read for Fezziwig?"

"But, of course," Mortie tilted his head to the side and nodded again slowly.

Ricky shook his head vigorously. "Of course," he squeaked, shuffling the pages in front of him.

In the back row, Maude gasped. "Fezziwig? The short, little, happy guy?"

Ruby elbowed her sharply. "Hush, Maude!"

"Well, alright then. Here you are," Ricky squeaked. He handed Mortie a piece of paper and began to call up the groups to read their scenes. When it came time for the next round of readings, Ricky called Mortimer up to read for Fezziwig and Eddie to read for Scrooge.

"Whenever you're ready," Ricky told them.

To his credit, Mortimer delivered each line with his characteristic monotone drawl, although on one occasion when there was humor involved, he turned toward Ricky and curled the edges of his lips upward into a painful attempt at a smile. When this happened, Ricky cowered a little bit further into his seat.

"Dear God, that'd scare the hair off a cat," Maude whispered with a grimace.

"Hush, Maude," Ruby smiled, trying to keep from giggling.

When Eddie and Mortimer finished their scene, Ricky straightened himself in his chair and fidgeted with his papers some more. He cleared his throat loudly. "That," he began to stutter, "that was certainly the most interesting interpretation we've heard this afternoon." He cleared his throat again. "Thank you, Mortimer."

"Richard," Mortimer bowed again before returning to his seat.

Ricky began fanning himself quickly. "Okay," he said once he caught his breath, "Edward, please stay here and read again as Scrooge, and Lionel, please come read for Marley."

"Let's scoot out the back before Opal has us reading for Tiny Tim," Maude whispered to Ruby.

"How in the world could we read for Tiny Tim?" Ruby asked her.

"If Mortimer can be Fezziwig, anything is possible," Maude replied. "That was the scariest thing I've ever seen."

Ruby agreed. "It was worse than when Opal went skinny dipping in Graceland!"

They both doubled over in laughter as they walked back to the car.

~Chapter Nine~

Ruby was worried sick. She wouldn't admit it out loud, but Opal could see it in the way she scrubbed her mother's cast iron skillet. Opal shot Maude a look, but Maude shook her head slightly.

"Leave her be," Maude whispered.

Ruby sighed heavily and dried the skillet before putting it away. "I need to run and get Mavis from school. Y'all want to meet us for dinner later this evening?"

"Better yet, how about we bring y'all dinner and after you put Mavis to bed, we can crack open a bottle of wine and gossip like the Baptists we are!" Maude laughed.

"That sounds fine," Ruby said dully. She dried her hands on the nearby dish towel and grabbed her keys from the hook by the front door.

Opal and Maude followed Ruby out of the door. "I've got a cut and color this afternoon followed by a perm for Mrs. Lavonia, but those shouldn't take me long. What are your plans?" Opal asked Maude.

"I figured I'd come up there and let you touch up my roots," Maude replied.

"Oh goody," Opal smiled. "Always a pleasure." Opal rolled her eyes at Ruby hoping to make her laugh, but Ruby got into her car silently and backed out of the driveway without a wave.

"Want to ride over to the shop with me?" Maude asked.

"On your death mobile? Absolutely not. Come on or we'll be late," Opal said.

Maude begrudgingly got into Opal's car. Opal had just enough time to touch up Maude's graying roots before Mrs. Ethel arrived for her weekly cut and color.

"She always comes on Friday afternoon," Opal explained.

"I don't know why. It's not like she has a thriving social life," Maude whispered to Opal as they heard the bell chime on the front door.

"You haven't seen the way that ol' widower Johnson eyes her every Sunday at church," Opal winked.

"Really? Oooh, then maybe we should do something extra special. In the name of true love and all." Maude clapped her hands together.

Opal was already off rummaging through her cabinet full of her new and, as of yet, not thoroughly tested hair care products. It looked as if Color Me Crazy was about to get its first victim. Maude watched in excited suspense as Opal set out to work on the poor unsuspecting Mrs. Ethel. It was almost like waiting for a train wreck to happen all the while hoping for a miracle. Opal chatted on and on until she finally turned the conversation toward the nice Mr. Johnson and how sad it was that he was still single after all this time alone. Mrs. Ethel heartedly agreed with a sly little smile.

"You know, rumor has it that he cast his eye over in your direction once or twice at church," Maude offered casually.

"I don't know what you're talking about," Mrs. Ethel replied with a school girl giggle.

"I think we should go something extra special this week. Make sure he can't take his eyes off of you!" Opal said.

"What do you have in mind?" Mrs. Ethel was all ears.

"I know just the thing. You just sit back and relax," Opal said, spinning the chair around away from the mirror.

A few hours later, she locked up the front door of the beauty parlor while Maude watched Mrs. Ethel get into her car. Mrs. Lavonia had long since been permed and sent on her way, but Mrs. Ethel's situation called for extra time.

When they were safely in Maude's car heading back to Ruby's, Maude turned to Opal and asked. "Granted, I've never understood why little ol' women insist on dying their hair purple, but why did you add the green highlights?"

"It wasn't purple. It was lavender. And now she looks like a beautiful flower," Opal explained as though it was the most natural reason of all.

"She looks like she's been smoking some flowers," Maude replied.

By the time Maude and Opal got dinner from Mike's Seafood, Mavis and Ruby were seated at the table waiting for them. They ate quickly and Ruby put a sleepy Mavis to bed. Ruby turned the lights off in the kitchen and joined Maude and Opal in the living room.

"Jameson will be home in a few hours," Ruby sighed. "I haven't wanted to bother him about my suspicions, but Wilbur hasn't come by at all these past two weeks. I'm worried about him. What if Pete has hurt him or something?"

"I wondered the same thing, so I had Teddy drive by there this afternoon. He said Wilbur was out in the front yard when he rode by. Pete's truck was out back, so everything looked normal. He said the boy looked fine, or at least like he always does," Maude shrugged.

The news seemed to calm Ruby's nerves some, but she couldn't shake the ache that she felt nonetheless. She missed him bounding in through the front door. She missed his smile when Mavis asked him to play dolls with her. She missed the sounds of him laughing when Opal did something funny. If truth be told, it hurt her that Wilbur was absent while Jameson was gone. Did the boy only want to spend time at the Manor when Jameson was around? She best not think about all of that now.

"Did you hear that Nadine went on a date last night?" Opal said. She hoped that by changing the subject, Ruby would feel better.

"With who?" Maude asked. "Who'd want to date that old cow?"

"Elton Judson," Opal laughed.

"Do what?" Maude guffawed. "Elton? Oh Lord, I bet that was a fun one!"

"Elton's always been real sweet," Ruby said. "He's a nice fellow."

"I wouldn't say nice," Opal laughed. "He's so sleazy."

"I hope he buttoned his shirt," Maude laughed. "Every time I see him around town he has his top three buttons wide open. Nobody wants to see that."

"I think he does that on purpose," Opal said. "When he came by the salon last week for a shave, he had all the buttons undone. I accidentally spilled some root powder and well, I think he got the message."

"Opal!" Ruby exclaimed.

Elton was the only insurance salesman in Rhinestone. He considered himself quite the ladies man. He had the shiniest bald head and could bench press a Buick if he wanted to, according to him. He wore tight white pants everywhere he went, but didn't seem to like tight shirts. He wore the baggiest button down shirts he could find and had trouble keeping them buttoned up.

"Well, are you going to give us the details or not?" Maude asked.

"It was for my line of natural products. Powdered root from the hickory trees over yonder. I ground them up and added them to the paste I made from the pine needles," Opal explained.

"Not the powder stuff! I want details on the date!" Maude huffed.

"Oh! Well, I don't know anything really. Eddie told me that Elton came by his flower shop and bought a bunch of red roses to be delivered to Nadine. Guess the date went well," Opal shrugged.

Maude cut herself another big slice of pound cake and asked how rehearsals were going.

"Fine, fine," Opal said. "Once everyone finally accepted their roles. Speaking of Nadine."

"Did you hear about that Ruby?" Maude asked.

Ruby shook her head and picked at her piece of cake.

"Oh yea, it was rough for a bit. When Ricky posted the cast list Thursday night, some people weren't too happy about it. Poor Ricky agonized over it for days before he felt comfortable announcing it," Opal said. "Of course some were no brainers. Eddie is the perfect Scrooge. His voice is perfect for the part. Ricky is Bob Cratchett obviously and I'm the Spirit of Christmas Past and Ricky's wife. You know, since I can handle double roles."

"I think those are all perfect. Who was upset though?" Ruby asked.

"Nadine for one. Mortie wasn't too happy at first either, but he accepted it after I talked to him," Opal smiled sheepishly.

"Fezziwig?" Ruby asked.

"Not quite," Opal explained. "Ricky thought he would make a better Spirit of Christmas Yet to

Come. Mortie didn't quite agree. He said the character was a little too dark and creepy. Plus he doesn't have any lines, which I think really bothered him. That particular spirit just stands around and points a lot. So, I persuaded Ricky to also let him be Jacob Marley which Mortie was agreeable to. Nadine on the other hand wasn't as easily persuaded. For some reason she got it in her head that she was supposed to be my role. Can you imagine?"

"Well, what part did she get?" Ruby asked.

"The fat ghost!" Maude interrupted. She couldn't control her laughter.

"The Spirit of Christmas Present," Opal sneered. She will have to wear a fat suit and a wig. She has a decent amount of lines though, so I'm not sure why she got her panties in a wad. But she eventually came around."

"What changed her mind?" Ruby asked.

"I told her if she didn't want to be in the show, Maude would gladly take on the role. I knew she'd never give up her time to shine to Maude. Even if it is in a heavy costume," laughed Opal.

"You didn't tell me that!" Maude gasped.

"I can't wait to see this show," Ruby announced in between fits of laughter. "I'll be front row!"

"You better be! This is going to be a hit for sure," Opal said.

"What time did you say Jameson would be home?" Maude asked.

"He said it'd be later after I went to bed, but I may stay up. I don't sleep well when he's not home," Ruby said. "I have a couple of crosswords and a new book to keep me busy."

Opal yawned loudly and elbowed Maude. "I think it's about time we head home. I'll follow you so you don't run me off the road," Opal told Maude.

"I reckon you're right," Maude said.

"I have to work all day tomorrow, but I'll see you Sunday after church," Opal told Ruby. "Maude, I'll need your help tomorrow at the shop. I've got a full book and Molly can't answer the phones and check people out while she's shampooing."

Maude nodded and grabbed her purse from the table. "Free labor is all I'm good for," she winked at Ruby.

Ruby locked the door behind her friends and settled into her recliner to wait for Jameson to get home. By the time he arrived, Ruby had long since dozed off. He put away his suitcase, checked on Mavis, and sat down in his own recliner to eat a piece of cake. It was good to be home.

"Ruby, it's time to go to bed, sweetheart," Jameson said once he had put the plate in the kitchen sink.

Ruby looked up. "You snuck in without me hearing you."

"Yeah, I think we need to invest in a guard dog for you and Mavis. You can sleep through a hurricane," Jameson laughed.

"Oh, hush, we have enough cats," she said. She stood up and gave him a big hug. "It's good to have you home. I've missed you."

"I missed you, too. New York is fine and all, but they don't have your pound cake," Jameson laughed.

Ruby shook her head and rolled her eyes. Ruby filled him in on the adventures at home and around town while he had been away. Together they walked up the stairs to their room.

"That play is going to be a hoot," Jameson laughed.

"Yeah, can you imagine?" Ruby shook her head.

"So, how was Wilbur while I was away? You haven't mentioned him. Did he eat you out of house and home?" Jameson asked.

"No. As a matter of fact, he hasn't been by since you left," Ruby turned out the lamp on her side of the bed.

"What?" Jameson asked.

Finally, she began to tell him everything that had been bothering her these last two weeks. She told him about Teddy checking on him and about her fear. She didn't mention how hurt she had been, although he knew her well enough to know how much she missed the boy.

"I'm sure he's alright," Jameson comforted her. "All the same, if we don't see him tomorrow morning first thing, I'm going to take a ride out there and see about him."

For the first time in two weeks, some of the tension seemed to leave her shoulders and she slept soundly.

The next morning, Wilbur walked up the back porch steps of the Manor. For some reason he felt a bit nervous as he knocked on the door. He hadn't been here in two weeks. There was no reason to come over since Mr. Jameson was out of town and there were no projects to work on together. He hated to admit it, but he had really missed this place. He missed the smell of something delicious baking in the oven. He missed sounds of Mavis chasing after the chickens and the cats in the yard. He missed the creaking of the swing as they sat in the afternoon breeze whittling. Most of all, he missed the Montgomerys. He missed feeling like he might be part of something more, a part of a family.

"Wilbur!" Jameson greeted. "I was starting to wonder about you. I was just about to drive over to your house and see if you were alright."

Wilbur looked around for the clock on the wall. "But I thought I was supposed to come over around eight o'clock."

"Ruby said you didn't come by once while I was gone. She's been about to climb the walls. If you hadn't shown up on time, we were going to have to send out a search party for you." Jameson smiled at him. "What's been keeping you so busy?"

Wilbur shrugged. "I didn't know I was supposed to come when you weren't here." He looked down at his feet uncomfortably.

"Supposed to?" Jameson asked.

"I mean, you didn't tell me there was anything you needed me to work on while you were gone. I didn't know I was supposed to come over," Wilbur explained without looking up at Jameson.

"Wilbur," Jameson knelt down beside him. "You don't have to come over here because you're supposed to. That's not what any of this is about. You are welcome here anytime, day or night."

Wilbur finally met his eyes.

Jameson smiled, "I hate to be the one to break this to you, but Ruby long ago decided you were one of her people. She and those friends of ours claimed you long ago."

Wilbur began to smile.

"And so have I," Jameson continued.

Wilbur felt a tear trickle down his cheek and he turned quickly to wipe it away. Jameson waited patiently until they were once again face to face.

"You're always welcome here. Okay?" Jameson smiled gently as the boy absorbed the words.

Wilbur nodded and smiled. Jameson turned at the sound of Ruby and Mavis coming into the kitchen.

"Honey, look what the cat drug in!" Jameson said to Ruby. He stepped aside so she could get a clear look at Wilbur.

"Wilbur!" Ruby and Mavis exclaimed. Ruby ran over and gave him a rib shattering hug. "I've been so worried about you."

Wilbur hugged her back equally as tight. She finally let him go and held him out at arm's length to look at him properly.

"You didn't come visit me not once while Jameson was gone," Ruby said as she brushed some loose hair from his eyes.

"I'm sorry," Wilbur said, looking down at his feet again.

"It's alright, sweetheart. As long as you're okay, that's all that matters." She gave him a quick kiss on top of the head. "Have you eaten yet?"

"No ma'am," Wilbur answered.

"Well, breakfast will be a little bit. I'm getting a late start this morning. I was up half the night reading a book that Jameson's mother gave me," Ruby smiled. She turned to the stove and continued to ramble on about the book she had been reading.

Wilbur wasn't really listening. He was simply glad they wanted him back. He would make sure not to miss another weekend.

"Sit here," Mavis instructed. Wilbur slid into the empty chair next to her and helped her peel the orange in her chubby hand. "Big Mama's making waffles this morning. Waffles and bacon!"

Waffles and bacon sounded perfect to Wilbur.

Chapter Ten

The holidays usually had Magnolia Manor bursting at the seams. This Thanksgiving was no exception. The Manor was full of people, just like Ruby liked. A full home meant a full heart.

Jameson had woken up early to smoke the turkey and bake the ham. Maude and Opal arrived early Thursday morning to help Ruby prepare for so many guests. A few minutes after ten, Wilbur walked in carrying a sack full of pecans. All of Ruby's favorites were now present.

"Oh perfect! Thank you honey," Ruby said. Wilbur scampered off to help Jameson with the turkey outside.

"Alright, Ruby, let me find a place for my Jell-O salad in the refrigerator. Then, tell me what we need to do," Opal announced after she pulled all of the ingredients for the day from the full fridge.

"I keep telling you, Jell-O is not a salad," Maude told her. She moved the box she had brought with her that contained her signature green bean casserole and sweet potato soufflé off the table to make room for more pans. She reached in her purse and pulled out a small bag of candy.

"That's because you have no couth. I made this just for you. It's about time you started eating healthy," Opal told her. "Hey! Don't eat that. Wait for the other guests to arrive." Opal snatched the candy wrapper from Maude's hand and ate the candy instead.

"Hey! That was my last one. How in the world is that Jell-O stuff supposed to be healthy?" Maude asked.

"It's a secret," Opal smirked.

"That woman is going to be the death of me yet," Maude mumbled as she went to the hallway to hang up her jacket.

"What exactly did you put in it?" Ruby had to know.

"Nothing much. I just ground up some prunes and mixed them in there." Opal turned to see Maude walking back into the kitchen. "And like I was saying, Ruby," she winked at her friend, "it's got a jar of cherries, some marshmallows, chopped nuts, and a can of pineapple. Then you just fold in the tub of whip cream."

"And that's supposed to be healthy?" Maude asked.

"The cherries are organic," Opal shrugged.

Maude rolled her eyes. She was already fed up with Opal and her crazy fad diets.

Ruby stifled a laugh and continued to make the pies. "Y'all hush. We've got to get this dinner on the table or we'll never eat."

"Right you are Ruby!" Opal rolled up her sleeves to get to work. "Have you mixed up the dressing yet?"

"Not yet. I made the cornbread for it yesterday. It's on the big dining table along with the cake. I was just about to boil the macaroni noodles," Ruby said, reaching in the cabinet for a large pot.

"I'll grab the cornbread," Opal said. "Maude, you start grating the cheese."

Maude was pulling a large block of cheddar out of the refrigerator as Opal spoke. "I'm already ahead of you, bossy."

Ten minutes later, Maude was layering the macaroni and cheese to go in the oven and Ruby stirred the corn on the stove.

"Good lord, Ruby. How much cornbread did you make? There's enough for three pans of dressing here?" Opal asked.

"It might have grown a little more than I intended," Ruby told her.

"What did you feed it? Miracle Grow?" Opal replied.

"It's organic!" Maude smirked. "That's why it grew so big. It's healthy!"

"You wouldn't know healthy if it bit you on your backside! Why don't you stick to what you know best, Maude? Like donuts and pound cake!" Opal sassed back.

"Will you two stop it," Ruby told them. "It's Thanksgiving. We're all supposed to be happy and thankful."

"I am plenty thankful. Thankful you two have me around to keep your life interesting," Opal smiled.

Ruby laughed and tossed the dish rag at Opal.

"And it's a time to eat and not care what anyone else thinks! Anyway, what time's everyone getting here again?" Maude asked sulkily.

"Jameson is going to pick up his mother around two and Opal's guests should be arriving before three, right Opal? So there's no time to waste," Ruby answered. "When is Teddy coming?"

"He said he should get off around four today, so he should be over not long after that," Maude replied. "That's the plan at least."

"We can make him a plate if something comes up," Ruby said.

"Will all of your escorts be arriving together?" Maude asked Opal.

Opal rolled her eyes. "Of course not. Eddie and Ricky should be here around three like I said earlier, but Mortie will be on call all day long. It's a lonely, but busy calling being the only embalmer in town. He said be sure not to wait on him," Opal said solemnly.

"Jameson said the Cowboys kickoff at four, so we should be able to eat before that ruckus starts," Ruby laughed.

Jameson took Mavis to pick up his mother and by the time he returned, Eddie and Ricky had arrived. Every time the front door opened, all heads turned towards the noise to see who was entering. When the last dish came out of the oven a few minutes after three, Jameson said the blessing and everyone dug in.

The kitchen was host to a full feast. There was an entire turkey and ham to be devoured. Potato soufflé, sweet corn, green bean casserole, butternut squash, dressing, macaroni and cheese, cranberry sauce, buttered rolls, and a table full of desserts also lay in wait. Pecan and pumpkin pies, lemon bars, pumpkin cheesecake, Opal's Jell-O salad, a hummingbird cake, and a bowl full of cinnamon spiced applesauce had already been sampled throughout the morning.

When everyone had their fill, Ruby, Maude, Opal, and Mrs. Montgomery covered all of the dishes in case anyone got hungry later. They tidied up the kitchen and retired to the front porch to eat their dessert away from the loud yells and cheers coming from the room full of men watching their football game. Mavis swung on the old tire swing not far from the porch without a care in the world.

By the time Teddy arrived, the Dallas Cowboys and Seattle Seahawks had already kicked off. He made himself a heaping plate and sat on the floor in front of the television in the living room with Jameson, Wilbur, Eddie, and Ricky.

"If Landry has any sense, he'll put Hershel Walker in there," Jameson told Wilbur. "Dallas will have this game in the bag!"

"You're crazy," Teddy said. "Seattle's going to beat Dallas by a landslide."

"I don't know. I'm with Jameson on this one. Dallas is going to come through," Eddie said.

As the game went on, Mrs. Montgomery decided she was ready to go home. Ruby went to get the car keys and tapped Jameson on the shoulder. "We're going to go on and take your mother home," Ruby whispered.

"It's almost half time," he said. "I can take her in just a few minutes."

"It's fine," Ruby said sweetly. "She's ready to get on back home to check on the dogs. You know how she is. I've already made her a few plates to take back with her. I'm taking Mavis, too."

Ten minutes later, as the seconds ticked off the game clock to signify half time, Teddy and Jameson stood up to stretch. "About time for round two," Jameson laughed. Wilbur followed them back to the kitchen to eat some more of the delicious Thanksgiving food.

"I think I'm going to get a slice of pumpkin pie," Eddie announced. "You want anything, Ricky?"

Ricky shook his head and kept his eyes glued to the television screen. The Dallas Cowboy cheerleaders had arrived in the center of the field for their halftime show.

"On second thought, I think I better stay right here," Eddie said. He sank back down on the couch next to Ricky to watch what Ricky called the most exciting part of the whole afternoon.

Ricky moved to the beat of the songs and seemed to know their routines by heart. "I always wanted to be a cheerleader when I was younger," Ricky explained.

By the time the second half kicked off, Ruby, Maude, Opal, and Mavis returned to the Manor. They ignored the loud cheers from the living room and sent Mavis upstairs to get ready for bed. The three women settled around the dining room table already exhausted from the events of the day.

"Well I'll be!" Maude exclaimed. "Who knew cooking and eating all day could be so tiring!"

"Well, you sure ate enough for all of us," Opal laughed.

"Oh hush, I'm too tired to even argue with you," Maude replied.

Suddenly there was a loud succinct knock on the back door.

"Who in the devil could that be?" Ruby asked.

Maude jumped to her feet and cracked the door open slightly. "Who goes there?" she asked in a deep voice.

"It is I, Mortimer Raven," the voice on the other side of the door said.

"Mortie!" Opal laughed. "Why'd you come to the back door? You scared us!"

"My apologies," Mortimer replied. "I tried the front door, but no one answered. I assumed it rude to enter one's property without invitation. Good evening, my dear. And good evening, Ms. Cooper and Mrs. Montgomery."

"Hello!" Maude and Ruby squeaked. "Happy Thanksgiving!"

"Let's get you fed," Opal said. She took Mortimer by the hand and led him to the kitchen.

A few minutes later Maude and Opal heard the loudest collection of screams they had ever heard. They jumped up and ran through the kitchen to the living room where they found Opal curled up on the floor laughing hysterically. Ricky was in Teddy's arms, Jameson and Wilbur were wide eyed in the recliners, and Eddie was crouched behind Jameson's chair.

"What in the Sam Hill is going on here?" yelled Maude.

"I suspect I gave them quite a fright," Mortimer said.

"Ahh!" Maude screamed. "I didn't see you there!"

Mortimer emerged from the corner of the room holding his plate of food in one hand and his glass of iced tea in the other. "My apologies, madam," Mortimer said.

"He damn near gave me a heart attack," Eddie said. He stood up and shook his head. "Came up right behind me and asked what we were watching. I thought it was a ghost!"

"Specters and apparitions only exist in the mind, Edward. And in the theatre, as Richard can attest to," Mortimer smiled.

"Um, right," Ricky nodded.

"Oh Mortie, so wise!" Opal smiled.

Maude helped Opal off the floor and told the men to get back to their football game. She clutched her chest and walked back to the dining room followed by Ruby. Opal joined them a few minutes later still laughing.

"You should've seen them," Opal said. "I swear! A group of grown men afraid of little old Mortie."

Maude and Ruby both stared at Opal like she had three heads.

"I tell you, those three are a full time job. Once I got Ricky away from Teddy and calmed down Eddie, Mortie said he would just eat in the kitchen. I told him I'd sit with him, but he said he would need to eat quickly and get back to the funeral home. He works so hard," Opal sighed. "I'm going to see him off and then I'll be right back."

Ruby smiled politely as Opal went back to the kitchen with Mortimer.

"He still freaks me out, Ruby," Maude whispered.

Opal returned a few minutes later. "I let Mortie out the front," she said. "I hate that he didn't get to spend more time here tonight. At least we have rehearsals all next week together."

"You really like him, don't you?" Ruby asked.

"Of course! What's not to like?" Opal smiled.

"What about Eddie and Ricky?" Maude asked.

"What about them?" Opal asked.

"You said you liked Mortimer, so?" Maude said.

"That doesn't mean I can't equally like Eddie and Ricky." Opal replied. "I like them all in their own special way. I don't expect you to understand."

Ruby shook her head and silently begged Maude to let it go. By the sound of the noise coming from the living room, it sounded like the football game was finally over.

"If they wake up Mavis, I'm going to tan their hides!" Ruby yelped. She scurried to the kitchen.

"I kind of want to see that!" Maude laughed. She clapped Opal on the back and said, "I guess we better help clean up. It's getting to be my bedtime, too."

Thirty minutes later, Maude and Opal offered to drop Wilbur off at his house on their way home and surprisingly Wilbur accepted their offer. Though they weren't surprised when they were a little less than a quarter of a mile from his house, he said he would just walk the rest of the way.

"See you Saturday," Opal called after him.

Once Wilbur was out of sight, Maude yawned and said, "I'm going to sleep all day tomorrow and wake up refreshed Saturday morning!"

"I have to work all day tomorrow. The Friday after Thanksgiving is always a busy day. You'd be surprised at how many singed eyebrows there will be to wax. Keeping Rhinestone beautiful is a tough job," Opal sighed.

"Then I'll make sure I sleep extra long for you then," Maude laughed. Opal dropped Maude off at her door and then pulled through the grass to her own driveway. They both climbed straight into their beds and fell fast asleep.

While Maude slept and Opal worked to keep the residents of Rhinestone beautiful, Ruby, Jameson, and Mavis spent all Friday relaxing around the Manor. After Mavis went to bed, Ruby herself nodded off several times during Dallas. It was harder and harder to stay awake once she got comfortable in her chair. Jameson, who never cared about the Ewings that flashed across the television every Friday evening, sat in his recliner content to read a biography about Abraham Lincoln. Once the late night news had finished, he nudged Ruby on the arm and told her it was time for bed.

"I missed my show," she yawned. "What happened?"

Jameson shrugged. "Oh, you know. One of them slept with the other one and now somebody is mad about it."

"Jameson, you are no help. Now I'm not going to know what's going on next week," she told him.

"Don't worry. You can sleep through that one, too," he laughed.

They had only been in bed for a half hour when the phone rang. Any call at midnight was a bad sign. Jameson answered on the second ring. His end of the conversation was short. Ruby couldn't tell what was going on.

"I'll be there in a few minutes," he finally said.

"What's wrong?" she asked him as soon as he hung up the receiver.

"That was Teddy. Pete Reynolds has been arrested. They need someone to take temporary custody of Wilbur," he said. "It must be bad this time." He stood up and walked over to the closet to find fresh clothes to wear.

"Oh goodness. What did Pete do? Wilbur's not hurt is he?" Ruby asked.

"Don't think so. Pete got into a bar fight from what Teddy said. Don't know the details, but I'm guessing Wilbur was at home at the time," Jameson buckled his belt then sat down to tie his shoes.

"What in the world is Pete doing out this time of night anyway?" Ruby fumed at the idea of it.

"Seems like he was getting himself arrested. It'll be okay. I'll go get Wilbur and bring him home," Jameson smiled over at his wife.

"I'll go and make sure the guest room is ready. I don't know when I changed those sheets last. I need to open up the vent and let it warm up a bit before he gets here. Do you think he'll be hungry? Where is Wilbur now?"

"Teddy said they sent Leroy over to his house to get him. I'm going to meet them at the station. I don't think Wilbur will care about the sheets, but he'll probably want a little snack." He leaned over and kissed her on top of the head. "I'll be back as soon as I can."

Jameson met Teddy at the police station. Teddy gave him the details of Pete's arrest. Apparently, there had been a dispute over a rather heated game of cards. Words were exchanged and Floyd McAllister found himself flying through the front window of the Tipsy Toad. Pete proceeded to fight against two other patrons who were trying to restrain him. By the time the deputies arrived, several tables and chairs had been broken in the melee.

As they walked down the hallway, Jameson looked into the booking area where Pete was being photographed. The man had not come out of the fight unscathed. There was a noticeable cut over his swollen right eye. His nose appeared to be broken and his lip had a gash. Jameson thought he saw Pete sneer at him, but the man might have been grimacing in pain.

"We tried to get the paramedic to look at him, but he was fighting so much, he wouldn't let anyone get close. He refused all medical attention," Teddy shrugged.

"He'll feel it when the alcohol wears off," Jameson said.

"Yep. That'll be fun," Teddy agreed.

They continued walking down the corridor until they came to the last room on the left. Wilbur was sitting in the metal chair across the table from Leroy who was about to thump a triangular folded paper through a makeshift goal post.

Leroy looked up to see Teddy and Jameson standing there. "You got here just in time. This young man was beating me something bad," he said, trying to coax a smile out of the boy.

Wilbur looked up at Jameson.

"Thanks Leroy. Thanks Teddy. Come on, Wilbur. It's time to go home," Jameson told him. He took the boy back down the hallway without a glance back at Pete.

Chapter Eleven

Ruby woke up early to make homemade buttermilk pancakes, bacon, and a mixed fruit salad. When Jameson came down the stairs with a drowsy Mavis, she poured tall glasses of orange juice for them all.

"Where's Wilbur?" Ruby asked.

"I showed him how to turn on the shower water and told him to come on down when he was done," Jameson responded. "After we eat, I'll run him over to his house to pick up some of his things. Then I'll need to run by the office and sign some papers. It looks like Pete's going to be in there for some time."

"That man," Ruby started to say. She scrubbed the sink and let that thought fizzle out.

Jameson cut up Mavis' pancakes and added just the right amount of syrup. When Wilbur came down the stairs a few minutes later, they all gathered around the table for breakfast.

"These sure are good honey," Jameson smiled at Ruby. "Wilbur, when we finish eating breakfast, I'll take you by your house to pick up some things and then swing by my office. When we finish, we'll come on back here and work on some things. Remember that project I was telling you about." Jameson winked at Wilbur who smiled slyly.

"What are you two going on about?" Ruby asked.

"Nothing dear. Don't you worry your pretty little head about it," Jameson smiled. "Did you sleep well, Wilbur?"

"Yes sir," Wilbur said.

"Wilbur, did you sleep here?" Mavis asked.

Wilbur swallowed what was in his mouth and looked at Ruby before nodding to Mavis.

"Wilbur is going to be staying here with us for a little bit, sugar," Jameson smiled.

"You can sleep in my room if you want!" Mavis said. "I can share my toys with you."

"Thanks Mavis," Wilbur said. He smiled ear to ear as he poured more syrup onto his pancakes.

When they were all finished eating, Jameson turned to Wilbur and asked, "Ready to go?"

Wilbur nodded and pulled on his shoes. "We'll be back directly," Jameson said to Ruby.

Ruby watched them walk outside to Jameson's truck and pull out of the driveway.

"Big Mama, is Wilbur gonna live here forever?" Mavis asked.

"He'll be staying with us for the time being, sugar," Ruby smiled. She kissed Mavis on the top of her head. "What do you think about that?"

"I think he should stay forever. He's nice," Mavis mused. Before Ruby could respond, Mavis hurried up the stairs to her room to play.

Ruby cleaned the kitchen and mopped the downstairs floor while the boys were gone. A few minutes before eleven, Maude and Opal arrived. Ruby could hear them before she saw their heads poke around the corner of the kitchen.

"Yoo-hoo Ruby!" Opal crooned.

Maude walked in behind Opal and stretched loudly. "I'm so tired," she yawned.

"I don't see how! I practically had to peel you out of bed this morning. Thank God you agreed to shower before coming here because Lord Almighty, you smelled!" Opal said.

"I don't know what it was, but something near about killed me. I reckon something I ate had me up and down all night Thursday. When I finally fell asleep, I didn't dare move," Maude shrugged.

"Well, you did eat a lot," Opal said.

"I felt fine until I ate the rest of your Jell-O salad before we left Ruby's Thursday night. I thought it was supposed to be healthy," Maude said.

"It was, but you're a walking toxin. It had a lot of work to do," Opal explained.

"I thought you were kidding about the prunes?" Ruby said aghast.

"What prunes?" Maude asked.

"Oh, don't worry Ruby! A few bites wouldn't hurt the average person. But Maude ate half the dish by herself," Opal smiled.

"What? So you were trying to kill me!" Maude shot back at her.

"If I wanted to kill you, you'd be dead," Opal told her calmly before turning her attention to Ruby. "Anyway, how goes it Ruby?" Opal changed the subject.

"Oh goodness, I've been waiting for y'all to get here. It's been one crazy thing after another," Ruby said. ""Let's sit down. I've been cleaning all morning and I'm already out of breath."

"Where's Jameson and Wilbur? He's usually here round this time," Maude interjected.

Ruby looked over at her. "They had to go down to Jameson's office and take care of all the paperwork," she told her.

"Paperwork for what?" Opal asked. Maude looked just as confused.

"You haven't talked to Teddy? I thought sure he'd tell you," Ruby was surprised.

"No, I haven't talked to him since Thanksgiving evening. Since he was off Thursday evening, he had to work all day Friday. We're going out tonight though. If I feel better, of course. Anyway, what's going on?" Maude asked.

"Well, Jameson got a call late last night and had to go pick up Wilbur from the police station. Pete got himself arrested and it looks like he'll be in for awhile. I don't know anything other than that right now. Jameson took Wilbur to get his things and to sign some temporary papers. Looks like he'll be staying with us for the time being." Ruby said.

"Teddy is as quiet as the tomb when it comes to his work. He never breathes a word of anything to anybody," Maude told them.

"That must be so hard for you," Opal said to Maude. "With you being an old busy body and all."

Maude shot Opal a dirty look and pursed her lips.

"I'm just saying," Opal replied.

"That explains why y'all weren't over here any sooner," Ruby said.

"Why didn't you call us? We'd have been right over here this morning. Or last night even," Maude ignored Opal and focused her attention on Ruby.

"I didn't want to say too much around Wilbur. Pete gets me so mad I'm liable to say something ugly," Ruby gritted her teeth.

"Well, that would be a first," Opal said.

"Don't worry; I've already said enough ugly stuff for both of us. That man could make the Pope cuss!" Maude told her.

"And he's such a nice man. It's really hard to get him mad like that. Y'all remember when we met him that one afternoon in Rome," Opal added.

"For the last time, you ain't met the Pope!" Maude snapped at her.

"Age hasn't been kind to you, Maude. That's ok, I can remember enough for both of us," Opal patted Maude on the arm.

The home phone rang on the wall across the kitchen and Ruby jumped up to answer it.

"Hello? Ok. Oh goodness. Absolutely. I'll see y'all when you get home," Ruby answered.

She hung up the phone and returned to the table. "That was Jameson," Ruby said. "They're finished at the office. Jameson said when they went to the house, Wilbur ran in and Jameson waited in the truck. When he came back, he had a small trash bag with two shirts and a pair of jeans. He had a couple of pencils and his toothbrush. Jameson said he's going to run him by the store to pick up a few things. Jameson said he's been living in filth, y'all. I just can't bear it."

"I'm not surprised," Maude said. "I'm glad he'll be in a home where he has everything he could ever need."

"Or ever want," Opal chimed in. "I'm glad I took the day off. Looks like we have work to do!"

"We can't do anything," Ruby laughed. "Best not to rock the boat."

"Y'all don't know how long he'll be here?" Maude asked.

Ruby shook her head and then shrugged her shoulders. "As long as the good Lord will allow," she sighed.

"Where's Big Daddy and Wilbur?" Mavis asked. She was carrying her doll's bicycle that was now missing its front wheel.

"They've gone into town for a little bit, sugar," Ruby explained.

"But I need them to fix the bike," Mavis showed Ruby the broken toy.

"I'm sure they'll take a look at it once they get back," Ruby told her.

"Wilbur is living here now," Mavis told Opal and Maude. "Is he going to be my new brother?" Mavis climbed in Ruby's lap.

"We'll just have to see, sweetheart," Ruby said.

"Ok. I'm hungry," Mavis announced.

"I'll fix us up some lunch," Opal said. "Maude, come help me. Let's see if I can teach you a thing or two!"

"No, you are not cooking for me twice in one week. I'll fix lunch, that way it'll be safe!" Maude told her.

"Oh stop it, I'm just going to reheat some of these leftovers," Opal said. "Plus, you ate all the Jell-O salad."

"I know how to warm up leftovers," Maude said.

"Well, well, well, I see you have been paying attention!" Opal smiled. "You'll snare Teddy soon enough with that knowledge."

"Don't you go on saying that. I ain't ever getting married again. Been there, done that. Teddy feels the same way. We're too old for that mess again," Maude laughed. "Speaking of marriage, when are you going to settle down with one of your beaus?"

"Oh Maude, there's enough of me to go around. Of course, no one could ever tie me down forever. I need to run free and stay wild," Opal smiled. She twirled around the kitchen using the whisk as a microphone. "I'm untamable!"

"Let's eat!" Maude said. She sat at the table with Opal, Ruby, and Mavis.

When Jameson and Wilbur pulled into the driveway two hours later, Wilbur went straight upstairs loaded down with shopping bags.

"Big Daddy! What did you bring me?" Mavis asked as she jumped into Jameson's outstretched arms.

"Well I did see something that I just knew you needed. Take a look in this bag," Jameson said.

"Another bow!" Mavis squealed. "This one is purple!" She hugged Jameson tightly before running upstairs.

"Where all did y'all go?" Ruby asked.

"I took him over to Junction to get some new slacks and shirts. He needed socks and underpants, too. I got him a new pair of shoes and new things for school. I told him to take them upstairs and put everything away in the dresser and closet. Ruby, if you'd seen his house down there by the creek, well, let's just say we can't let him go back there," Jameson said.

Ruby hugged Jameson and made him a plate. He sat down next to Opal at the table.

"What's the news with Pete?" Maude asked.

Jameson took the handkerchief out of his pocket and began wiping his glasses. "It doesn't look good for him. It's not exactly his first run in with the law." Jameson put his glasses back on. "Oh, he's mostly got drunk and disorderly charges. Nothing too violent, but that all changed a few months ago. Seems like he got arrested for a burglary over in Junction. He got off on some kind of technicality, but Mitch is pretty tired of seeing him in court. Told Pete the last time he was there that if he got in any more trouble, he was going to throw Pete under the jail," Jameson sighed heavily.

"So what's going to happen?" Ruby asked.

"Well, it looks like Mitch meant it. He denied bond which means Pete is going to be in jail until there's a hearing. Floyd's wanting to press charges. And Pete isn't making it any easier on himself," Jameson said.

"What do you mean?" Maude wondered aloud.

"Well, let's just say that Pete didn't choose the most diplomatic words when he was referring to Mitch and the entire legal system. Granted, he was nursing one heck of a hangover, but still, he didn't help his cause any," Jameson explained.

"Well then, how long will he be in jail? Won't he have to go to trial or something?" Opal asked.

"They'll revisit bond when he has his preliminary hearing. That usually takes a few weeks, but with the holidays, it might be a bit longer. We'll know more about what will happen after that. In the meantime, Pete will have the opportunity to finally sober up. That won't be pretty. Sobering up is a rough process, especially behind bars. He's in for a tough time," Jameson nodded.

"Serves him right!" Ruby told them. They all turned to her in surprise.

"Well, it does," Ruby continued. "After the way he's treated Wilbur. And his only son at that. Wilbur is such a good kid. He deserves someone who will raise him as his own. He deserves a family and Lord knows Pete's never given him anything close to that."

"You're not wrong, honey. Let's go see how it's going upstairs," Jameson said.

"Y'all run along. We're going to have another one of those lemon bars," Maude said.

Ruby followed Jameson upstairs to check on Wilbur's progress.

"How's it going up here?" Jameson called in the doorway.

"I've just about got everything settled in," Wilbur said.

Ruby peeked in through the door and saw that Jameson had not only bought Wilbur new clothes, but a stack of books, a new comforter for the bed, and a small suitcase. She kissed Jameson on the cheek and peeked in across the hall at Mavis' room. The little girl was brushing her doll's long black hair in the center of her pink bedspread. She asked her to put on her shoes so they could run to the store.

When Ruby and Mavis came back downstairs ten minutes later, Maude had already worked her way through two lemon bars.

"Jameson and Wilbur are going to get all of the Christmas stuff down from the attic this afternoon while I run into town. Y'all want to come?" Ruby asked.

"I better get Maude home so she can get ready for her date later this afternoon," Opal laughed. "And I've got rehearsal this evening. We took the last two nights off, so who knows how it's going to go. Ricky and I are going to a quick dinner beforehand so he can get all his jitters out before rehearsal. This show has been so hard on him already."

"I can't imagine," Ruby said. "It's such an iconic show and the cast sounds so, um, eclectic."

"It's definitely a classic. I just cannot wait for y'all to see it!" Opal said. "Anyway, we'll let y'all get settled. Let's have lunch at Chubby's Monday while the kids are in school."

"That sounds good to me," Ruby smiled. She collected Mavis' coat and ushered her out of the door to the car. "I'll see y'all Monday around noon." She waved goodbye to Maude and Opal and told Mavis they were going to pick up some groceries.

Ruby managed to find more than just groceries while she and Mavis were out. She bought four new red stockings to hang on the mantle along with a new wreath for the front door.

While Ruby and Mavis were out, Jameson and Wilbur took some quick measurements for a project they had been talking about for Ruby's upcoming Christmas present. Jameson had hired a company in town to construct a wall sized fish tank for Ruby who had always loved exotic fish. They were scheduled to install it in a few weeks.

For all Ruby knew, Jameson and Wilbur spent much of the afternoon hauling boxes out of the attic. By the time Ruby and Mavis returned home from town, they had the tree assembled and almost had the string of lights fully untangled.

"I don't know how in the world this thing ties itself in so many knots every year," Jameson muttered.

"Oh good, you remembered to get my nativity set down," Ruby said, clapping her hands together in anticipation.

"Of course. How could I forget that?" Jameson smiled. "Alright Wilbur, let's plug these in and make sure they all work."

Wilbur obliged. Of the four different light strands they had connected, one was blinking randomly, one stayed on continuously, one came on for a few seconds and promptly died, and the last one never lit up at all.

"Two of them don't seem to be working," Ruby said, looking at the lights stretched out across the floor.

"I see," he said. "We might have to get some new ones next week if I can't get these working. Hmm." He walked over to the box of miscellaneous light bulbs and proceeded to search for the right bulb to fix the problem. An hour later, he had all the strands on, although one still blinked randomly of its own accord.

Ruby looked up from the nativity set she had been arranging. "Oh good, the lights are working. Once we get those on the tree we can start decorating. Then, how does some hot cocoa sound?"

Jameson and Wilbur were definitely ready for some cocoa.

Chapter Twelve

"How'd it go this morning?" Maude asked. She was already picking the chicken from the bone of her deep fried wings.

"Just like Jameson said, Mitch denied Pete's bond. They set the next hearing for the thirtieth of December. Wilbur will be with us at least through Christmas," Ruby said, taking a sip of water.

"He should stay with y'all from now on," Opal said.

"I wish we could do that, but you know how the law is. It moves at its own pace," Ruby said.

"Well, I meant how did school drop off go, but we can jump ahead to that," Maude laughed.

"Oh! It went just fine. I pulled up to the front of the school and they both walked in together. They looked so cute walking into the school doors. You know he walked every day back and forth to school. Pete never once took that sweet child to the school. I doubt he even knows who his teachers are," Ruby fumed. Every time she thought about the way Pete treated Wilbur, she got madder than an old wet hen.

"Of course Pete never goes up to the schoolhouse. There's no whiskey in there," Maude shrugged and picked up a drumstick and took a huge bite. "There's got to be a way they can get him help."

"Jameson said he's about to sober up the hard way," Ruby said. She reached for one of the mini cheese biscuits.

"Yeah, but what about after he's out? That's when he needs to be sober," Maude said.

Opal nodded. "Ten to one he'll be back up at the bar before he goes home."

"If they let him back in," Maude nodded.

"They'll let him in," Opal said knowingly. "I heard from one of my customers, in strictest confidence of course, that the Tipsy Toad loses more than half their night's revenue when he's otherwise indisposed. They're all chums. They'll welcome him back with open arms."

"I don't know, Opal. Jameson said he tore that place up something bad during that fight," Ruby said.

"Once their tempers settle on down, they'll all make nice and it'll go back to normal," Maude said. "Plus, they need his money."

"How in the world can that be? I've never known Pete to do a day's work in his life," Ruby shook her head.

"Well, not an honest day's work anyway," Opal added quickly.

"What's that mean?" Ruby asked.

"He gets his disability every month, but he squanders it at the race track and at the bar mostly. I can't say specifically, but I hear he makes enough money from shine and other enterprises to more than pay for a few broken chairs."

"Opal, you know more about people in this town than they know about themselves!" Ruby exclaimed.

"I do hair, Ruby. What else are people going to talk about under the dryers if it ain't other people's business," Opal shrugged.

"Let's change the subject," Ruby said. "How did rehearsal go?"

"Rehearsal Saturday night was a rough one, I'll be honest. We have less than three weeks to tighten things up and I just don't know if we can get there," Opal lamented.

"Why do you say that?" Ruby asked.

"Nadine can't seem to stop complaining long enough to learn her lines, but rest assured she knows everyone else's. She calls herself the understudy to everyone, but she can't get her own blocking down to save her life. Eddie is a saint. I tell you, he's the main one in the scene with her, so he's having to work even harder to coax her along. Ricky finished her costume ahead of schedule and she had a fit once she put it on. She said no one would be able to recognize her in it, which I don't reckon is a bad thing," Opal explained.

"How's Mortie doing?" Maude asked.

"Perfect as always. He's always the calm and steady one at rehearsals. He's been helping Eddie with his lines on our nights off. I'm telling you, he really is an angel," Opal beamed.

"That's not exactly the word I'd use, but ok," Maude replied. "Ow! Why'd you kick me?"

"I didn't!" Opal fussed.

Maude glared at Ruby who continued to eat her chicken tenders. "I'm sure it's going to be amazing. We'll be there opening night for sure," Ruby said sweetly. "Right Maude?"

"I'll be there alright," Maude replied. She rubbed her sore shin underneath the table. "But I do have a question?"

"Yes?" Opal asked.

"Ain't it a little strange that all your boyfriends are together all the time? You just said Mortie's helping Eddie and Ricky's making their costumes and, damn't Ruby!" Maude yelped. "If you kick me one more time, I swear!"

Ruby ignored Maude's outburst and finished her coleslaw.

Maude pulled her legs up and said, "Like I was saying, ain't it weird that they're all buddy-buddy?"

"They're all perfect gentlemen, if that's what you mean. They aren't going to throw down and fight in the theatre for God's sake. They're professionals and they all respect me," Opal said aghast. "We theatre people have a bond."

"They have a bond alright," Maude muttered. "And trust me, it ain't the theatre."

"What's that supposed to mean?" Opal asked.

"You're a wild card, Opal, that's all I'm gonna say," Maude shrugged.

"Don't be jealous because I'm a free spirit and you're an ol' stick in the mud," Opal told her.

"Oh goodness, Maude. Leave Opal be. Let's change the subject again," Ruby said exasperated. "How did your date go Saturday?"

"It was ok," Maude said. "We ate at The Salty Cactus over in Junction and then saw a movie. I don't even remember the name of it. Teddy and I both fell asleep not long after it started," Maude laughed.

"I know the feeling. I'm tired nearly all the time," Ruby agreed. "I haven't seen a whole episode of Dallas in months. I'm going to have to wait until the reruns come on so I know what's going on."

"Why don't you ask Jameson? Y'all always watch TV together," Maude asked.

"He's too busy reading to pay attention to anything important happening on the television," Ruby shook her head.

"Y'all need more fiber in your diet," Opal explained. "I've got just the thing for you both."

"Thanks, but I'll pass," Maude sneered. "Last time I ate one of your concoctions I near about died."

"You didn't die, Maude. I swear, the older you get the more dramatic you get. My colonic seemed to work just fine. You're welcome," Opal shrugged.

"How many subjects can we keep changing to," Ruby said. "Goodness!"

"It is hard to keep Maude on track," Opal agreed.

"What plans do y'all have for Christmas? That should be a safe enough topic," Ruby joked.

"I can't focus on anything besides the play right now. I don't know if I'll ever get around to decorating this year," Opal said.

"Opal! You have to decorate! It's Christmas," Ruby exclaimed.

"Between the shop and the Christmas play, I barely have time to sleep. I had to hire a new girl just to help during the holiday rush. Emily does a good enough job sweeping up and shampooing, but let's just say her future isn't in hair," Opal said.

"You have to find some time to decorate. The Comb Over always has the prettiest window displays every holiday," Ruby replied.

"Y'all want to take over the decorating festivities this year?" Opal asked.

"Yes!" Ruby squealed.

"No!" Maude yelped at the same time.

"Perfect, then it's settled. All the decorations are in the back room. Maude has a key," Opal said.

"Wonderful. This is going to be so much fun, isn't Maude!" Ruby said in a high pitched voice.

"That's not the word I would have chosen," Maude stared from one to the other.

"Let's meet tomorrow morning after I drop the kids off at school. I can't wait!" Ruby squealed. "See you then!"

Opal skipped back over to The Comb Over and Ruby walked to her car in the parking lot leaving Maude to order another round of wings for herself.

As promised, Ruby walked through the doors of The Comb Over twenty minutes after dropping the kids off the next morning. Maude was already there. She had been enlisted in tidying up the supply closet while they waited for Ruby to arrive. Opal's first appointment wasn't until ten, so she had just enough time to direct where the boxes should go before her cut and color arrived.

Maude and Ruby spent nearly an hour going through the boxes full of lights, greenery, door wreaths, and window paint. "Good Lord, there's more stuff here than over at Ruth's Department Store!" Maude huffed.

Opal peeked around from Brenda Trotter's beehive and studied the scene in front of her. "Wait a minute? There's gotta be some more boxes in the back. I know Ms. Belva's reindeer collection and light up Santa are back there somewhere," she said.

"Maude, can you go look?" Ruby asked.

"Use the ladder and check in the upper storage," Opal directed.

Maude disappeared into the storage room and came out ten minutes later with three boxes stacked on top of each other. "A little help!" she yelled.

"Maude! Don't break anything!" Opal and Ruby yelled. They each took a box from her and set them down gently on the floor.

"Yep, these are it! Be careful with them. Ms. Belva collected these from the North Pole," Opal explained.

Maude rolled her eyes and began to unpack the boxes in front of her. She was tasked with putting the sleigh and reindeer for Santa's display on the table in front of the main window.

"Maude! What are you doing?" Opal asked. She startled Maude so badly that she almost dropped the reindeer she was holding.

"What?" Maude asked.

"You've got Dasher where Vixen should be," Opal shook her head. "And look at this! You've got Donner and Prancer completely mixed up. Honestly! It's like you've never decorated for Christmas before."

"Maude! This is serious business," Ruby said.

"They're toy reindeer! What difference does it make what order they're in?" Maude snapped back.

Opal and Ruby were appalled. "Sometimes I really wonder about you, Maude. How in the world could you not know something so important?" Opal asked her.

"I'll do them," Ruby said. She took over the reindeer scene and directed Maude to hang the wreaths on the double doors.

"Your lack of Christmas cheer is probably why we didn't get to meet the real Saint Nicholas in Italy, Maude," Opal huffed.

"I have plenty of Christmas cheer, thank you very much!" Maude snapped.

"I can see," Ruby said sarcastically.

"It's the naughty list for you," Opal said. "Again."

"You don't have that kind of power!" Maude snapped back.

"We'll see," Opal shrugged.

Maude continued to hang the wreaths on the front doors just in case Opal really did have connections. She was a wild card after all. It was usually better to stay on her good side.

Ruby pronounced their progress as moving in the right direction. "We've got to get the paint on the windows next," she said.

"I'll do it," Maude offered.

"Absolutely not," Ruby said at the same time that Opal swore.

"You have the handwriting of a serial killer. You ain't writing on my windows!" Opal said.

"I ain't done it!" Maude retorted. She pouted in the empty chair underneath the nearest dryer. "Then who's gonna do it?"

"Well, you aren't going to like it, but the person who has done it every year is who you need to call. She's on my naughty list right now, too," Opal sighed.

"Who?" Maude asked.

"Nadine," Opal sighed again.

"That old cow?" Maude barked. "No way!"

Opal nodded. "Ms. Belva always said she had the prettiest handwriting of anyone she knew. She was right. Nadine is an old cow, but she's a talented artist. She does all the windows on this street and the next," Opal said.

"Well, I ain't calling her," Maude said. She looked at Opal who shook her head.

"I'll call her," Ruby said. Sometimes being the only mature adult around was hard work.

Ruby walked over to the counter and picked up the receiver. She flipped through the rolodex that Opal kept by the phone until her fingers found the number for Nadine Waters. She dialed the number and waited.

"Hello," Nadine answered a few minutes later.

"Hello, Nadine. It's Ruby Montgomery. How are you doing?" Ruby said with a bit more enthusiasm than necessary.

"Oh hello, Ruby. I'm fine. How are you?" Nadine gushed with equal excitement.

"I'm fine. Well, the reason I called is that I'm at The Comb Over helping Opal with her Christmas decorations and we were wondering if you'd be able come over and letter her windows for us," Ruby said.

There was a long pause. Ruby thought for a moment that they had been disconnected.

"Hello? Nadine?" Ruby asked.

Finally Nadine sighed loudly, "I just don't know, really."

"What's wrong?" Ruby asked against her better judgment.

"It's just that I'm not exactly sure I'll be able to get over there this year. I know where one of y'all is, the others aren't far behind. Maude has made it clear that she doesn't appreciate my many talents," Nadine huffed.

"What does Maude have to do with it?" Ruby asked.

"Well, I know she's over there. It's rare to see one of y'all without the other two. Maude is tied at the hip to both of you. I really don't know how you two put up with her so much. You both must be saints," Nadine sighed.

"Now wait just a minute!" Ruby huffed.

"Now Ruby, Maude has made it quite clear that she isn't my biggest fan. She practically threatened my life at the last play," Nadine shuddered.

"To be fair, I don't remember Maude threatening you," Ruby began.

Maude suddenly turned her attention to the conversation Ruby was having. "Threatened? I haven't yet, but I'm about to!" she yelled.

Ruby held up her hand to hush Maude's commentary. It did little to calm the situation.

"See, she's doing it again, isn't she? I can hear her in the background," Nadine said.

"But Nadine," Ruby began again.

"That wasn't a threat Nadine; that was a promise!" Maude yelled next to Ruby.

Ruby pushed Maude away from the desk and glared at her.

"Hush! Both of you! I can see that this is getting us nowhere," Ruby sighed. "We can just call someone else. You have a nice day Nadine."

"It's fine. I'll be there in about thirty minutes," Nadine replied. "Otherwise her window won't match the rest of the street. The whole thing will look awkward."

"What?" Ruby asked.

"I'll be over there in a few minutes," Nadine said again.

"Are you sure?" Ruby asked.

"Yes. We are all adults here and it is Christmas, after all," Nadine said. "Well, some of us are adults anyway."

"If you're sure. We'd really appreciate it," Ruby told her.

"Of course, Ruby," Nadine said. "Of course."

"Alright, well, thank you, Nadine," Ruby said.

"No problem, Ruby," Nadine said sweetly. Ruby hung up the phone and turned her attention to Maude who was fuming over by the dryers.

"I think it's best you and I let Nadine paint in peace, don't you think?" she asked.

"I swear, that woman is a demon straight from hell," Maude pouted.

"I just don't understand what it is with you two anyway!" Ruby said. "When did all this start?"

Opal rang Brenda out at the desk and held the door for her to leave. She turned to Ruby and said, "Oh, Maude's never forgiven her for spreading that rumor about her and Jethro and her aunt's fortune."

"Jethro Thompson?" Ruby asked. "That was almost a decade ago!"

"You know Maude don't let things go," Opal laughed.

"Everyone who knows you knows that you came into that money legally. Jethro was a good attorney. Jameson thinks real highly of him," Ruby said.

"He's also forty years older than me, four foot two, and bald! I ain't never been that desperate in my life!" Maude fumed.

"Well, I wouldn't say that," Opal mumbled.

Maude shot her a dirty look.

"Nadine was just jealous you came into all that money," Ruby said.

"I can't help that my aunt died and left everything to me. I also can't help she used Jethro Thompson as her attorney, but it worked out in the end," Maude said.

"It sure was a nice surprise," Ruby agreed. "I don't know why Nadine is still hung up on all of that though. Why does she care?"

"Because I used that money to buy that land next to Opal. She had her eyes on it, but I bought it fair and square," Maude huffed.

"It's been tit for tat ever since," Opal said.

"Well, she started it. And I aim to finish it," Maude said.

"You know how it goes, Ruby. Maude put the rotten tuna fish underneath the seats in Nadine's new corvette and then Nadine dumped those crickets into Maude's backseat. Maude spilled molasses on Nadine's head at the library's raffle, so Nadine told Joe over at the Pig not to sell Maude any cigarettes or caffeinated coffee on account of her doctor's orders, so then Maude changed our Nadine's hair dye one afternoon here, to which Nadine put a feral cat in through the window of Maude's kitchen, and well, it's been going on for awhile now," Opal explained.

"Maude, you didn't," Ruby looked at her.

"I repay what I'm given. Kindness for kindness. And sometimes otherwise for otherwise if necessary," Maude admitted.

"I swear, between you and Opal and all of y'all's shenanigans, I'm going to need a vacation," Ruby laughed.

"Oh good. Where are we going?" Opal asked.

"Oh lord. You started something now," Maude chuckled.

Chapter Thirteen

"You look so pretty in your dress, Mavis!" Ruby crooned. "And Wilbur, that shirt brings out your eyes so nicely. We are going to have such a lovely evening at the theatre tonight."

"Y'all about ready to head on out?" Jameson asked. He straightened his tie in the hall mirror and made sure his billfold was in his back pocket.

"I think we're ready," Ruby said. She smoothed down the back of Mavis' hair and ushered the little girl out of the front door to the car. Wilbur settled in next to Mavis in the backseat. Ruby closed the door and settled into the front passenger seat. The drive to the theatre took no time.

"It looks like it'll be sold out," Ruby said. If the cars in the parking lot were any indication, she was right.

"There's Maude," Jameson pointed out.

"Let's hurry inside. It's chilly out here tonight," Ruby said. She helped Mavis and Wilbur out of the car and the four of them hurried to the theatre steps where Maude was waiting for them.

"I have been looking forward to this!" Ruby squealed.

"Oh, so have I," Maude cackled.

They handed their tickets to the man at the door and found their seats. The stage looked beautiful. Even Maude had to admit that it looked like something out of a magazine.

"Ricky sure does have an eye for design," Ruby said.

"Maude, I think you ought to try out for the next play. See if you can get Ruby up there, too," Jameson said. He winked quickly at Wilbur.

"Not a chance," Maude replied. "I ain't getting up there."

"Shh, y'all, this is Opal's thing. Just a few more minutes," Ruby whispered. She loved attending the annual Christmas show. She was like a kid in a candy store when it came to anything Christmas.

Ruby followed Maude into the row of seats. Mavis was sitting next to her with Jameson to the young girl's right. Wilbur sat in the aisle seat. Maude reached in her purse to take out a piece of butterscotch. She handed a piece to Ruby before offering a piece to the rest of the party. Mavis loved butterscotch and for a moment was tempted to keep Wilbur's piece for safekeeping until she felt Jameson's watchful eye bearing down on her. She quickly decided that Wilbur could probably be trusted with his own candy. The lights flickered to signify that the show would be beginning in a few minutes.

"Ohh, here we go!" Ruby exclaimed.

Ricky walked to center stage with Opal next to him. Both of them were in full stage makeup and wore long travelling cloaks to conceal their costumes underneath. Once the clapping died down, Ricky cleared his throat and began his usual announcement.

"Thank you all for coming here tonight. We are honored and delighted to have you here with us on the opening night of "A Christmas Carol." We have worked very hard to be able to bring you this production this weekend. We hope you fall in love with the characters the way that we have and perhaps come back for the next two showings. Tell all your friends!" Ricky smiled.

There was a rustling behind the curtain that was directly behind Opal and Ricky. They tried to ignore it, but the rustling got more noticeable.

"Yes, yes, thank you all for coming tonight. We ask that there be no flash photography as it burns out our eyes up here," Opal grinned. "Anyway, we are about to begin. I present to you," she trailed off. She was again interrupted by whoever was behind the curtain.

"What in the devil?" Opal hissed.

Nadine peeked her head out between the slit in the heavy curtains and said, "And please keep your noises to a minimum. Maude, I know you're somewhere out there and I hear you always get excited on nights like this. Hopefully you didn't bathe in that awful perfume again, but please maintain some polite decorum."

Opal snatched the curtain shut causing Nadine to stumble behind the curtain.

"I'm going to kill her!" Maude whispered.

"Oh God. Thank you for that Nadine," Ricky smiled nervously. He was thankful he could not see into the audience because of the bright stage lights. He was sure Maude looked murderous. "Anyway, as my lady was saying, we present to you A Christmas Carol: Rhinestone Edition."

"This means war," Maude whispered loudly to Ruby. "And what the hell does Rhinestone edition mean?"

"No idea!" Ruby said. Jameson shrugged his shoulders. Ricky and Opal exited the stage and the lights went out. When the music started, everyone looked around in confusion. Jameson caught Ruby's eye and could tell she was just as befuddled as he was.

"I don't remember the movie starting like this," Maude whispered loudly.

"Shh, Maude!" Ruby hissed. But Maude was right. This certainly wasn't in the movie.

"Ruby! I'm pretty sure old timey England didn't have banjo music!" Maude retorted.

Mavis clapped along to the beat and Jameson had to hold back a laugh. This was certainly going to be interesting.

"I'm sure it's just an artistic choice," Ruby offered diplomatically.

"What? Jolly ol' England meets Deliverance?" Maude asked.

"Shh," Ruby whispered again.

Eddie walked onstage. He was clearly Ebenezer Scrooge. The audience couldn't quite determine what time period this certain edition was set in, but it was definitely not modern. It was, however, very colorful. His electric green scarf shrouded his black cloak that was buckled up to his neck. His black boots were stiff and tapped against the hard wood of the stage. The sound effects coming from the sound and light booth were those of a howling wind and light music to add to the atmosphere. The narrator's voice boomed out and over the audience startling both children and Ruby.

"I wonder who's in the booth." Ruby whispered loudly to Maude.

"I don't know, but dang. It's all a little loud for my taste," Maude replied.

Jameson turned around and cupped his hands over his eyes. "I think I see Bill and Levi up there, but it's hard to tell," he whispered.

"Why is he yelling?" Mavis asked, still smacking on the butterscotch candy.

"Must be a problem with the sound system, sweetheart. I'm sure they'll have it fixed in a jiffy," Jameson assured her.

The sound never quieted, but eventually the audience got used to things and settled in for the show. While the fashion choices and setting of the play had been updated, they had chosen to use the script in its original form language wise. The English accents sounded more southern than anything else and the word choices were very out of place against the backdrop of such neon costume pieces. There were also a few issues with the timing of things. Jacob Marley, played by Mortimer Raven, was already on stage and speaking when the sound of his chains echoed throughout the theatre. Someone in the booth clearly had a cold, because every few minutes the audience could hear sniffles and quiet sneezes,

"I think they need some help up there," Jameson casually whispered to Ruby.

"I think you're right," she whispered.

Opal delighted the crowd with her rendition of the Spirit of Christmas Past. However, when The Spirit of Christmas Present entered the stage, Maude could not contain her laughter at the sight of Nadine in a fat suit and heavy wig.

"Oh! This is good!" Maude howled.

But before Nadine could deliver her first line, the lights on stage flickered.

"ACHOO!" Suddenly the entire theatre went dark, including the lights on the stage.

"Ahh," Mavis screamed. She climbed into Jameson's lap and held onto his neck for dear life.

"It's ok," Jameson sputtered. He unwrapped Mavis' vice-like grip and took a deep breath. "Surely they'll get the lights fixed soon, everyone stay calm."

Though no one in the audience could see anything happening around them, there was a commotion on the stage in the form of a loud crash followed by screaming.

"What are you doing? Get off me!" Nadine yelled.

"I'm sorry!" Eddie yelled back. "Oh!"

"Don't put your hands there!" Nadine said. They heard a loud thud and Eddie let out a yelp of pain.

"Eddie! Don't get handsy with Nadine," Opal shrieked from somewhere offstage.

"I'm sorry!" Eddie said.

"I can't see anything!" Nadine shrieked. "Get this thing off of me."

What or who was on her, no one knew exactly. Someone ran across the stage and once again crashed into something because there was another loud yelp.

"What's going on here?" Maude yelled loudly.

"I'm trying to fix it! I'm so sorry!" Bill said over the speakers.

"Push the other button," Levi said into the microphone. A blood curdling screech split the air.

"Who's running this thing?" Maude demanded.

"Turn on the lights!" Nadine shouted. "I can't see anything and I'm trapped under this costume! At least turn on the stage lights!"

"I'm trying!" Bill from the booth replied.

"I told you it's the other button!" Levi said again.

"Someone help me!" Nadine screamed dramatically. "I can't see a thing up here!" She was wailing uncontrollably.

"We can't see anything out here either, you old goat!" Maude yelled back at her.

"Maude? Is this your doing? It ain't funny!" Nadine hollered.

"It ain't me! Geez!" Maude yelled back.

There was another crash and a few yelps uttered on the stage, followed by a few choice curse words from a stagehand. Another blur of a shape ran across the stage. "Nadine! Where are you?" Ricky called out.

"Over here!" she yelled.

"I can't get to you," he yelled back. "I can't see a thing."

"I'm over here!" Nadine shrieked.

"It's pitch black, you idiot! No one can see you!" Maude yelled to Nadine who was still wailing.

"Maude! This isn't funny! Turn on the lights!" Nadine yelled.

"OW! What in the hell!" screamed Maude. She fell into her seat and flung off the sweaty hair piece that Nadine had flung into the audience off of her. "Ahh! She's trying to kill me!"

Ruby jumped up out of her seat and landed in Mavis' empty seat next to Jameson. "Y'all! What's going on here?"

"Maude, is that you?" Opal yelled. "I can't see you! Where are you?"

"Opal? Opal! Is that you? I can't see you either!" Maude yelled. "Nadine attacked me!"

"Somebody help me!" wailed Nadine.

"Can it Nadine!" Opal yelled. "Maude needs my help! Maude? Where in the world are you?"

"I'm being attacked in this funny farm!" Maude yelled.

"Maude! Stop it! You're embarrassing me!" Ruby hissed. "Y'all just sit down and stop carrying on!"

"Embarrassing you! I'm the one who's being attacked by flying critters!" Maude yelled, still fighting off Nadine's sweat soaked hairpiece.

"I'm coming, Maude!" Opal shouted again.

Ruby shielded herself and Mavis from Maude's flailing.

"Levi? Bill? Everything ok up there?" Jameson yelled to the sound booth.

"Yes, yes. We'll be back on in a few minutes," Bill responded.

"Alright," Jameson said. "Y'all just sit tight and let's let them get it all situated."

"I'm coming Maude!" Opal yelled. "Ouch! Sorry, oops! My apologies! Ow! Sir! I'm not your wife!"

"Opal! Is that you?" Maude shouted.

"I'm coming!" Opal replied. "At least I'm trying to!"

Before Opal could reach Maude, the lights suddenly came back on just as quickly as they had gone out. The audience began to clap.

"It is fine," a low gravelly voice resonated through the theatre from the sound booth.

"What the devil was that?" Maude shouted.

"Mortie! Is that you?" Opal called out.

"It is I," the voice responded. Every head snapped to the back of the theatre to see Mortimer Raven descend from the sound booth wearing a long black travelling cloak that obscured his face. He was dressed as the Spirit of Christmas Future. He walked down the center aisle towards the stage and deliberately ascended the steps to the stage and disappeared behind the thick velvet curtain.

"Mortie saved the day!" Opal cheered. She skipped over to where Maude was still crouched behind the seat in front of her and picked up Nadine's wig. "She'll be needing that, I suppose. Y'all act right and get back up in your seats. I'll see to it that this wig doesn't come off again."

Opal sprinted back to the stage and disappeared behind the same thick maroon curtain that Mortie had moments before.

"We're going to take um, a short fifteen minute, um, break and uh, see you all back in your seats then," squeaked a high pitched voice. A series of soft sneezes followed.

"I told you it was that button," Levi said, in what was clearly supposed to be a whisper in the booth.

"All these buttons look alike!" Bill snapped back.

"Fellas? We can still hear you down here," Jameson called out.

"Mute us!" Levi huffed. There was another loud screech. "This button!"

"Well, I have never in my life," started Ruby. She dusted herself off and reclaimed her original seat. "Are y'all ok?"

Wilbur nodded and grinned at Maude who was sweating bullets. Jameson deposited Mavis into her empty seat with Maude's bag of candy that had flown out of her purse in the scuffle and stood up to stretch. He extended his hand to Maude and helped her back to her seat. "Are you alright?" he asked her.

"No! How could I be? That cow tried to kill me with her hair!" Maude howled.

"Maude, shh!" Ruby said. "I'm sure it was an accident."

"Are you deranged?" Maude snapped. "She knew exactly where she was throwing that weapon!"

"It was pitch black, Maude. I reckon she just got lucky," Ruby smiled.

Maude folded herself into her seat and crossed her arms. She was not going to easily forget this evening. Ruby looked over and Jameson and shrugged. He smiled back and turned towards Wilbur who had remained in his seat during the debacle. He couldn't help but chuckle at the chain of events and commotion around him.

"What's got you so tickled?" Jameson asked, although he was smiling now, too.

"This show is a lot funnier than when we read it in school last year," Wilbur said.

"That's because this was the Rhinestone edition, son," Jameson said with a hearty laugh.

"I should have known the Rhinestone edition was going to try to kill me," Maude huffed.

She pulled a silver flask from her purse and hastily took a gulp. Not completely convinced that one gulp would completely work, she took a second one just in case.

"Feeling better now?" Ruby asked.

Maude shrugged and took a third sip just to be on the safe side.

They watched the stagehands fix the set that had gotten destroyed during the intense blackout.

There was no way to quickly repair the large hole in the freeform wall of Ebenezer Scrooge's office, but they did manage to reset the furniture and pick up the discarded costume pieces and return them to their owners.

When everyone was settled back down and the stage was reset, the play resumed where it had left off. Nadine was visibly shaken, more so from Opal's refitting of her wig than the actual hullabaloo on stage. Maude, for her part, continued to stare daggers at her. With the flask from her purse emptied, she rarely moved until the odd sneeze or cough came from the booth overhead. When the show ended, she gathered up her purse and the small bouquet of flowers that she had brought for Opal. She followed the Montgomerys down to the foot of the stage to form a line to greet and congratulate the cast. Ruby was impressed at how well Maude had gathered herself. By the time they got to Opal in line, Maude had a big grin on her face.

"Here, these are for you. Lovely as always," Ruby smiled. She handed Opal her bouquet of flowers that she had brought and motioned for Maude to hand Opal the bouquet she carried.

"Oh yes, great job," Maude said. She smiled at Opal and then at Ruby.

"Aren't you going to give Opal her flowers?" Ruby whispered.

"Huh? Oh these? No, these are meant for someone else," Maude replied with a pasted grin on her face.

"Oh God," Ruby whispered.

Maude moved past Ruby to Nadine and stood in front of her.

"Maude," squeaked Nadine. She was still wearing her heavy costume and bulky wig.

"These are for you," Maude said. She went to hand the flowers to Nadine, but before Nadine could grab them, Maude whacked her on top of the head with them repeatedly. "That's for embarrassing me and for attacking me with your disgusting wig and that's for being an overly annoying buffoon!"

Maude straightened her coat and walked briskly out of the side doors into the cold evening air leaving everyone stunned in her wake.

"Well, that was dramatic," Opal laughed.

⟿Chapter Fourteen⟿

Ruby looked out of the kitchen window at the strong magnolia tree in the front yard. She was not so secretly hoping for snow on Christmas. Christmas was only two days away and Jameson said there was little to no chance of having a white Christmas this year. She knew in her heart that one of these years she would be able to look out of the window and see snow.

Even as a little girl, she would stay up late on Christmas Eve, long after her older brother and sister had fallen asleep and pray for snow. There were many Christmas mornings where she would run downstairs and bypass the Christmas tree in the den and fling open the front door wishing for drifts of thick white snow to blanket the ground. It had never worked. Rhinestone never got any snow. The only snow Ruby had ever seen was from her trip to Tennessee with Maude and Opal. Seeing Graceland coated in white made for the prettiest pictures, but Ruby still willed it to snow in

Rhinestone every December. She was always on the lookout for a Christmas miracle.

"See any flurries?" Jameson asked.

"Not a one," Ruby sighed. "Maybe next year."

"You and Mavis about ready to head on out?" he asked.

"As soon as she comes down the stairs," Ruby replied.

"I'll see what she's up to," Jameson smiled. He walked up the stairs quickly and called out for Mavis. "Sugar, what are you doing in there?"

"My dollies want to come, too," Mavis said sweetly. She had three of her most loved dolls wrapped up in one of Jameson's giant sweaters. She dragged them behind her like a dog on a leash towards the stairs.

"Let me help you with them," Jameson laughed. He picked up Mavis and her dolls and gently descended the stairs. "Alright, Ruby, Mavis is ready. Hope there's room for three more."

Ruby looked confused and shook her head. "We're going in Maude's new car. I'm so glad we finally convinced her to get something besides that motorcycle. At our age, well, never mind that. I just don't think with the four of us and the rest of the gifts that there'll be any more room for three more people," she said.

"Oh no!" Mavis cried. "But they have to go!" She clutched her dolls to her chest.

Ruby finally realized what Mavis was referring to and chuckled. "Oh yes, sugar, they can go. Big Mama was confused for a minute."

Jameson bundled Mavis in her coat and opened the front door as Maude reached for the door handle to walk in. Opal was smiling ear to ear about to ring the bell. "We're here!" she yelled gleefully.

"I see that," Jameson laughed.

"Well, Maude's all in a tizzy because she hasn't started her Christmas shopping yet, but I told her that's what today is all about," Opal said. Thankfully Ruby missed the animated wink she gave Jameson.

"I said I hadn't finished my Christmas shopping yet," Maude grumbled.

"Well, that's the same thing," Opal shrugged. Maude rolled her eyes to heaven.

"Well, y'all have fun. No need to hurry on back," Jameson smiled. He kissed Mavis on her head and kissed Ruby on her cheek. "Be safe out there."

"Ruby and Mavis will be fine, but I can't guarantee this one," Maude pointed at Opal with her thumb, "will survive."

"Good thing you know the best lawyer in the county," Jameson said with a chuckle. "Just promise you'll make it look like an accident."

"It'll be a case of temporary insanity!" Maude said.

"You sure you two will be ok?" Ruby asked Jameson.

"Of course! Wilbur and I have a list of things to get to before we can have Christmas here at the Manor. Don't you worry about it one little bit. You'll be too busy making sure Maude doesn't strangle Opal with some loose tinsel," Jameson laughed.

"The very first chance I get!" Maude called over her shoulder as she and Opal climbed in her car. Ruby and Mavis climbed into the back seat with Mavis' dolls.

He and Wilbur waved goodbye until Maude's car was no longer in sight. "Ok, Wilbur, let's get down to business. It's going to take a Christmas miracle to get all this finished by the time they get back."

Wilbur was giddy with excitement. Jameson had been planning to surprise Ruby with a giant fish aquarium for months. Ruby had no idea what she would see this evening when she walked in through the front door. Wilbur knew she would be plumb excited.

"Thomas should be here around ten to oversee the install. He says he can have it all put together and curing by the time she gets home. By next week, Mrs. Ruby can pick out her fish and whatever other creatures she wants to put in there," Jameson grinned. "It's a salt water system, so we'll probably have to order the fish from overseas, but that'll be up to her."

Jameson was just as giddy with excitement. He had wanted to have the fish stocked by the time Ruby got home, but Thomas was already working overtime to fit this install into such a short window of time. With Maude and Opal's help, they were able to get Ruby out of the house today, but Ruby was a hard one to surprise usually. She had an eagle eye and nothing got past her for the most part. Jameson and Wilbur had worked meticulously with Thomas to get measurements and pick out colors any time that Ruby wasn't home. They had even gone over to Junction one afternoon to Thomas' workshop to see the final product. This was going to be the surprise of the century.

When Thomas arrived with his crew, Wilbur and Jameson had already pushed back the furniture in the living room and removed all of the pictures and frames that hung on the wall. They were covering all the items that would remain in the area with large sheets to prevent any dust from settling.

"Right on time," Jameson said as he opened the front door for Thomas and his crew.

Thomas had brought three of his best workmen with him in order to make sure that everything was done well before six o'clock in the evening. That was the time that Jameson had guaranteed Ruby would be out and about. Maude had told him they would keep Ruby out of the house until at least seven o'clock, but Jameson liked to err on the side of caution.

Wilbur watched the men unload large boxes and pipes and tubing. He held the door for them as they made their trips back and forth to their work trucks. Once everything was unloaded, he and Jameson made sure to stay out of the way as best they could.

Meanwhile on the way to Junction, Maude weaved her way in and out of traffic in her new car.

"So Maude, how much more shopping do you have to do?" Ruby asked while Mavis played with the dolls in her lap.

"Just a few more things. I've got to find Teddy something. Lord knows that man is hard to buy for," Maude replied.

"I thought you said you hadn't even started your Christmas shopping?" Opal implored.

"I never once said that. You make stuff up," Maude said.

"I have not. It's not my fault your memory is slipping," Opal said. She turned to the backseat. "Sure sign of old age, you know." Opal winked at Ruby.

"We're the same age!" Maude snapped.

"Ain't done it! You're older than me by four months," Opal explained.

"That don't mean nothing!" Maude huffed.

"Some of us are retaining our youthfulness while others like you have embraced a more mature and settled lifestyle," Opal explained.

"Mature and settled?" Maude asked.

"It happens, Maude. It's okay. Nothing to be ashamed about," Opal said. She patted Maude's arm sympathetically.

"I swear one of these days," Maude began. She could hear Ruby laughing in the backseat.

"And with old age comes a lot of changes. We'll have to get you a book to better explain all of that," Opal said.

"I'll show you changes," Maude said.

"Oh, quit it, you two," Ruby laughed. "Back to what I was asking. What are you going to get

Teddy? Oh Maude! What's he getting you? What if he proposes? A Christmas proposal!"

"God, I hope not!" Maude said. "I'd hate to have to hurt his feelings at Christmas."

"Maude! You wouldn't!" Ruby gasped.

"I sure the hell would. I ain't gettin' married again. Teddy knows that," Maude explained.

"Well, Maude, like I've already explained to you, you ain't getting any younger. We need to find someone who's going to take care of you in your golden years," Opal mused.

"If you want to live to see your golden years, I suggest you shut your yap," Maude sneered. "Actually, open up that yap and spill the beans on your three. What are you getting your beaus for Christmas?"

"Oh, I've got it all planned out!" Opal smiled.
"

"You've got it planned what they're getting you?" Ruby asked.

'Of course!" Opal gushed. "This is important stuff. Ricky is such a charmer. I got tickets to a show. Yes sir, I'm going to let him take me to Atlanta in January to see A Chorus Line when it comes to town. It's his favorite, besides West Side Story, of course, but that's another story. Anyway, for my Christmas present he's getting matching costumes for us to give an impromptu performance for Easter next year."

"How is it impromptu if you're planning it?" Maude asked.

"You obviously don't understand high art, Maude," Opal told her.

Maude stared at Opal, but refrained from comment.

"What about Eddie and Mortimer?" Ruby asked.

"Eddie really is the dearest," Opal continued. "I don't have any idea what he's getting me, but I got him that golden pocket watch he's been eyeing over at Jan's Jewelry & Diamonds.

"Oooh, Jan's, they only sell the nicest jewelry in there. You can never go wrong with stuff from there," Ruby said approvingly.

"And Mortie, now he's the true romantic! He knows how much I've been missing John since I was coerced into relocating him. Mortie painted John on canvas! I'm not sure what all he used to paint it, some kind of oil paints, but it's beautiful. Can you believe it?" Opal exclaimed.

"Oh my, that does sound, um, lovely," Ruby agreed. "What did you get Mortie?"

"I got him a new hi-fi. He gets lonely down at the funeral home and it's mostly so quiet there. He was thrilled of course! He's so in tune with his emotions," Opal explained.

"I thought he had one. I would have sworn there was some music playing at the last visitation we went to," Ruby said.

"Well," Opal began. "He did, but alas, it's no longer with us. The eight track went out on it. Started eating the tape right in the middle of one of the services. Sounded like someone was conjuring and contacting Satan. You would have thought the dead had sat up and the coffin sprang open when all that caterwauling started. Near about had a stampede for the door."

"Oh dear God!" Maude gasped.

"Brother Matthis near about keeled over himself," Opal sighed. "Almost had two funerals for the price of one."

"Oh, that sounds awful!" Ruby said.

"It was entertaining!" Opal said.

"What about you and Jameson?" Maude asked. She wanted to change the subject from that creepy old funeral home as fast as possible.

"A couple of new outfits for court. You know he wears those slacks until they start to get holes in them. I don't know what it is about men and their clothes. They just wear them out and hate to shop for new ones," Ruby said.

"Not all men," Opal interrupted. "I have to practically pry Ricky out of the stores."

"I could see that," Ruby said. "Anyway, I also got him a new briefcase with his name on it"

"Oh, that sounds real nice," Opal agreed.

"Get out of my spot!" Maude suddenly roared.

"Jesus Maude!" Opal cried. She was grabbing the handle above the door and bracing for impact.

"I had my blinker on waiting and this cow! Are you kidding me?" Maude yelled. She slammed the car into park and snatched open her car door. "Nadine! I know you saw me waiting!"

"Maude, Jameson was kidding about being able to get you off from murder charges. Don't do anything this close to Christmas!" Opal warned, trying to hold her friend back.

"Oh, hello Maude. I didn't see you there. Is that a new car you're driving?" Nadine asked sweetly.

"You know damn well it is. I couldn't get the smell of sulfur out from under the seat of my old Chevette, no thanks to the rotten eggs you smeared across the back end!" Maude hollered.

"I don't know what you're referring to, Maude. I would never," Nadine said.

Opal ran around the driver's side of the car and pushed Maude to the passenger seat. "I'll find us another one, don't you fret. Have a good day Nadine! Next time leave the wig at the theatre!"

"I ought to run her over!" Maude yelled.

"Maude! Stop it!" Ruby hissed from the backseat. People passing by had stopped to stare at the impending cat fight. Ruby could have died of embarrassment. Thankfully Mavis had not been paying attention. "There are people around, Maude. You can't let Nadine keep getting your goat like that."

"She ain't nothing but an old goat. That's right Ruby," Maude agreed.

"Now I didn't say that," Ruby whispered.

Nadine was fuming in the rearview mirror as Opal sped off to the other side of the parking lot. "See. There's a good one right over there." she told Maude.

"That ain't the point. That old cow did that on purpose," Maude huffed.

"Let's just put that behind us. We're going to have a good time today," Opal said. "Who's hungry?"

"Mavis and I ate already," Ruby said.

"I'm starving," Maude said.

"Shocker," Opal smiled.

"I'm hungry, too!" Mavis whined.

"Then that settles it!" Opal grinned. "Let's go to Patsy's Diner over yonder."

"I wish Rhinestone could get a diner. There's a real need for one. One would fit real nice over there by Jim's Quickstep," Maude pondered.

"Rumor has it Sammy and his wife are opening one soon," Opal said.

Maude perked up at the news. After a full breakfast of pancakes, bacon, eggs, and grits, she led them over to the mall for a day full of shopping.

"First things first, what are you getting Teddy?" Opal asked.

"I said I don't know," Maude replied. "Any ideas in the big old head of yours?"

"Fuzzy handcuffs!" Opal exclaimed. "Never know when you might run up on a suspect and need them. And they're bound to be more comfortable than the ones you use, Maude."

"The ones I use?! What in the world has gotten into that crazy head of yours now?" Maude demanded.

"Y'all quit that mess right now," Ruby hissed. She glared from one to the other and quickly cupped her hands over Mavis' ears.

"I'm just saying. Anyway, act right Maude. He's your fella. What does he like? Besides old crotchety ladies who act all scrappy in the mall parking lot?" Opal smiled.

"When he's not working he likes to watch football or play cards or work on his old Chevy," Maude shrugged as they walked into the nearest open store.

"What about this?" Opal asked. She handed Maude an ornate box with a handle.

"A poker set? Hmm, actually, that's pretty good. Good one," Maude said.

"See! One down. This is easy," Opal said.

"Now all I have left is you two," Maude announced.

"Same!" Opal said. "Well, you and Ruby, that is."

"I have you two left on my list as well," Ruby smiled.

"Well, this is going to be a grand adventure after all!" Opal exclaimed. "Come on Mavis, how about you and I go on a little adventure and let these two old ladies finish their shopping."

Chapter Fifteen

"Well look who's back!" Jameson said. Wilbur followed him down the front porch steps to help unload the shopping bags from the trunk.

"Sorry we stayed out so late," Maude said. "You wouldn't believe how crowded those stores were."

"Oh, I can imagine," Jameson said.

"Well, we had to stop and eat every two hours between these two," Opal laughed. She pointed between Maude and Mavis.

"And if Opal hadn't gotten lost in the book store, we would have been home sooner," Maude announced.

"I didn't get lost. I knew exactly where I was," Opal said.

"Anyway, enough about our adventures, what did you boys get into while we were gone?" Ruby asked.

"Oh, nothing really," Jameson smirked. He turned to Wilbur who was eating an apple. "Right, Wilbur?"

"Oh, not much at all," he smiled.

"Hmm," Ruby said. "Y'all are both grinning ear to ear. Something's up."

Jameson laughed and hurried behind Wilbur up the steps to the front door and held it open for Mavis and Ruby.

"Oh my goodness!" Ruby gasped. "Jameson!"

"Do you like it, honey?" Jameson asked.

Ruby was speechless. The life-size aquarium took up the majority of the wall that separated the living room and the informal dining area of the kitchen.

"I love it. I'm, wow, I'm so surprised!" Ruby exclaimed. She turned towards Maude and Opal and asked, "Did y'all know about this?"

"We'll never tell!" squeaked Opal. Maude shrugged innocently.

Ruby walked to the other side of the aquarium in the living room and waved through the clear panels. She studied every inch of the tank and marveled at the size of it.

"Mavis knows how to swim?" Opal asked Jameson.

"Of course. With the creek over yonder, we made sure she could swim from the time she started walking. She's a strong swimmer," he said.

Mavis looked up at the giant tank in awe. Opal knelt down and smiled broadly at her.

"Just imagine all the things that are going to get to swim in that," Opal told her. "It's almost like an indoor swimming pool, except without so many people."

"Good grief, Opal! Don't tell that child it's a swimming pool. You'll have all the kids in town in here bobbing for fish," Maude chided her.

"Well, that'll make for a good story," Opal laughed heartily.

Mavis looked up at Big Mama's best friends. She didn't understand what all the fuss was about. That pool was way too small to swim in. Even she knew that. Plus, it was empty. There wasn't any water or any critters in there. She bounded up the stairs and left the grownups to marvel at the empty tank that took up most of the wall.

"Jameson, I just can't believe it," Ruby said again. She had walked back to the dining area and ran her hands over the glass. She had not taken her eyes off of the tank. "I can't believe it's mine in my very own home."

"Well, believe it honey. Thomas left a catalog on the kitchen table for you to pick out your own fish. It's a saltwater system, so you have a lot more options," Jameson explained.

Opal walked to the table and found the thick catalog on the table. She handed it to Ruby who sank down in the nearest chair. Opal stood over her shoulder and oohed and awed over the pictures of tropical creatures on each page. "Ruby! Look! It says these are found off the coast of Italy! We probably swam with them after we went cliff diving! Remember Maude!"

"I didn't dive. I was pushed," Maude grumbled.

"She always says that," Opal grinned, with a quick wink to Jameson. "Her memory gets worse and worse with each passing year."

"Lies!" Maude hissed.

"We'll have to go back and do some more diving. Ruby, you can dive this time! You really missed out. And Jameson, you can come, too. You can't even imagine the fun we had that day!" Opal sighed happily.

"I've heard some stories," Jameson laughed.

"Maude, look! This fish is so tiny. He's a cute one," Opal said. "I remember seeing this one in the water for sure. I know you would remember this one!"

Maude hurried over and looked over Ruby's shoulder. "I don't remember them. Of course, I don't remember much since you were trying to drown me!" Maude said.

"No one tried to drown you," Opal smiled.

"The hell you didn't! You pushed me off the cliff!" Maude reminded her.

"Now Maude, I remember things differently," Opal explained.

"Surprise, surprise," Maude rolled her eyes.

Ruby ignored the squabble and turned to look at Jameson.

"Really Jameson? You think I could get some fish from where we were in Italy?" Ruby asked. She was as excited as Jameson had ever seen her.

"That was the trip of a lifetime," Opal said.

"Life changing for sure," echoed Maude.

"It really was. Oh Jameson, can we?" Ruby asked.

"I don't see why not! If they're in that book, Thomas said he could get them," Jameson replied.

"That way that trip will always be a part of our home!" she said.

"I would love that, Ruby," Jameson grinned. "You circle all the ones you want and I'll let Thomas know. He said he'd make sure what all you pick will be compatible with the system and each other, so pick a few different ones for him to look through."

"This is so exciting!" Ruby squealed. Maude produced a bright red pen and Ruby began to circle fish on the different pages. "Ooh, look at this one! It's bright blue!"

"We'll help you name them!" Opal shrieked. "I'm so good at naming things. It's a true gift."

"Oh God, I can see it now. Your fish will all be named after Shakespeare characters!" Maude laughed.

"That's a great idea, Maude! I'll let you have this one," Opal applauded. "Wilbur, you can help, too. You two sure did a great job with this!"

"Did you really jump off a cliff, Ms. Opal?" Wilbur asked.

"Of course we did. Life is all about the adventures you take, Wilbur. Never be afraid to make the jump. I've been trying to tell this one that for years," Opal said, pointing her thumb at Maude who was still looking through the catalog of fish.

Maude looked up. "I spend all my time trying to keep us from dying," she said.

"She always exaggerates!" Opal laughed. "I'm sure you've picked up on that by now."

Wilbur stifled a laugh and shook his head. He knew better than to egg on Maude.

"We've got an old photo album around here somewhere," Maude said. "I haven't looked at it in years. Ruby, where's that picture book at?"

"I'll get it," Jameson said. He reached for a weathered photo album on the top shelf next to the television. "Here you go."

"Oh, the stories these pages could tell!" Maude said. "Look at how good I looked. Damn!"

"Well, we'll say you looked better," Opal added quickly. "Thankfully there's no pictures from that nudie beach you wanted to drag us to."

"That I wanted to drag who to?" Maude gasped. "Again, I remember things differently."

Ruby, Jameson, and Wilbur were now howling with laughter.

"You went to nudie beach?" Wilbur whispered in shock.

"We went everywhere. Opal drug us half way around the world. That beach was almost the sanest thing we did that year," Maude told him but she was laughing despite herself.

"Oh that was a great summer," Opal added. "We need to take another adventure."

"That was the trip that changed all of our lives," Jameson added. He patted Ruby's knee and she smiled.

"Sure did," Ruby agreed. "What an adventure!"

"Oh yes, between cliff diving, Santa Clause, and the baby, we sure embarked on some kind of adventure," Maude laughed.

"Santa? A baby?" Wilbur asked.

"Yes, Maude kidnapped a baby on an international flight. It was quite the scandal, as you can imagine," Opal said dryly.

"Oh goodness," Ruby laughed. "No Wilbur honey, Maude didn't kidnap a child. Though Opal, you did catnap a kitten. But Lordy, let's start at the beginning."

"Almost got me arrested," Maude mumbled. "Over a damn cat!"

"No!" gasped Wilbur.

"Oh yes," Maude said. "Apparently it's against the law to smuggle live animals across the world. Who knew?"

"Well I certainly wasn't going to smuggle a dead animal across the world. Geez Maude! Sometimes your mind makes me wonder," Opal said.

"We're lucky we made it to Italy and back at all," Ruby giggled.

"Don't sound so dramatic," Opal pouted. "Naples and Nepal are spelled practically the same."

"If you rearrange the letters," Ruby laughed.

Wilbur's eyes were as wide as saucers. "Did you have fun too, Mr. Jameson?" Wilbur asked.

"No, I missed that one. I was too busy knowing everything to be smart," Jameson said. He smiled over at Ruby.

"What do you mean?" Wilbur asked.

"It was just us girls," Opal said.

"Let's just say that it took Ruby going halfway across the world for me to realize that I couldn't live without her. I wasn't as smart then as I am now," he chuckled. He patted Ruby's knee again.

"Oh my goodness! Will you look at Opal and those dang monkeys!" Maude cackled.

Ruby burst out laughing. "I had almost forgot about that. Lord, it's a miracle we didn't come home with a barrel of monkeys!"

"If it wasn't for these two, Magnolia Manor could've had monkeys running around it. Maybe on our next trip," Opal shrugged.

"Thank goodness we were there!" Maude laughed.

"Why so many pictures of feet and the sky?" Wilbur asked.

"Well, the locals didn't always take the best portraits of us, so we got some real nice ones of our shoes and look, here's one of Opal's arm," Maude pointed out.

"You got a tattoo, Ms. Opal?" Wilbur asked. He pointed to a blurry picture of Opal with tattoos on her arms and hands.

"Henna," she explained. "Maude's got a real one though. Right on her."

"Shut it!" Maude hissed. "Anyway, look at these. The finest hotel by the sea."

Opal, Maude, and Ruby giggled again.

"You've got a couple hidden in back behind the others," Wilbur noticed.

Ruby flipped the page quickly. "We don't need to look at those." She made a mental note to go back and remove the photographs of men from the nudist beach before Wilbur could make any further investigations.

"Where's the baby?" Wilbur asked as he flipped back to the beginning of the book.

"Oh, she's there. She's just well hidden," Maude said.

"Who's up for hot chocolate?" Ruby asked.

"Me!" Opal cheered.

"Wilbur, if you'll help Ruby in the kitchen, I'll unload the bags from the car with Maude and Opal," Jameson said.

Wilbur followed Ruby to the kitchen and Jameson held the front door open for Maude and Opal.

"You did good Jameson!" Maude said. She clapped Jameson on the back and handed him Ruby's shopping bags from the trunk.

"Thanks for all your help. Couldn't have gotten her out of the house without y'all," Jameson said. He shut the trunk and followed the women to the porch.

"This one is for Mavis' eyes only. She picked out some special Christmas gifts all on her own," Opal said. She handed Jameson a small bag and winked.

"I'll take it up to her directly," Jameson replied.

"Anything new on the Pete drama?" Maude asked.

"His hearing is next week," Jameson said. "I've got a bad feeling about it though."

"What do you mean?" Maude asked.

"I think Floyd's going to drop the charges. He and Pete are thick when they're sober, whenever that is. And Bobby knows Pete is his best customer.

The case is slowly losing momentum. Nothing we can do but wait," Jameson explained.

"What does that mean for Wilbur?" Maude asked.

"I don't know," Jameson sighed. "I don't even want to think about it."

"Have you told Ruby?" Maude asked.

Jameson shook his head.

"Well, we won't say anything to Ruby. We ain't gonna ruin her Christmas," Maude said. She gave Opal a knowing look. "When they make a decision we will work it all out. Nothing to fret about just yet."

"Yes ma'am," Jameson laughed.

He set the shopping bags on the dining room table and accepted the mug of hot chocolate from Wilbur.

"I put extra marshmallows, just like you like it," Wilbur smiled.

"Thanks!" Jameson said. "Ruby, I put Mavis' shopping bag on the table here." Opal said Mavis

"I'll take it up there," Wilbur told her. He picked up the bags and headed up the stairs. He stopped outside Mavis' door. She was sitting on her bed playing with the dolls and a stuffed teddy bear. Apparently they weren't behaving the way that she wanted them to because she was giving them quite the scolding. Wilbur walked in and sat down in the rocker opposite her.

"Hey Mavis," Wilbur said. "I heard this was yours."

"Don't look! These are for Christmas!" Mavis warned him.

"I'm not looking. I'm just bringing them up here for you," Wilbur told her.

"Oh, okay. You can do that," Mavis graciously told him.

"Do you know where the wrapping paper is? I need to wrap some presents and I can help you, too, if you want," Wilbur said. "They're not all nice and store bought like these are, but," Wilbur began.

"That's okay. Big Mama loves pretty paper. She doesn't care what's inside," Mavis told him. "It's in her closet. Come on, I know where it is."

She bounded off the bed and skipped down the hall to Jameson's and Ruby's bedroom. It only took a few minutes for her to find two giant rolls of Christmas paper from Ruby's closet.

"So, you want the snowman or Rudolph?" Mavis beamed.

"Rudolph," Wilbur smiled. They returned to Mavis' room.

"Turn around. I've got to wrap your present first," Mavis told him.

Wilbur smiled. "Okay, we'll turn around and wrap each other's presents then we can wrap the other ones together."

The adults sat around the table drinking their hot chocolate. Ruby opened a tin of jam cookies and passed them around.

"What time are you leaving in the morning?" Ruby asked.

"I'm going to head out around seven," Opal said. "It's a four hour drive."

"Tell your mama and daddy we said hello," Ruby said. "What about you Maude?"

"Teddy wants to leave around lunchtime. His mama lives about five hours south of here, so we should be there by supper, spend the night, and come back Christmas day. He's got to work that night, so we'll have to hurry on back," Maude explained.

"Stop on in if you want," Ruby offered.

"I may do just that," Maude replied. "Especially if you bribe me with another cup of this hot chocolate."

"When will you be back, Opal?" Jameson asked.

"I'll be back the day after Christmas. We can exchange our gifts then," she smiled.

"You know, I still can't over your parents going to Hawaii for Christmas. Good for them!" Maude interrupted.

"I know. They aren't getting any younger and mama has always wanted to go," Ruby said. "The house will be quieter without everyone here though. Mrs. Montgomery will be here for lunch, but she likes to be back home before dark. Guess it'll just be the four of us for a bit."

"That sounds right up your alley," Maude smiled. "Those kids are awful quiet up there. What do you think they're doing?"

"I'll go check on them," Jameson said. He set his empty mug down on the table and headed upstairs. He could hear them laughing as soon as he came up the landing, but he couldn't tell what they were saying.

"What are you two up to?" Jameson asked.

"Hey! Don't peek!" Mavis squealed.

She and Wilbur dove on the pile of paper and gifts between them to hide their progress from Jameson. He could see that there was tape and what looked like glitter all over her floor.

"Oh yes, ma'am," Jameson chuckled. He went back downstairs to report their progress to the others.

Chapter Sixteen

"WILBUR!"

Wilbur groaned loudly and rubbed his eyes.

"Wilbur! It's Christmas!" Mavis squealed. She burst through his door with a good running start. Before he could fully brace himself, she flew through the air and landed on his stomach before he could fully open his eyes. She started to shake him until he agreed to get out of bed. "I gotta go wake up Big Mama and Big Daddy. It's Christmas!"

Wilbur yawned and looked over at the alarm clock on his nightstand. He saw that it was six thirty in the morning. Mavis certainly wasted no time when it came to Christmas morning. He could hear Ruby and Jameson in the next room being startled awake by Mavis. He couldn't help but grin. This was going to be the best Christmas yet.

He surveyed his new outfits hanging up in his closet and got dressed. He brushed his hair in the bathroom and walked down the stairs to the kitchen. Mavis was still in her pajamas with her long hair sticking up in every direction. There may have even been a marshmallow from last night's hot chocolate in there. "Wilbur! It's Christmas!"

"I think you might have mentioned that," he laughed. Ruby walked over to him and gave him a big hug. "Merry Christmas, Wilbur."

"Merry Christmas," he grinned. He then allowed Mavis to drag him by the hand to the living room. His jaw hit the floor when he saw the piles of presents underneath the large tree.

"Merry Christmas Wilbur," Jameson smiled in the doorway.

"Come on y'all!" Mavis hollered. "Big Mama! Big Daddy! It's Christmas!" She was already seated in front of the tallest pile of presents. She had a sugar filled grin plastered across her face and she looked like she could barely contain herself. "It's Christmas!"

"Right you are, sugar!" Jameson said. He patted Wilbur on the shoulder and sat down in his recliner. Ruby came into the living room with two mugs of hot coffee. She handed Jameson his mug and sat down in her recliner. "Merry Christmas, everyone!"

"Here Wilbur! This one's for you!" Mavis handed Wilbur a small box and then scooted back across the floor to the largest box in the room. "And this one is for me!"

"For me?" Wilbur asked.

"Go on, Wilbur," Jameson encouraged.

Unlike Mavis, who was shredding the wrapping paper to bits, Wilbur slowly and methodically unwrapped the package. The box inside had the name Seiko written across the top. Opening the box, Wilbur saw a handsome wrist watch inside.

"For me?" Wilbur gasped.

"Of course! Every man needs a good watch," Jameson smiled.

Wilbur gingerly took the watch from the box and wrapped it around his wrist.

"Come here, let me help you," Ruby said gently. She fastened the watch around Wilbur's wrist and smiled warmly at him.

A piece of wrapping paper flew past Wilbur's head.

"Look! Look at this!" Mavis crooned. Wilbur turned towards Mavis and saw her standing in front of a tall wooden dollhouse.

"That's really nice Mavis," Wilbur said.

"It's all mine!" she said. "But you can play with it, too! Wilbur, you can be Betty and I'll be Martha Sue," Mavis giggled. She held up two small dolls that she had previously unwrapped.

"Here Wilbur, open this one next," Jameson said. He handed Wilbur a large box. Wilbur carefully unwrapped it and his heart skipped a beat. It was the fish he had caught with Jameson from their first fishing trip mounted against a log.

"Wow! This is amazing," Wilbur said. "Thank you!"

Jameson smiled and set the fish off to the side so it wouldn't get lost in the mountain of wrapping paper and empty boxes. In no time, Mavis and Wilbur had worked through their piles of gifts and waited patiently while Jameson opened his gifts from Ruby and surprised Ruby with a set of new pearls earrings.

"Mavis, would you like to give Wilbur his present from you?" Ruby asked.

Mavis looked around the base of the tree and found a box. "Here you go, Wilbur! Open it. Hurry up, let's see what you got!"

Wilbur carefully pulled the wrapping paper from the misshapen box and found a teddy bear inside. "Thanks Mavis!"

"You're welcome. Big Mama said you might want something more grown, but you ain't grown yet. I knew you'd love it. I know how to get the best presents," Mavis assured him.

"I love it," Wilbur smiled. "Here, I've got something for you, too.'"

Wilbur found one of the boxes he had wrapped and handed it to Mavis. She tore through the wrapping paper and Jameson used his pocket knife to open the box for her. Inside was a handmade picture frame that Wilbur had made. Inside the frame was a photograph of Mavis' favorite orange cat, Elephant.

Mavis hugged Wilbur and he patted her head. "I have something for you, too," Wilbur said to Jameson and Ruby. He handed them a box from behind the tree and watched them open it together. Inside was a handmade frame that resembled Mavis'. Instead of a photograph of a cat, there was a picture of the four of them: Jameson, Ruby, Mavis, and Wilbur. It was from the opening night of Opal's play in October, the first time that Wilbur had gotten dressed up and gone out with the family.

Ruby passed the frame to Jameson as she stood up to hug Wilbur. She squeezed him harder than she had ever hugged him before. "Thank you," she whispered. "I will treasure this forever."

Jameson smiled and echoed, "This is magnificent, Wilbur. Thank you." He laid the frame back in its box. Not to be outdone, Mavis dove under the tree. Wilbur rushed over to it and caught it before it could fully tip over. Mavis ignored the falling tree and shouts from Ruby and Jameson. She found her gifts for them and hurriedly climbed into Jameson's lap.

"Me next!" she said. "Ms. Opal helped me find these treasures!"

"Oh my goodness," Jameson whispered back. With Opal helping Mavis shop, anything was possible.

"Open it, Big Daddy!" Mavis said. "I wrapped it all by myself!"

"You first, honey," Jameson said to Ruby.

Ruby took the oblong and somewhat disheveled package gingerly from her granddaughter. As she opened it, she remembered to steal her face against any surprises which may be lurking inside. To Ruby's surprise, once she finally ripped through the four layers of tape and snowman paper, she found the ceramic figurine of a beautiful ginger cat. It was bigger that she would have thought.

Ruby examined the cat carefully. "Hmmm, what's this exactly?" She asked with a fair amount of trepidation.

"Oh, that's where the tissue comes out!" Mavis beamed.

"Do what?" Ruby needed clarification.

"You put the box of tissues in here and then the tissue comes out the back. Ms. Opal said it was pretty and practical." Mavis was giddy with the delight of her gift. "She said we had plenty of tissues here to stuff in it."

Jameson was in tears at the thought of Ruby displaying a cat with Kleenex coming out of his hindquarters. "We can put that right here on the coffee table," he said, wiping a tear out of his eyes.

"It looks just like Elephant," Mavis said.

"Oh my, well, that sure is, nice," Ruby said.

Jameson pulled out his handkerchief and coughed into it. "I can't wait to see what's inside my box!"

He picked up the small box from his lap and carefully unwrapped the paper. Inside the box was a crumpled ball of paper. He looked over at Mavis who was wide eyed.

"Open it!" she said excitedly.

He smiled at her and pulled the ball of wadded up tissue paper out of the box. As he unrolled the layers of protective paper, he felt the item get less heavy.

"Well, would you look at this," he said. "A dragon. Just what I always wanted!" He held up the tiny glass figurine for all of them to see.

"I knew you'd love it!" Mavis shouted. "Everyone needs a dragon. You can take it to your office and all the other mans will want one, too. You have to share, Big Daddy, but it's yours to keep."

"Thank you, sugar," Jameson said. He hugged Mavis tightly and winked at Wilbur who was trying hard not to laugh out loud.

"Wait 'til you see what I got Grandma Montgomery. She's going to love it so much," Mavis squealed.

"Ruby, honey, do you have any idea about that gift?" Jameson asked.

Ruby shook her head and her face lost all color.

"Oh, well, that's good," Jameson said. "Here's to hoping it's as great as that cat gift!"

They finished opening up the gifts. Jameson got a large trash bag and collected the pieces of wrapping paper that Mavis had so expertly shredded. Ruby started to work on lunch and sent Mavis upstairs to try and do something with her hair before Mrs. Montgomery came over for Christmas lunch.

"Want to ride over with me to pick up my mother?" Jameson asked Wilbur.

Wilbur nodded and followed Jameson to Ruby's Buick. The ride out to Mrs. Montgomery's house didn't take long since the roads were free of traffic. Wilbur waited in the car while Jameson helped his mother down the porch steps.

"Merry Christmas Wilbur," she smiled.

"Merry Christmas, Mrs. Montgomery," he replied.

Jameson put the bag of gifts in the trunk and made sure the covered dish was secure in the floorboard before backing out of her driveway. Mrs. Montgomery chatted the whole drive back to the Manor.

"We're here," Jameson called through the front door. He settled his mother in the living room and checked on the food cooking in the kitchen before going upstairs to check on Ruby and Mavis. He found them in Mavis' bedroom sitting on the floor. Mavis had her arms crossed as Ruby carefully combed through her wet hair.

"Ouch!" Mavis said. "That hurts!"

Ruby sighed heavily. "I found three marshmallows in her hair," Ruby said. She's been bathed and once I get her hair good and brushed, we'll be downstairs. The ham should be coming out of the oven in a few minutes."

"I'll go and check on it again. I pulled the biscuits out already," he said.

"Can you ask Wilbur to set the table, please," Ruby said. She was having trouble getting the comb through Mavis' wet hair.

Jameson winked at Mavis who continued to scowl. He went back downstairs and asked Wilbur to set the table while he got the ham out of the oven. Mrs. Montgomery walked into the kitchen and looked around.

"Where's Mavis?" she asked.

"She's upstairs. Ruby had a time getting something sticky out of her hair earlier, but she'll be down directly," he replied.

"Peanut butter," his mother said. "That'll work every time."

"I'll keep that in mind for next time," Jameson said. "How's the table coming along Wilbur?"

"Just finished," Wilbur replied. He had set the last of the Christmas china in place and got the Christmas tree glasses out of the cabinet. He could hear Mavis and Ruby coming down the stairs.

"Grandma!" Mavis yelled as she bounded into the kitchen and sprang into the awaiting arms of her great grandmother. Grandmother Montgomery braced herself for Mavis' excitement. Thankfully there was a chair waiting behind her in case she fell back. She had experience with Mavis' bursts of excitement before.

"Oh my goodness, sweetie. Look how pretty you look! Like a little angel in that dress," Mrs. Montgomery complimented her.

Mavis twirled around in her new Christmas dress to show the full effect of her outfit.

"I don't know about the rest of you, but smelling that ham is making me hungry. Let's sit on down at the table," Jameson said.

Ruby added some more salt and pepper to the gravy. "Everything's ready. Jameson will you say grace?" Ruby asked.

They bowed their heads as Jameson offered the Christmas blessing. A few minutes later the conversation was drowned out by the sound of forks and knives scraping against the plates of food. By the time Jameson pushed away from the table to loosen his belt, Mavis was already in Mrs. Montgomery's lap telling her all about the presents she got for Christmas.

"Speaking of presents, we should go out to the living room to exchange gifts with Grandma Montgomery," Ruby said.

"Yes! Let's go, Grandma! It's Christmas!" Mavis shouted with joy.

Mrs. Montgomery allowed Mavis to half drag her to the living room where the presents were. Once everyone was settled in the living room in their assigned spots, Mavis dug through the small stack by her feet until she found the one she was looking for.

"I picked it out all by myself!" Mavis said cheerfully. "I even wrapped it, too."

"I can see that," Mrs. Montgomery said happily. She took the box from Mavis and admired the snowman wrapping paper.

"Go on!" Mavis encouraged.

"Yes, Mother, go on. We're all anxiously waiting to see what Mavis picked out," Jameson smiled.

She peeled the wrapping paper that was still damp with glitter and glue off of the rectangular box and took off the random pieces of tape that held the box together. Inside was a folded up Christmas sweater. It was neon green.

"How precious," Mrs. Montgomery exclaimed.

"Show Big Mama!" Mavis said. "They have more if you want one, too, Big Mama!" She clapped her hands and jumped up and down.

Mrs. Montgomery pulled the sweater out of the box and Jameson started to choke on his molasses cookie at what was printed on the front of the sweater. "Oh, sugar, you've outdone yourself with this one," Jameson said. "Ruby, look who is on the front!"

In the center of the blazing bright lime green jumper was a vaguely familiar face wearing purple eye shadow and an oversized cherry hat similar to the kind worn by Roman Catholic priests. The face was framed with braided dark hair with feather extensions.

"Is that...Boy George?" Wilbur asked in disbelief.

"A Boy George Christmas sweater, boy howdy!" Jameson laughed.

Ruby silently reminded herself to never let Opal help with Mavis' Christmas shopping again.

"It sure is plum precious," Mrs. Montgomery said. She was trying her best not to laugh at the pure comedy before her. Mavis was certainly delighted in her gift choices and had no idea that the adults were holding back laughter.

"And look! If you press this button here, his feathers light up!" Mavis announced proudly. "Put it on, please!"

"Oh my," Mrs. Montgomery said. She pulled the sweater over her head and smiled for Mavis.

"You can't beat that, Mother. I expect to see you in that in your next Christmas card," Jameson howled.

"Where did you, um, find this, um, treasure at?" Mrs. Montgomery asked.

"At the mall!" Mavis squealed. "Ms. Opal and me picked it out real good!"

"I can see that!" agreed Mrs. Montgomery. "Did y'all get such beautiful sweaters, too?"

"Oh no, but I'm quite content with my glass spun dragon and Ruby here loves her tissue holder," Jameson said.

"How nice," Mrs. Montgomery replied. "Everyone needs a good tissue holder."

"Look Grandma! It's orange, just like Elephant!" Mavis said. She found the box that contained the ceramic cat tissue holder and shoved it under Mrs. Montgomery's nose. "Look! Ain't it precious?"

"Oh my!" Mrs. Montgomery exclaimed. "That certainly is one word that could possibly describe it. Wilbur, did you receive such a rare find as well?"

"No ma'am," Wilbur giggled. "Mavis surprised me with a handsome teddy bear."

"I wanted to get everyone a sweater, too, but Mrs. Opal said that each person needed something distinctive. Whatever that means," Mavis added sagely, as though Opal was the voice of authority for all present giving.

Ruby groaned and sank back into her recliner.

"Opal certainly has a flair all her own," Mrs. Montgomery said.

~Chapter Seventeen~

"Pete was released earlier this afternoon," Jameson said solemnly. He laid his briefcase down on the table and went to wash his hands at the sink.

Ruby turned to face him and held her breath for a moment. "What does that mean for Wilbur?"

"I don't know yet," he replied.

"What do we tell him?" Ruby asked.

"We'll tell him in the morning. No need to get into all that tonight," Jameson said. "I'll have to wait and talk to Mitch in the morning."

"But what do we tell him? He's been so happy here, Jameson," Ruby said. "It's only five days after Christmas; it's still the Christmas season."

"I know honey. We have temporary custody of him, but now that his father is out, I don't reckon that will hold up much. If Pete wants him home, he'll have to go. And if Wilbur asks to go home, we need to respect that," Jameson replied.

"He is home," Ruby said with spirit.

"I know, honey," Jameson said. He hugged her tightly before walking up the stairs. He heard laughter as soon as he reached the top step.

"Wilbur!" Mavis giggled. "That's not how you play!"

Jameson heard Wilbur chuckle and Mavis giggle. He peered around the corner into the room and saw them huddled around the dollhouse. Before he could speak, he heard a loud noise downstairs.

"Jameson!" Ruby called up the stairs anxiously.

Jameson closed the door to Mavis' room and hurried down the stairs. There was a loud pounding coming from the front door.

"Pete's here!" she swallowed hard. "He's on the porch."

Jameson looked out of the front window and saw Pete Reynolds pacing on the front porch. Jameson slipped out of the front door and closed the heavy door behind him.

"Good evening Pete. Can I help you with something?" Jameson asked.

Pete sniffed and rubbed his nose with the back of his hand. "I'd say so," he hissed. He spit a wad of tobacco at Jameson's feet.

Jameson ignored the tobacco on the porch and leaned against the door frame. He stayed silent and eyed Pete who cleared his throat before continuing.

"I know Wilbur's here," Pete said.

Jameson didn't say anything, but nodded. He pulled his handkerchief from his pocket and cleaned his glasses methodically.

"Well," Pete said.

"Well what?" Jameson asked.

"Damn't Jameson, don't act all high and mighty with me now," Pete replied. He leaned over the porch railing and spit the rest of the tobacco onto Ruby's mums. He lit a cigarette and blew the smoke out of his mouth slowly.

"You been drinking, Pete?" Jameson asked.

"What's it to you?" Pete answered.

"Just a question," Jameson said.

"I ain't gotta tell you nothin," Pete hissed. "Now, where's my boy? We've got places to go and people to see."

"Where you off to?" Jameson asked.

"That ain't none of your business," Pete replied. He tossed the cigarette into Ruby's flower beds and tried to reach around Jameson to get in the front door.

"Now, just you wait a minute," Jameson said. "Courthouse is closed for the day and will be for the next few days. Tomorrow's New Years Eve. Why don't you let me drive you home and get you settled in? We can revisit this next week once everything opens back up."

"I don't need your charity, Jameson Montgomery," Pete hissed.

"You know it's not like that, Pete," Jameson started to say. "You're just getting home and all. You have a lot of things to sort out and take care of, I'm sure.

"Tell Wilbur to get on down here. Tell him his daddy's here and it's time to go home," Pete snapped.

"Pete, let's not do this today. You're not exactly in the best condition," Jameson began. He put his hand up to stop Pete from pushing past him.

"Wilbur! Get down here boy!" Pete hollered.

"Now Pete, let's talk about this calmly," Jameson started again.

"He ain't your son!" Pete yelled. He grabbed the front of Jameson's collared shirt and snarled.

Jameson politely shook Pete off of him and straightened his collar before replying, "He's as good as. Now Pete, it's time for you to leave. Get off my property before I call Sheriff Owens out here to talk to you." There was sternness in Jameson's voice that was usually reserved for court.

"You think you can scare me with all your friends. That's the only reason you was able to steal my boy is cause you got friends in the police! I know Judge Dean and you is friends. You and your wife and her gaggle of girlfriends. All y'all got it in for me down there!" Pete yelled. He staggered backwards a little too far and tripped on the first step.

"Pete, this is the last time I'm going to tell you. It's time for you to leave," Jameson said sternly.

Pete wiped his nose once again on the back of his hand. "You ain't seen the last of me," Pete warned. He stumbled off the front porch. Jameson watched him walk unsteadily down the drive stopping occasionally to kick a rock that seemed to offend him.

"What in the world?" Ruby asked as soon as Jameson had come inside and locked the door behind him.

"Can't say I wasn't expecting it," Jameson sighed. "I'm afraid we're going to have a battle on our hands. He said we haven't seen the last of him."

"What does that mean?" Ruby asked.

"With Pete, it probably means exactly that. I'm sure he'll be back with a vengeance next time," Jameson said. "I'm going to let Ben and Teddy and everyone know that Pete's made contact."

Jameson picked up his briefcase from the table and retired to the small study just off the front staircase and closed the door behind him.

Later that evening, Opal called to remind Ruby about the bonfire at her house to ring in the New Year tomorrow night. They had even gotten some sparklers for the kids.

"I'm afraid the plans have changed," Ruby sighed. "Pete came by a little bit ago and made a small scene. We think it's best if we just stay in for the night and try to keep things quiet."

"Pete's out of jail? I thought his hearing wasn't just yet," Opal said.

"Pete's out?" Maude yelled in the background.

"Hush, Maude. I can't hear Ruby!" Opal chastised her.

"Fine!" Maude

"Jameson said the charges were dropped. I really don't know much else. You know the courthouse is closed for New Year's," Ruby replied.

Maude picked up the receiver in the living room to join the conversation. "You don't think he'd try anything, do you Rubes?" she asked.

"He wasn't very pleasant when he stopped by today," Ruby admitted.

Maude huffed loudly. It sounded more like a low growl. When she got her dander up it was hard to distinguish between the two.

"I understand," Opal said. "Of course, you know we'd never let anything happen to y'all down here. Teddy will be here, Ricky, Eddie, and Mortie are coming, too. And with me and Maude, Pete won't even dream of trying anything."

"At least, he better not," Maude added quickly. "This won't be my first rodeo!"

"I know, but Jameson and I really want a quiet evening at home after all that," Ruby said. "I know y'all will have a good time."

"Call us if he shows back up. I mean it, Ruby! You call me and I'll make sure he learns to behave," Maude said.

Ruby laughed and hung up the phone. Talking to Maude and Opal always lightened her stress level. It had certainly been an interesting holiday season thus far.

Ruby, Jameson, Wilbur, and Mavis spent the next evening eating pizza and popcorn while they counted down to the New Year. When the clock struck midnight, they all cheered and hugged.

"Happy New Year everyone," Jameson said.

"This year is going to be the best one yet," Mavis said sleepily.

Jameson and Ruby tucked Wilbur and Mavis into their beds and headed to bed themselves. They all slept peacefully and soundly until the next morning.

Early New Year's morning, Maude barely had time to open her eyes before Opal shook her out of bed.

"What in the devil?" Maude shouted.

"Get up! We've got to go," Opal hurried her.

"What?" Maude yawned. "I already said Happy New Year to you last night!"

"Maude! I've been robbed!" Opal shouted.

The news jarred Maude awake. Suddenly she was wide awake. She threw a robe on and slid her feet into the nearby slippers. "Are you hurt?" She focused her eyes on Opal who was half dressed in front of her. "Did they take anything?"

"I'm fine. Oh Maude, Eddie called me. Someone's broken into the salon. He said the police are already there. Come on!" Opal shouted again.

They made the drive to Main Street in three minutes with Maude driving. She always made good time, but when she was stressed, she made great time.

"What in the world?" Maude yelled.

The front window of The Comb Over was shattered. The lights were off in the store, but a large brick was visible in front of the nearest hair dryer. The back shelf had been knocked off the wall and Opal's merchandise table had been overturned.

"Y'all stay back," Teddy whispered. The front door was still locked. Opal handed him the keys to the shop from her purse and Teddy opened the front door. He disappeared into the shop and came back a few minutes later. "It's clear. There's no one in there."

"I bet it was Pete," Maude said.

"We don't' know that for sure, Maude," Opal said, more diplomatically than usual.

"You know as well as I do, this is something that ol' drunk would do," Maude fumed.

"Why do you say that?" Sheriff Bennet Owens asked.

"Just a feeling," Maude replied.

"Hang on a minute," Ben said. He walked back over to his Sheriff's car and listened to the radio for a moment. He motioned for Teddy and one of the other deputies to join him. Not to be excluded, Maude followed behind them to listen.

"Front window of Montgomery, Abernathy, & Associates has been smashed, too. I'll call Jameson," Bennet sighed. "Looks like the whole lobby has been trashed. Things are upturned and papers are everywhere."

"I'm telling you, it was Pete," Maude whispered to Teddy.

Teddy ushered Maude back over to Opal and Eddie who were sweeping up the broken glass. "Just wait here a minute," he said.

Maude pushed some of the furniture out of the way so Eddie could sweep under the dryers. She didn't hear Teddy come up behind her. "Opal, anything missing?" he asked.

Opal shook her head. "The register is fine and nothing is out of place besides the window and this mess. The shelves are broken, but it doesn't look like anything's been taken."

"Ok. That's good. Ben called over to the Montgomery's and Jameson's tires have been slashed. Looks like the truck's been keyed, too. Malcolm and I are about to ride over there and see what's going on," Teddy explained.

"I'm going to kill him!" Maude told Opal through gritted teeth.

"Well, thankfully I didn't hear that," Teddy said. "You two wait until I get back before you try to settle any accounts."

"I need to get this window boarded up," Opal said.

Maude walked over to the phone and quickly called her ex-husband, Larry. Larry was still the go to plumber and handyman in Rhinestone. Regardless of their history, he still jumped when Maude said to.

"Good morning," Larry answered. "This is a surprise."

"Morning, Larry. I'm sorry to call you so early in the morning, but I need your help," Maude began. She quickly explained what was going on and asked if he could help them put a temporary patch on the window.

"I'll be right over," Larry said.

"Oh Opal, my love. I just heard the news!" Ricky squealed. He pushed past Eddie and hugged Opal tightly. "This is so awful. Who would do this?"

"I saw it this morning," Eddie explained. "I had to come check on the cooler. It's been on the fritz all week and I couldn't risk losing my carnations."

By the time Larry arrived with the plywood, Ricky, Eddie, and Opal were in a full blown discussion about the complications of fixing the front window. Eddie had volunteered to stand guard on the premises, but Ricky insisted that was a ludicrous idea. Opal tried to referee between the two, but she was still in a bit of shock over her damaged window. Larry looked from one to the other without so much as a comment. There was no need for him to jump into that fray. Maude walked over to his truck to help him and between the two of them, they had the front window patched in twenty minutes.

"That oughta hold it until she can get someone out to replace the glass," Larry told Maude.

"Thanks Larry. I really appreciate you coming over here so fast," Maude told him.

Larry stood up a little taller. "You're always welcome," he smiled.

"Larry, thank you so much for fixing this," Opal said. She threw her arms around him and gave him a giant hug. She had always had a soft spot for Larry even when things didn't work out between him and Maude.

"No problem. You know I'd do anything for you," Larry said with a wink. "Any idea who would have done something like this?"

"Pete Reynolds," Maude mumbled.

"We don't know for sure, Maude, but it does kinda look like it might have been him," Opal said, again offering a diplomatic answer.

"Oooh, Pete. He's a bad bad man," Ricky said. "Don't be messing with Pete Reynolds, my love. You just call me if you need me!" He kissed Opal on the cheek and waltzed away.

"Everything good here?" Maude asked Opal.

Opal looked around and nodded.

"Then let's go," Maude said. Opal hugged Eddie and thanked him for calling her about the break in before following Maude back to the car.

"Didn't Teddy tell you to stay put?" Eddie asked Maude.

Maude stared at him. "When do you think I've ever listened to him?"

"Fair point," Eddie smiled.

Maude made the drive to Montgomery Manor in half the normal time. Opal held on for dear life and jumped out the moment Maude laid on the brakes.

"What are y'all doing here?" Teddy asked. "I told y'all to stay put."

"Did you really think I'm going to listen to that?" Maude asked. "Where's Ruby?"

Before Teddy could answer, Maude had pushed past him and headed for the front porch. Opal shrugged and followed on her heels.

"Ruby! Move Malcolm, let me in," Maude huffed. She pushed Malcolm out of the way and barged in the front door. "What's going on here?"

Ruby was sitting at the table drinking a cup of coffee. "Oh Maude! Did you see Jameson's truck out front?" she asked.

"I didn't even look. Was it Pete? I'll ruin him," Maude gritted her teeth.

"That's the common consensus," Ruby said. "Whoever it was backed into the magnolia tree, too. I sent Mavis and Wilbur over to Mrs. Montgomery's house. Malcolm and I just got back from dropping them off. There's no need for them to be here in all this mess. Come on out and see for yourself."

Ruby led Maude and Opal back outside past Malcolm who was still at the door writing in a notebook. She showed them Jameson's truck and the injured magnolia tree next to it. "Is the salon ok?"

"Just a smashed window and some broken bits. Nothing was taken. Larry came by and boarded it up," Opal said.

"Cecil went down there to the office and boarded things up there, too. He said the offices were all locked, so nothing was taken. Whoever it was tossed around some papers and knocked over the chairs in the lobby, but nothing that can't be fixed," Ruby said.

They walked back to the front porch where Jameson was now standing. Teddy joined him and shrugged his shoulders. "Pete's not at home," Teddy said to Jameson. "Sheriff just rode by there and the house is empty. We've got a BOLO out on him. He can't get too far."

"It's Pete. That man disappears for weeks at a time," Maude grumbled.

Jameson took his handkerchief out of his back pocket and began to wipe off his glasses. "Speaking strictly from a legal aspect, is there any proof that Pete did this. I mean, I think we can all agree that he is the prime suspect, but usually a little more than that is needed in a court of law. Is there anything other than our suspicion here?"

"His old truck is already pretty battered. I don't imagine we can tie him to this damage, if that's what you're asking. Just be careful, Jameson. If he contacts you again, or any of y'all, we'll take care of it," Teddy said.

"I'm sure I'll be hearing from him as soon as the courthouse opens back up. He's bound and determined to get Wilbur back," Jameson said.

"We'll burn that bridge when we get there," Teddy replied.

Chapter Eighteen

"Honey, I don't like this any more than you do, but my hands are tied," Jameson said.

"It isn't fair," Ruby cried. "None of this is right. Mitchell has to be able to do something about this."

"His hands are tied, too, honey. Believe me, we've tried everything. Pete's threatened to sue us all and there's no letter to the law that says he isn't allowed to have his son back. Cecil and I have tried everything we know to do," Jameson explained.

"But he destroyed the salon and your office. And your truck! And my tree!" Ruby cried.

"Well, he swears he doesn't know anything about that," Jameson sighed. "There's nothing any of us can do about any of that now. By law Pete will be able to get Wilbur back. At least for right now."

"What do you mean?" Ruby asked. She wiped her eyes with the hem of her dress.

"If history is anything, Pete will slip up again. If it weren't for Bobby over at the bar dropping his charges and Floyd McAllister suddenly dropping his, this wouldn't be happening right now. I'm sure it will only be a matter of time because Pete's walking on thin ice. As much as I don't want to, we're going to have to follow the rules here," Jameson sighed deeply.

"It's not right," Ruby said again. "He should have to pass some kind of drug test or something. Don't they know how he neglects his own son?"

"Unfortunately the law can't terminate a parent's rights so quickly. It's not an easy process. Technically now Pete hasn't done anything to be held. Once the charges were dropped, he became a free man again. And even to begin with, he wasn't arrested for being a bad parent," Jameson said.

Ruby didn't say anything, nor did she act like she had even heard what he said. She knew that Jameson and his partner, Cecil Abernathy, had been working nonstop since Pete was released a few days before. As soon as the courthouse opened Monday morning, Jameson filed a petition with Judge Mitchell Dean. As expected, Pete and his attorney pushed back. There was nothing more that Jameson could do. Pete was Wilbur's father and the temporary custody order had expired.

"Ruby, Pete's getting him from the police station on Friday morning," Jameson said.

"But, but that's in two days!" Ruby cried.

Jameson held her tightly as she cried. Tears slipped from the bridge of his nose into Ruby's hair. Dinner that evening was subdued. Even

Mavis picked up on the dismay of the evening. When dinner was over, Jameson sent Mavis upstairs so they could talk to Wilbur alone.

"Big Mama and I need to talk to Wilbur for a little bit. Run along and play and one of us will be up to get your bath ready," Jameson said.

"Is Wilbur in trouble? 'Cause he didn't do nothing. And I didn't either," Mavis said.

"No sugar, now run along," Jameson replied.

Mavis took her time on the stairs. Once she was fully out of earshot, Wilbur broke the silence.

"When do I have to leave?" he asked quietly.

Ruby looked at Jameson and swallowed hard. This was yet another conversation that she had been dreading. It had already been a week of difficult conversations. Once the police cleared out last week on New Year's Day, Jameson and Ruby had driven to Mrs. Montgomery's house to pick up Mavis and Wilbur. When they got back home, there was no way to hide the damage to the magnolia tree or the damage to Jameson's truck. No one brought up Pete as a suspect, but they had a feeling that the boy knew. Jameson sat him down and told him that Pete had come for a visit the night before, but he was in no state to take Wilbur home that evening.

Wilbur nodded. "I know. I went to my room and opened the window. I heard everything."

Jameson hadn't expected Wilbur to hear that conversation. It wasn't something he wanted to burden the boy with. He quickly regained his train of thought and explained that the temporary custody order from the court was still being upheld while the courthouse was closed for the holidays. Jameson said that once the courthouse opened back up on Monday, they should know more. He told Wilbur that if it came down to it, he would have to go back with his father. Wilbur took all of the news quietly. He didn't ask many questions or offer any suggestions.

"Do I have to leave right now?" Wilbur asked.

The directness of Wilbur's question brought Ruby firmly into the present.

"Your father is going to be waiting at the police station Friday morning. While Ruby takes Mavis to school, you will ride in with me to my office. He's meeting us at nine," Jameson said slowly.

Wilbur looked down at his plate and nodded, but didn't say anything. Neither did Ruby. She was trying her hardest to hold back the tears that had been escaping all evening. She gathered up the plates and moved them to the sink. When Wilbur brought the empty drinking glasses to her, she reached over and hugged him tightly. He didn't want her to let go.

No one slept well that night or the following night. Ruby had made sure all of Wilbur's dirty laundry was clean and Mavis had become inconsolable when she found Wilbur packing his suitcase Thursday after dinner. No matter how many times Wilbur promised to come back and visit, Mavis wouldn't stop crying. She even offered to pack her new doll, Betty, in Wilbur's suitcase so he wouldn't forget about her.

"He can't go. He's our family. He's mine," Mavis kept saying.

"I'm afraid that's not how it works, sugar. You can't keep people. Sometimes they have to do what they have to do," Jameson tried to explain. Logically he understood why Wilbur was leaving, but his own heart was having a difficult time, too.

"You can if they're family. And he's my family. Like Big Mama keeps Ms. Opal and Mrs. Maude. He's just as much family as they are!" Mavis argued. She made a point that neither Ruby nor Jameson could refute, not that they even wanted to. Eventually, she fell asleep on Wilbur's bed while he and Ruby folded his shirts. When Jameson carried her to her room, he thought he saw Wilbur wipe a tear from his eye.

Ruby woke up Friday morning earlier than usual. No one said much that morning while they ate their oatmeal and drank their orange juice.

"I don't want you to go Wilbur," Mavis whimpered. She put on her shoes by the front door and dragged her backpack behind her.

"It'll be ok Mavis," Wilbur said. "I'll still come over and we can play sometimes."

"It won't be the same," Mavis whispered. She turned around suddenly and almost knocked Wilbur down with the force of her embrace. Jameson gave her a minute, and then pried her away from Wilbur who was struggling hard to maintain his composure.

They all knew that Mavis was right. The four of them walked outside in the cold morning air. Wilbur hugged Mavis and Ruby in the driveway one last time as Jameson loaded his suitcase in the truck. Jameson had had it towed to Coop's Tire Outlet the past weekend where Maude's nephew put on all new tires and managed to buff out most of the scratches. It had a brand new paint job and looked better than ever.

Wilbur waved as Ruby and Mavis backed out of the driveway. He climbed into Jameson's truck and didn't say anything on the drive to Jameson's office. The front window was still boarded up. Across the street, the front window of The Comb Over was also boarded with plywood. Both offices had appointments early next week to have the panes replaced.

It was the first time Wilbur had been back downtown since the evening of the Christmas play. He had not seen the windows that had been broken out. As badly as he wanted to think otherwise, he knew deep down that his daddy had done it. Maybe it really was best that he go back home. At least then his dad wouldn't hurt Ruby, Jameson, and their friends anymore. It wasn't right for anyone to get hurt on account of him not going home.

Jameson parked the truck in his usual parking spot. They sat in silence for a few moments. Finally Jameson spoke. "Wilbur, I want you to know that if you need anything, anything at all, you can always come to me or Mrs. Ruby. We will always take care of you, no matter the time of day, no matter what it is."

"Yes, sir," Wilbur mumbled. He looked down at his hands, but said nothing more.

Jameson looked down at his watch. "We had better go in," he sighed.

It was the longest walk either of them had ever taken. The entire process only took a half hour. When Jameson walked back out to his truck, he was lost. It was a feeling he hadn't felt since Melanie's passing.

No one said it aloud, but Ruby and Jameson both watched the front door anxiously all weekend in hopes that Wilbur would walk though it for a visit. Anytime the phone rang, Jameson answered it in a hurry to see if it was Wilbur calling. But no such call or visit happened. Even Mavis lost the interest in playing with her new dollhouse and sat in front of the fireplace idly.

Ruby called Opal and Maude over for a visit Monday morning to break the monotony. They had given her the space to privately mourn all weekend and were chomping at the bit to see her. They found her in the kitchen eating leftover molasses cookies and drinking lukewarm coffee.

"I need to pack up his stuff that he left and get it over to him. I thought he'd come get it this weekend, but he must have been busy. It just feels so quiet," Ruby said. "I know he and Mavis would both be at school at this time of day anyway, but there's still something missing."

"We'll help you, if you want us to," Maude offered.

Ruby nodded and the three of them walked up the stairs to Wilbur's room. There was an empty box sitting on the floor next to his bed.

"Oh my goodness, he left his coveralls. I thought he had thrown these things away," Ruby smiled.

Maude patted Ruby on the shoulder.

"I remember when I first brought him here with me for lunch after he helped me gather ingredients for my hair dye line. He was covered in mud and wearing those too short coveralls. It feels like ages ago, but really it was just a few months ago."

Ruby smiled at the memory.

"Speaking of the hair stuff, how's that going?" Maude asked. She was hoping to change the subject away from Wilbur.

"Fine, just fine. Can hardly keep the shampoo and conditioning bottles on the shelves. I added the lotion bottles and the hair paste yesterday. I hope to unveil the accompanying tea and supplement line in a few weeks. I'll have to wait 'til spring to really get the soap line going because I can't get my hands on the necessary ingredients for that right now," Opal explained.

"Y'all look at this," Ruby whispered. She held up a piece of white construction paper with a pencil drawing of four people. Wilbur's artistic hand had drawn Jameson, Ruby, Mavis, and Wilbur. He had even included Mavis' fat cat, Elephant. In the bottom corner he had signed his name and written the word Family across the top.

"He's a good little artist," Maude said.

"We haven't heard from him since Pete took him," Ruby said.

"Not at all?" Opal asked.

Ruby shook her head.

"How are we going to get him this stuff?" Maude asked.

"Jameson said he'd take it to his office and Pete's lawyer would come get it," Ruby said. "I don't guess it's a good idea for us to drop it by."

"How long are you going to wait to hear from him before you go down there?" Opal asked.

"I don't know," Ruby answered. "I just keep hoping he'll come by or at least call. Maybe Pete's turned over a new leaf and they're doing well together. I just don't know."

For Wilbur's sake, they hoped that was true, although none of them would have bet on it.

The next few days passed uneventfully. There was no contact with Wilbur still, which worried Ruby tremendously. Jameson kept his stress to himself, but the tension in the room was palpable. Mavis asked every night at bedtime when Wilbur would be coming home, but neither Jameson nor Ruby had an answer for her. No one had called the office to pick up Wilbur's boxes either, but Jameson did not relay that information to Ruby. She had not gone back into Wilbur's room since she packed it up. The bedroom door remained closed.

By Friday, Ruby was walking around in a fog. She was unable to concentrate on anything she was doing. Twice she poured salt in her morning coffee by mistake and had to get a new cup. Jameson watched her as he ate his breakfast. Something had to be done. He decided to stop by the beauty parlor and talk to Opal and Maude after he dropped Mavis off at school. He knew they would both be there early this morning because the new window panes were being installed at The Comb Over and at his office. They were the only ones who were guaranteed to help Ruby snap out of it

Two hours later, The Stone Sisters were once again gathered in Ruby's kitchen. Maude brought a half eaten cake and set it on the cluttered counter. She took one look at the thick coffee Ruby was drinking and poured it out. A new pot was brewing before Ruby could protest. Opal stirred a large boiling pot on the stove. She had brought a bag full of herbs and Lord knows what else with her. She claimed that her specialty tea would help cure Ruby's depression.

"What's the cake for?" Ruby asked.

"I got it for Opal on Tuesday. We had a nice dinner and ate cake and drank wine. Nothing fancy," Maude answered.

It suddenly dawned on Ruby that she had forgotten Opal's birthday on Tuesday.

"Oh God, Opal! I'm so sorry!" Ruby cried. She jumped up from her chair and hugged Opal.

"It's ok," Opal smiled. "There will be other birthdays."

"Ruby, I'll cut you a slice of cake to go with Opal's witchy brew while you go get dressed," Maude said.

Ruby went upstairs to get dressed. Maude was rinsing out Ruby's coffee mug when the phone rang. She answered it without hesitation.

"Hello," Maude said. "Oh? Um, hold on a minute." Ruby was still not back downstairs, so she would have to handle this herself. "Yes, how can I help you? Oh. Well, um, yes. I will have to get back with you on that. What? We'll have to call you back. Yes, I'll call you back. I'll call you back!"

Opal stared at Maude like she had two heads. "What in the world was that about?"

"That was the school secretary. You know Belle Jenkins. Well, she asked how Wilbur was doing because it was odd for him to miss so much school. Hasn't been there all week," Maude said in a whisper.

"Oh no!" Opal gasped.

"What are we gonna do?" Maude asked.

"Well, we'll have to go investigate, of course," Opal said matter of factly.

"What are we going to investigate?" Ruby asked.

Neither Maude nor Opal answered her right away.

"What's going on?" Ruby demanded. When no one answered, she crossed her arms and asked again more sternly. "What is going on? Who was on the phone? Who is being investigated?"

"That was the school calling to ask about, um," Maude started.

"Will someone please tell me what's going on?" Ruby all but yelled. "Is it Mavis?"

"No, no, Mavis is fine," Opal said meekly.

"Then why is the school calling?" Ruby asked.

"They want to know why Wilbur hasn't been to school all week," Opal blurted out.

✑ Chapter Nineteen ✑

"He what?" Ruby demanded.

"That's what Belle said. She wanted to know how he was feeling because he had missed a whole week of school," Maude told her. "I told her we'd have to call her back."

Ruby grabbed her keys from the hook by the front door.

"Wait a minute. Where are we going?" Maude asked.

Ruby looked at her and said, "Where do you think?"

"Hell yes! I love a good sting operation!" Opal yelled. "Come on Maude, let's go!"

"Hold on a minute, you didn't turn off the stove!" Maude shouted after them. "I swear, without me they'd burn the damn house down."

Ruby and Opal were already at the car by the time Maude turned off the stove and moved Opal's boiling concoction from the hot stove eye. She locked the front door and hurried down the front steps.

"Move over, I'll drive!" Maude said.

"Buckle up, Ruby! You know how Maude drives when she's on the warpath," Opal hollered from the backseat.

"She's not the only one on the warpath," Ruby said.

Pete's house wasn't far from the Manor as the crow flies, but there was no direct road connecting the properties. Maude pulled out onto the county road then turned on the dirt road after the creek. As they neared Pete's place, she slowed down more than usual.

"What are you doing?" Opal asked, peering over the Maude's shoulder.

"Making sure Pete ain't out there about to do something stupid," Maude told her. "I'd hate to have to run him over in Ruby's nice car."

"I have good insurance," Ruby replied.

Opal looked over at her friend. Ruby was generally the calm and collected one of the three, except when it came to her family. Nothing could bring the fight out of Ruby quicker than someone messing with her loved ones. She would have to be the voice of reason now that Maude and Ruby were both wound up.

"I don't see his truck," Opal said. "Maybe he's not home." She hopped out of the back seat as soon as Maude put the car in park.

"Opal! Get back here!" Maude yelped. "You can't just run up to the door!"

"Why not? Maybe I'm a door to door salesman," Opal shrugged. She skipped to the front door and knocked three times. "Hello!" she called out.

No one came to the door.

"She could be a regular secret agent," Maude mumbled as she got out of the car.

"I don't reckon anyone is home," Opal yelled over her shoulder.

"We'll see about that!" Ruby huffed.

Ruby joined Opal on the rickety porch and knocked hard on the door. "Pete? Wilbur? Open up!"

They could hear someone or something behind the door. Suddenly the door opened a tiny bit and Wilbur peeked out through the sliver. "Hello?" he whispered.

"Wilbur!" Ruby exclaimed. She pushed open the door and grabbed the boy into a big bear hug.

"Howdy Wilbur?" Opal sang. "Is your daddy home?"

Wilbur mumbled something incoherent.

"Lord Ruby, let the boy breathe!" Maude said.

Ruby let go of Wilbur and saw his bruised eye. "Wilbur! Did he hurt you?"

Wilbur didn't answer. He swallowed hard and looked at Maude.

"Is your daddy home," Maude asked.

He shook his head. "He's not here," he said.

"Good. Because he ain't gonna like what I've got to say," Maude growled. She pushed up her sleeves and looked around the porch.

"May we come in?" Opal asked softly.

Wilbur looked like a deer caught in the headlights. "I don't know, I mean, I don't think he would like that."

"Where is he exactly?" Ruby asked.

"I don't know," Wilbur responded.

Opal looked over Wilbur's shoulder into the house. It was in shambles and had an unpleasant smell emanating from it. The paper was peeling from the walls and there were stains around the front window. The couch was sunken in the center and there was a broken coffee table in front of it. She couldn't see past the living room, but she didn't imagine the rest of the small house looking any better.

"What happened Wilbur? How come you missed school this week?" Maude asked him.

Wilbur shrugged and looked down at his shoes. "I, well, I hope you're not mad," he said.

"No one's mad honey, at least we're not mad with you," Ruby said. "What's going on Wilbur?"

"Daddy left. He said he had some business to take care of and he'd be back after a while. He told me not to leave the house. I haven't left to go anywhere, I promise," Wilbur explained.

"Did he do that to you?" Opal asked gently.

Wilbur nodded slowly.

"When did he say all that? How long has he been gone?" Ruby asked.

"Sunday," Wilbur answered.

"Sunday?" Ruby repeated.

"Yes ma'am," Wilbur quickly wiped his nose on the back of his hand. He had a few scrapes on his lower arm and elbow.

"Two days after you came back," Ruby began, but she stopped herself before she lost her religion.

"You've been here all by yourself since Sunday?" Opal asked him.

Wilbur nodded, "yes ma'am."

Ruby steadied herself. "Go get your things, Wilbur. You're coming home with us."

Wilbur looked up at her in disbelief. Maude and Opal glanced in her direction, but said nothing.

It would be best to let Jameson work out all of the legal details. It would not be the first time they let Jameson in on the plan late. Right now, Wilbur needed a hot bath, some good food, and lots of love. That they knew how to handle.

"Really?" Wilbur asked. "I can go with you?"

"Yes, really. Now go get your stuff. Hurry up because Opal's got a special soup on the stove. It's supposed to make everything better," Ruby told him.

"Well, it's more like a tea, but," Opal interrupted. She was silenced by Ruby's glare. "We can call it a soup, that's fine."

Wilbur knew all about Opal's cooking, but even that didn't deter him. "Yes ma'am!"

"Don't worry, Wilbur. Ruby's been baking for a solid week. It's the only thing that calms her nerves. Those cookies she made should counteract any concoction Opal's making," Maude laughed.

A giant smile split Wilbur's face.

"Hurry on up, now," Ruby nodded. Wilbur scurried off into the shack and reappeared quickly with his suitcase. It didn't look like he had even unpacked it.

Maude went down the rickety steps and opened up the trunk to make room for Wilbur's things. She put the suitcase inside and opened the door for him to climb into the backseat with Opal.

"All aboard?" Opal called out.

Maude drove them back to the Manor without one look behind them. When they arrived, Wilbur got his suitcase out of the trunk and hurriedly carried it up the front porch steps.

"Wilbur, go on and take your things up to your room. I'm going to call Jameson and let him know what's happened," Ruby told him.

"I'll get lunch started," Maude offered.

"You didn't pour out any of my tea, did you?" Opal asked as she followed Maude into the kitchen.

"No, I didn't," Maude replied. "That's why it smells like death warmed over in here. What in the world did you put in there?"

"These are secrets from the ancient world. A mere mortal like you wouldn't understand," Opal said, examining the brew on the stove. She took a small spoon from her shirt pocket and tasted the liquid. She rummaged through her bag and added the contents of a small glass vial. "That should do it. Let me bring it back to a boil and it'll be ready."

"As I recall, you had some of those ancient world remedies over in India once, too. You better not have brought any of that mess over here," Maude grumbled.

"I never had anything of the sort," Opal told her.

"You did too! What in the world do you think they were smoking on that bus?" Maude reminded her. "Not that you probably remember."

Opal looked at her in disbelief. It really was sad how uncultured Maude could be at times. "Now really, Maude. I've told you time and again, they were my friends and that was a peace pipe. It's an international symbol of good will."

"Oh it was a pipe alright. We almost never got you on the plane," Maude said.

"You always exaggerate about everything," Opal shook her head. "But to answer your question, this tea is my own recipe. It's designed to bring not only peace, but prosperity, too."

"Well, we're gonna need a lot of peace and prosperity. I think Ruby has leapt off the deep end and Jameson's going to have to tread some deep water if this goes south," Maude replied. She peeked into the living room where Ruby was on the phone with Jameson.

Jameson listened as Ruby told him everything that had happened that morning. When she was finished, he took a deep breath. "And Wilbur is there at the house with you now?"

"Yes. We're all here. Wilbur needs a bath and then he will need to unpack. It looks like Pete roughed him up, Jameson. Maude and Opal are in the kitchen fixing lunch. We'll go get Mavis from school later on," Ruby said calmly.

"Y'all stay there at the Manor. I have no idea where Pete is, but if he comes home and Wilbur isn't there, he's not going to be happy. I need to make some phone calls to get this sorted out,"

Jameson said. "My God, I'm married to a kidnapper."

Ruby didn't laugh at his attempt at a joke. "I'm not letting him go back there," Ruby said firmly.

Jameson sighed heavily on the phone. "I know."

"I'm not joking, Jameson," Ruby repeated.

"I need to make some phone calls about this, Ruby. Y'all stay there and let me handle it from here. I'll pick up Mavis when it's time from school and bring her home," Jameson said.

Ruby agreed. She hung up the phone and walked upstairs to Wilbur's room. He was sitting on his bed looking through the boxes of his things.

"We were going to take these to you, but that didn't work out, did it? Why don't you jump in the tub real quick and after lunch we can fix your room back like you had it," Ruby told him. She gently brushed his hair out of his eyes.

Wilbur shrugged. "Won't I have to go back anyway?"

"We're going to do everything in our power to make sure you stay with us," Ruby assured him.

Wilbur nodded. "Okay." He slowly opened up the suitcase and pulled some clothes out for his bath. Ruby kissed him on top of his head and then went downstairs to join Opal and Maude.

"What did Jameson have to say about our little adventure?" Maude asked.

"He said he would handle it," Ruby shrugged.

"Let's hope he does," Maude said. "I don't imagine being married to someone who commits felony kidnapping would look too good for an attorney."

"Plus, Maude doesn't look good in orange stripes. Stripes bring out that extra weight she carries in her hips," Opal said.

"You're one to talk!" Maude said.

"No one is going to jail," Ruby said calmly.

Maude and Opal looked at each other and raised their eyebrows.

"I have to say Rubes, I like this new personality. This devil may care attitude is a nice look," Maude laughed.

"The devil shouldn't have messed with one of my kids," Ruby said.

Jameson and Mavis walked through the door three hours later. Ruby met them at the door and picked up Mavis and held her close. Jameson dropped his briefcase down by the door and stared at his wife.

"Mavis, why don't you go over to the living room and turn on the television? I'll bring you a snack in just a minute," Ruby said.

Mavis wandered into the living room and climbed into Ruby's recliner. She pulled the soft blanket that was draped over the top of the chair and wrapped it around her. She turned on the television and found a rerun of The Flintstones.

Once she was out of earshot, Jameson continued. "The next time you decide to randomly kidnap a child, let me know in advance so I can start the paperwork a little earlier," he said with a sigh. "And you two," he glared at Maude and

Opal. "I suggested you come for a visit and try to talk to her, not encourage her to commit a felony."

Opal and Maude didn't say anything right away.

"I mean, I know you three like to go off and have a good ol' time, but this is on a whole other level," he said. "Do y'all realize how bad this could get?"

"Jameson, you've got it all wrong. We never intended to," Maude said.

"I am perfectly capable of making my own decisions Jameson," Ruby interrupted. "Maude and Opal did not suggest or encourage any of this. This was my idea and I'd do it again."

"Ruby," Jameson said.

Ruby simply stared back without blinking.

"Well, I'll be damned. I'm sorry y'all, I just didn't see this coming," Jameson said.

Maude shrugged and Opal laughed. "I told you, Ruby was always the one who got us into trouble."

Ruby ignored them and asked Jameson, "You got everything taken care of didn't you?"

"Of course I did, at least for now. I got another temporary custody order signed until they can track Pete down. Who knows where he's at and when he'll return, but when he does, it's not going to be pretty. If you think you can stay around the house and not get into any more trouble, with Bonnie and Clyde here," he winked and pointed his thumb at Maude and Opal.

"You're Clyde," Opal whispered to Maude.

"Hush up," Maude said. She jabbed Opal with her elbow.

"I bet Mavis is famished after being at school all day," Ruby said. She grabbed a bowl and dumped a handful of chocolate chip cookies into it. She poured a small glass of milk and took them to Mavis.

"I assume Wilbur is upstairs?" Jameson said. He had pulled the infamous handkerchief from his pocket and cleaned his glasses thoroughly.

"He's upstairs catching up on his homework," Maude answered.

Jameson turned to the staircase and saw Wilbur standing on the third step grinning. Jameson crushed him in a hug and couldn't help but laugh.

"Oh Wilbur, you're in cahoots with some wild women," he said.

"Did I hear Mavis come in?" Wilbur asked.

"She'll be tickled to see you, Wilbur. She hasn't stopped asking about you!" Jameson said. "It's so good to see you. Come on."

Wilbur and Jameson found Mavis in Ruby's lap eating a cookie.

"Hey Mavis, can I have one of those?" Wilbur asked.

"Wilbur?" Mavis exclaimed. "Wilbur! It's you!" She jumped up so quickly that she knocked over the rest of the cookies.

Wilbur braced himself for Mavis' attack, but he was too late. She tackled him like a linebacker and he was crushed under her hug.

"You're home!" Mavis yelled. "Big Mama! Wilbur's home!"

"Yes Mavis, Wilbur is home. Now let him up," Ruby said, reaching down to help them both off the floor.

"Well, it's about time. I don't know why you were gone for so long. You've missed a lot, but don't worry. I'll make sure you get caught up," Mavis declared.

~Chapter Twenty~

"I love hearing Ms. Opal sing," Mavis said from the backseat of Ruby's car. "I'm gonna sing in the choir one day, too!"

"You have a lovely voice," Ruby said.

Mavis started to sing her own version of the hymns from church. Wilbur wasn't so sure that he could agree with Ruby's assurance of Mavis' angelic voice, but he smiled at her nonetheless.

Jameson turned into the driveway of Magnolia Manor and immediately stopped.

"What's?" Ruby started to say. "Oh my heavens."

Wilbur leaned around the headrest in front of him and saw his father's beat up truck in front of the Manor.

"Ruby, I'm going to drop you, Wilbur, and Mavis back off at the church and then come back down here to see about this," Jameson said. He backed out of the driveway and sped back to Beaver Crossing Holy Church for the Faithful.

Maude and Opal were still at the church talking to Teddy when Jameson pulled back up. When he quickly explained the sudden change of plans, Teddy offered to ride with Jameson back to the Manor. Pete's truck was still in the driveway when Jameson pulled back in. "Sure you don't want me to call for backup?" Teddy asked.

"Let's see what he has to say first," Jameson said. "I see him on the porch."

Jameson and Teddy exited Ruby's Buick and walked slowly to the front porch. Pete leaned over the railing and watched them approach.

"Afternoon Pete," Jameson said. "What can I do for you today?"

Pete didn't respond, though he eyed Teddy suspiciously. Jameson went up the porch steps first and sat down in the rocking chair by the front door. "What can I do for you today?" Jameson repeated.

"Imagine my surprise, comin' home and not seein' my boy at home where I told him to stay," Pete said dryly. "I know he's here. Ain't no need to bring the law with you. I'm here peacefully to take my boy back. Even though you's the one who came to my house and stole my kid." Pete put his arms up in the air and turned around in a slow circle.

"I'm afraid I can't let you do that, Pete," Jameson replied. "Wilbur's not here right now anyway. Judge signed another court order giving me temporary custody again. I'll be glad to meet with you in my office Tuesday to discuss some things. Monday is a state holiday, I'm afraid, so downtown'll be closed."

"So, just like that they let you take my boy again? I know you got friends in high places," he spit. "And I guess you just gonna stand there and let him do it, ain't you?" Pete looked from Jameson to Teddy.

"Pete, everybody just wants what's best for Wilbur. It's not right for him to be stranded all alone out there with no adult supervision. The judge didn't have much of a choice since he didn't know when you'd be back. We're talking neglect, abandonment, abuse. We're looking at what's best for Wilbur right now," Teddy tried to explain calmly.

"You serious? Best for Wilbur? I know what's best for him seeing as how I'm his father," Pete said.

"Nobody said you're not, but he needs adult supervision and right now it seems your business affairs are keeping you out of town a good bit," Teddy replied.

Pete glared at Teddy and looked him up and down. For a split second, his hand twitched near his front pocket.

"Now Pete, don't do something you'll regret," Teddy interjected.

Pete put his hand sup and said, "I'm just getting my keys." He spit over the railing and slowly put his hand in his pocket to fish out the keys. "I see that I've been bested," he snickered. "Guess I best be gettin' on with things then." He walked down the porch steps and didn't look behind him. When he got to his truck, he started it up and took one last look at Teddy and Jameson who were standing near the porch railing. He gave a semi-friendly wave and backed out of the driveway slowly.

"Glad that's over," Teddy said. He clapped Jameson on his back and hopped down the steps.

"I don't think we've seen the last of him," Jameson sighed. He followed Teddy back to the car and drove them both back to the church.

"I'll have someone drive by his place tonight and tomorrow. We'll keep an eye on this, don't you worry," Teddy assured him.

Jameson dropped Teddy back off at the church and took Ruby, Mavis, and Wilbur back home. He hoped Teddy was right about things being over with Pete, but if there was one thing that Jameson knew, it was that men like Pete weren't ones to ever go away quietly.

Jameson enjoyed sleeping in for an extra hour the next morning. It was a cloudy day with storm clouds that rolled in around noon. "I reckon I need to cancel the card game tonight," Jameson said to Ruby when she came to join him out on the front porch swing.

"Why do you say that?" she asked.

"Between the weather and Pete, I just don't have a good feeling," Jameson sighed. He eyed the dark clouds.

"Everything is fine," Ruby said cheerfully. "Maude and Opal are coming over this evening and once Mavis and Wilbur go to bed, Opal's going to do Maude's hair. She's got a new product line coming out soon and for some reason, Maude volunteered to be the tester."

"Volunteered or was told?" Jameson smiled. The rain on the roof began to keep time with the creaking of the old swing.

"Well, you know it goes," Ruby laughed.

"Then I think I better move the card game here," Jameson said. 'I don't like the idea of y'all ladies being here all alone."

"Oh no," Ruby interrupted. "Honey, we'll be fine. I promise. You need this time away. Relax and spend some time with your friends. Y'all tend to get a little loud and plus, the kids will be in bed. They've got school tomorrow, so don't worry."

Jameson mulled over what Ruby was saying and decided to call Teddy to see if he had heard anything.

"Haven't seen him since yesterday after church," Teddy told Jameson over the phone. "Looks like he probably went out of town again. His truck is nowhere to be seen in town. None of us have seen him."

"Well, that's good news, I guess. At least maybe it means things'll be quiet for a few days," Jameson said. "But, I can't help wishing I knew exactly where he was."

"I'm sure he'll show back up when the money for booze runs out or he needs something else from his science experiments out back behind his shed. Until then, we're going to keep a close eye out for him and make sure he doesn't do anything he shouldn't," Teddy assured him.

"I appreciate that, Teddy," Jameson said. He did appreciate the extra precaution they were all taking, yet that didn't stop the nagging pang of anxiety that continued to plague him.

When Maude and Opal arrived, Jameson was about ready to head over to Sheriff Owens' house for a poker game.

"I'll be at Ben's house. I'm going to pick up Cecil on the way. It ain't far. But if you see anything funny at all, call me over at Ben's and I'll be here in a few minutes," Jameson said.

"We'll be fine, Jameson. You go on and have fun," Ruby told him.

"Teddy's on call tonight, but I know he said he'll stop by the game. He won't miss any chance he has to beat Mitch at poker," Maude laughed. "We'll be fine," Maude assured him. "Plus, Ruby's a hardened criminal."

"That's what I'm afraid of," Jameson smiled and put on his coat. He kissed Ruby goodbye and opened his umbrella on the porch.

"Wilbur, grab that bowl of popcorn and Mavis, pick what cookies y'all want. Opal will get the movie started and I'll be right in there," Ruby said once Jameson left.

Maude followed them with a tray of sweet tea. "You coming Ruby?" she asked.

"Right behind you. Just making sure the front door is good and locked. Can't be too careful after all," Ruby said.

"What movie did you pick out?" Maude asked Ruby on the way to the living room.

"I didn't. With everything going on, I asked Opal to grab something on the way," Ruby said, turning back to her friends.

"Oh dear God!" Maude said.

"Don't start being pessimistic. I got two really good ones," Opal said in the doorway. She reached in her bag and pulled out the video cassette cases, each sporting a sticker that said, 'Be Kind, Rewind."

"Please tell me you didn't get something with subtitles like you did last time," Maude told her. She reached for the cases and looked at Opal in disgust.

"Of course not, I got something for the kids. Howard the Duck and Star Trek IV," Opal beamed.

Ruby and Maude stared at her.

"You got what?" Maude said sarcastically.

"The kid at the video store said these were great, especially since it's for kids," Opal explained. Sometimes Maude was slow on the uptake.

Maude turned to Ruby, "I'm going to let you decide between these two classics."

Ruby shook her head.

"Let's watch the duck movie," Mavis requested.

That settled things. Wilbur put the video in the VCR and pressed play. The first of the previews for upcoming gems began to play

"What in the world is this?" Maude asked. She picked up the ceramic orange cat that had been given a place of honor on the coffee table.

"Do you love it?" Mavis asked. She batted her dark eyes and smiled up at Maude.

"It's quite something," Maude said.

"I knew Ruby would love it. I helped her pick it out," Opal beamed.

"What does it have coming out of its? Is that a hole?" Maude whispered to Ruby.

"That's where the Kleenex goes," Ruby explained, stifling a laugh.

"The what?" Maude turned to Opal. "You got Ruby a cat with toilet paper coming out of its ass?" she said to Opal in a not so quiet whisper.

Opal huffed. "Really, Maude. Sometimes you can be so uncouth. It's not toilet paper. That would be crude. It's tissue paper. That's more sophisticated."

"Well pardon me," Maude rolled her eyes.

"Shh, the movie's starting!" Opal said.

Halfway through the movie, Mavis had fallen asleep on the floor with one of the couch pillows.

"This is terrible," Maude turned to Ruby. "Mavis has got the right idea."

"Shh, this is the best part!" Opal said.

"You've already seen this?" Maude asked.

"No, but I know when something exciting is about to happen!" Opal replied.

"Did you hear that?" Ruby asked. She jumped up from the couch and turned towards the kitchen. "Turn it down for a second."

"Probably just the storm," Maude said.

"There it is again! I think someone's outside," Ruby whispered. She looked through the giant aquarium that was full of water towards the kitchen. Thomas had come a few days earlier to get the water acclimated to the proper temperature.

"It's too early for Jameson to be back. He's only been gone an hour or so," Maude replied. "Probably just one of those blessed cats trying to get some cover from the storm. I'll go look out the window."

Maude returned a few moments later and shrugged. "Didn't see anything. The weather is getting worse though. May have to sleep on the couch tonight. You know my eyes aren't like they used to be."

"I'll say," Opal agreed. "I've got a tea for that though. I'll make you some tomorrow."

"You both are more than welcome to stay over tonight. In fact, I prefer that. I hear the wind getting louder. I hope it subsides long enough for the boys to all get home later," Ruby said.

A crack of lightning lit up the night sky followed by a crash of thunder.

"Did you see that? It got worse quick. We need to unplug the TV," Ruby said.

"I think some of that tea can't wait," Opal declared. "I'll be right back. Let me get some water boiling and then I'll get started on Maude's hair."

Wilbur stirred and started to pick up the snacks that Mavis had been working her way through before she fell asleep. "Let's get all this cleaned up and then I want you to go get in your night clothes," Ruby told Wilbur gently.

Maude collected the near empty drinking glasses and walked to the kitchen. She put them in the sink and watched Opal unpack a large bag full of bottles of differing shapes and sizes. Maude knew better than to ask what was in store for her this evening. Opal's potions would probably end up turning her hair green, but she knew better than to argue with Opal once she got into one of her kicks.

"Ruby, give me those bowls and I'll wash them real quick," Maude said in the doorway to the living room.

"Maude!" Opal called to her. "Let that cat in. Poor thing is probably half drowned."

Opal organized the bottles by color and waited for Maude to answer her. When Maude didn't emerge from the living room, Opal sighed and walked to the door. She flipped on the porch light and saw Pete standing there dripping wet. As soon as he saw Opal, he began pounding on the door with a gun. He was the picture of a savage with his hair matted to his face and eyes full of fury. He hadn't shaven in days and if Opal had to guess, this rain storm was the first bath he'd had since before he left town. His clothes were tattered and streaked with mud. Opal said nothing, but stared at him. She backed away slowly.

"Opal? Opal, is that you in there making all that racket?" Maude yelled. She had her arms full of plastic bowls and a half-eaten cookie in her mouth. "Oh my God!" Maude dropped the bowls and ran to the living room.

"Ruby! It's Pete. He's got a gun. Get the kids upstairs. Opal and I will head him off!" she shouted before returning to the kitchen.

"Wilbur, take Mavis upstairs to my room. Don't make a sound," Ruby ordered.

Wilbur nodded and shook Mavis awake. He led her upstairs as fast as he could get her short legs to move. Ruby watched them go up the stairs and she heard her bedroom door shut. She raced to the kitchen where Maude was shouting through the door for Pete to leave.

"Pete, you get on out of here! We've already called the police! Teddy and the other deputies are already on their way! They'll be here any minute!" Maude yelled at him.

Pete ignored their shouts. He continued to pound on the door with a gun in his hand before finally smashing his fist through the glass pane. He let out a guttural yell as blood ran down the gash on the side of his hand.

"Jameson is coming down the stairs now," Ruby shouted.

"No he ain't," Pete snarled. "There ain't no one else here." He was fumbling with the deadbolt lock on the door

"Pete, I swear to God, get out of here," Maude shouted. "Ruby, call the police. Go!"

Ruby ran to the phone on the other side of the kitchen and dialed 911. Pete pushed his way into the kitchen and swiped a row of Opal's glass bottles off of the table. They shattered into a hundred different pieces at Opal's feet. Opal grabbed the broom next to her and smacked Pete on the top of his head.

"You can't come into Ruby's house like this. And you darn sure aren't going to make a mess of my bottles!" Opal shrieked. "Not if you know what's good for you!" She whacked Pete across the face with the broom and he fell backwards. "Maude, watch your feet on the glass. He's set me back months with this mess!"

Pete managed to pull himself up and made to charge the door again.

⊶Chapter Twenty-One⊷

"Opal!" Maude shouted. "Hit him harder!"

"I'm trying!" Opal shouted. "Ahh!"

Opal slipped on the shards of glass and scrambled to stand back up. Pete grabbed one of the larger bottles from Opal's collection and broke it on the table. He swung it around like a sword and cut Opal across her cheek.

"Ahh! Maude! Help me!" Opal cried. She dropped the broom as blood spilled onto the floor. Pete continued to wave the broken bottle around wildly.

Pete pushed Opal against the wall and started to choke her. Maude grabbed the broom that had fallen from Opal's hand and hit him on his back. Pete swung Opal around to use as a shield and held the broken bottle to her throat.

"I'll kill her, I swear to God," he yelled. He backed out of the doorway into the night with the broken bottle still held against her throat. Maude could hear him cursing and Opal shouting as she fought to get away from him.

"Opal! Opal! You let her go!" Maude screamed. "Ruby, are they coming?" Before Ruby could answer, Maude rushed out into the night to save her friend.

Ruby dropped the phone and left it dangling on the cord. The voice on the other end of the line was asking a series of questions that went completely unanswered. Ruby rushed upstairs to her bedroom. She burst through the door and saw Wilbur peek his head out from the closet. "Shh!" she said. "You and Mavis stay quiet. Don't come out of this closet until I come get you myself." Wilbur covered Mavis with a blanket he had grabbed from Ruby's bed and nodded. Ruby looked like a wild woman. She shut the closet door and grabbed Jameson's shotgun that had been propped behind their bedroom door and flew back down the stairs.

Opal, for her part, wasn't going along quietly. She kicked Pete in the knee several times while continuing to flail about. She head butted him and caused him to stumble. When he stumbled, she picked up a rock in her reach and threw it at him. The rock caught the side of his face and he finally let go of her arm. She stood up and started to run back towards the porch when Pete grabbed her again and slammed her into the magnolia tree. She slid down to the ground and landed on her side. Pete stomped on her arm and she instantly felt sick from the pain. She curled into the fetal position and shivered.

Maude looked around for anything that would help her save Opal. She saw a garden shovel propped up against the porch railing and charged him.

"Opal! Get out of there, Opal! I've got him!" Maude yelled. She swung the shovel violently at Pete.

"Get off me!" Pete yelled. His attention was now on Maude and not the crumpled woman lying on the ground at his feet. He pulled the pistol out of his back pocket and aimed it at Maude.

Maude could hear Opal whimpering somewhere in the mud and called out for her. "Opal?"

"I'm ok," Opal cried. "He's got a gun!"

Maude swung the shovel wildly in the air again. She hit the magnolia tree with a thud. "Back off lady!" Pete hissed. "I'll kill you both, I swear!" He swung the gun like a bat towards Maude.

"I'm coming!" Ruby shouted. She kicked open what was left of the door and ran onto the porch.

"Ruby! Is that you?" Maude yelled. The porch light didn't illuminate the yard by the tree, so she was running into the situation blind.

Opal grabbed Pete by his ankle and tried to pull him down. Pete fired his gun and yelled at the top of his lungs, "Enough!"

The shovel landed with a thud against something solid. Pete fell hard onto Opal who was trying to get out of the mud with her shattered arm. Maude kept swinging wildly.

Another gunshot went off. Neither Maude nor Opal knew who fired the shot from Pete's gun, but they both feared the other had been hit. So did Ruby, who fired Jameson's shotgun into the night from the porch steps. Once again, the magnolia tree bore the brunt of the abuse. Her shots took out several of the top limbs that fell on top of Maude's head.

"Ruby!" Maude screamed.

"Maude?" Ruby yelled. She ran down the porch steps and bumped into Maude who was still clutching the shovel. "Where's Opal!" they both yelled. The rain was coming down like ice against their wet skin. To make matters worse, they couldn't see well between the dark and the cold rain.

"Help," Opal gurgled.

Opal was trapped beneath Pete's limp body. Maude threw down the shovel and rolled Pete off of her. "Ruby, I think he's dead."

"Oh my God! Are you sure?" Ruby said.

"Yeah, he ain't moving. And I think he's bleeding real bad," Maude said. The fear of the past few minutes was beginning to wear off and the reality of what had happened started to take hold.

Ruby dropped the shotgun and dropped to her knees next to Opal. "Opal, are you hurt?"

"Come here, get on up," Maude said to Opal.

"I can't," Opal whispered. "My arm."

"You're covered in blood!" Ruby yelped. She used the hem of her dress to wipe blood from Opal's face. "We've got to get you inside out of this cold. Come on Opal, let me help you."

Ruby gingerly helped Opal up and looked at her in the blurry lights from the porch. "Opal!" she cried. "Your face."

"He got me good," Opal replied.

"Are you sure you can walk?" Ruby asked.

"I think so," Opal grimaced.

Ruby helped Opal limp up the steps and turned back to Maude who was still examining Pete's body. "Maude, come back inside. You can't help him now."

Opal moved slowly and left a trail of blood as she walked across the porch and through the house. Her legs and arms were visibly cut up and she had grass and gravel stuck to her wounds. Opal's left eye had already closed and her arm was visibly broken. There was a deep jagged gash across her cheek that blood was seeping out of. She was lucky the bottle had somehow missed her eye. Her dress had also been ripped to shreds. Ruby helped her into the small bathroom off of the kitchen and heard Opal lock the door behind her. Ruby heard her whisper "I'm maimed for life."

"Opal, I'm going to check on Maude. I'll be right back. The police should be here any minute," Ruby told her through the bathroom door.

"Okay," Opal sighed. She turned on the water and started to wipe the blood from her face with one of Ruby's guest towels.

Ruby walked back outside to find Maude still standing over Pete's body. Ruby couldn't look down at him and Maude didn't seem to be able to look at anything else.

"Maude," Ruby said as she approached her. "You need to come on inside out of this rain. The police will be here any minute. We need to see about Opal."

"Where is she?" Maude asked solemnly.

"She's inside, in the bathroom. She's hurt pretty bad, but I think she'll be okay. They'll be able to patch her up at the hospital," Ruby told her. "I think her arm's broken and she's going to need stitches for sure, but it could have been so much worse."

"She could have died, Ruby," Maude said. "He could have killed her."

Ruby swallowed hard. "I know. He could have killed all of us."

"I never would have forgiven myself if she had gotten killed," Maude said. "I couldn't have forgiven myself if he had killed either of you."

"It's not your fault," Ruby said. "This isn't anyone's fault."

"He could've killed us," Maude reiterated.

"I know, but Maude, we're all ok," Ruby said.

Maude looked up at her. She opened her mouth to speak, but changed her mind and instead merely nodded.

"You need to come inside and get out of this rain," Ruby told her again. "And I need to see about the kids upstairs."

"Okay," Maude agreed.

Once again, Ruby led a friend up the stairs into the safety of her home, but this time the injuries weren't as visible. Maude was shivering and soaking wet, but as far as Ruby could tell, she was physically unharmed. She looked as though she had seen a ghost and her eyes were wide and unblinking. Maude was never one for theatrics and she wasn't normally the emotional one of the group, so seeing her like this was a bit frightening for Ruby.

Maude stopped at the front door and took a deep breath. Ruby led her to the kitchen table and helped her to her seat. She walked back to the living room to retrieve Maude's purse. Once she was back beside Maude at the kitchen table, she reached into Maude's bag and pulled out the small leather pouch that contained Maude's Virginia Slims and a lighter.

"Here. I know Opal and I've been on you to quit, but you probably shouldn't try to quit today," Ruby said, handing her the cigarettes.

Maude silently took the proffered gift and unclasped the top. Seconds later, she was taking a long drag from her cigarette.

Ruby washed her hands in the kitchen sink and heard a voice behind her. It was coming from the telephone that she had dropped in a hurry. Nadine's voice was still shrieking from the receiver.

"Nadine! Are you still there?" Ruby asked.

"Ruby! What's going on? What in the world? Are you alright?" Nadine asked.

"We need the police," Ruby said through forced calm.

"The police are on their way. They should be there any minute! Are you sure everything is ok?" Nadine asked.

"We need an ambulance. Opal's in bad shape and Nadine, better call the coroner, too," Ruby replied. She hung up the phone and turned back to Maude.

"Oh dear Lord," Nadine was saying as the line disconnected.

"I need to go upstairs and check on the kids," Ruby said. Maude nodded and continued to stare at the wall. Ruby hurried up the stairs and called out to Wilbur at the door. "Wilbur, it's me. I'm not going to turn on the light, so sit tight." She slowly opened her bedroom door and could hear Wilbur moving around in the closet. She grabbed a folded blanket from the foot of her bed and wrapped it around her. The closet's door was still shut and she quickly rushed over to open it. Mavis was still asleep, but Wilbur was sitting on the floor wide eyed.

She knelt down in the dark and pulled Wilbur closer to her. "Is he gone?" he whispered. Before Ruby could answer, Wilbur laid his head in her lap and she rubbed his back. "Everything is ok now. I want you and Mavis to get some sleep in my bed tonight, ok?" She walked Wilbur over to her bed and pulled the comforter back for him to climb in. She went back to the closet and picked up Mavis who was drooling slightly. She tucked her in next to Wilbur and kissed them both on the top of their heads.

"It was my daddy, wasn't it?" Wilbur whispered.

Ruby smoothed his hair and tucked the covers around him. "I'll be back in here shortly. Try and get some sleep. The police are on their way and an ambulance is coming for Opal."

"Did he hurt her?" he asked.

"She's going to be ok," Ruby answered him gently.

"Do I have to go back with him?" Wilbur asked.

"Never," Ruby replied. "He will never hurt you again."

"Ok," he said. She heard him sniffle before turning over to face the wall.

"I love you," she whispered. She closed the door to her room and knew that Wilbur wouldn't be able to sleep. She wasn't sure how much he had heard or what all he knew, but right now was not the time to explain it. He was safe and that was all that mattered.

When Ruby got back down the stairs, she saw headlights barrel into the driveway and heard a car door slam. Ruby walked onto the front porch and saw Jameson run towards her.

"Ruby! Are you ok?" Jameson yelled breathlessly. He pulled her into his chest and tried to catch his breath. "What's going on? You're bleeding!" Before Ruby could answer, Jameson looked past her into the kitchen. "Where's everyone? What's all the blood from? Ruby!"

"Shh, Jameson, I'm fine, the kids are upstairs. I'm not hurt. Maude's inside at the table. We need an ambulance for Opal and Jameson," Ruby stooped to take a breath. "Pete's dead."

Jameson's jaw dropped and his eyes darted around. "Where is he? Where's Opal? Did he hurt her?"

"He's over yonder," Ruby motioned with her hand. "He's under the magnolia tree. Opal's in the bathroom. She's hurt pretty bad Jameson, but she'll survive it. She needs to go to the hospital right now and I think Maude needs to go, too. I think she's in shock. I don't know."

Jameson turned and ran down the steps. He stopped in front of Pete's body by the magnolia tree and looked back at Ruby on the porch. The rain was still coming down in sheets.

Jameson knelt down and fumbled to find a pulse. Pete was lifeless. There was a shovel next to him and he could see his shotgun nearby in a puddle. This was not a good look. He stood back up and wiped blood and mud from his hands onto his wet pants. He found Ruby still on the porch.

"Ruby, what happened?" Jameson asked.

"He won't be hurting any of us ever again," Maude answered deliberately. She was standing in the door frame with a lit cigarette. She was as pale as a ghost.

A flood of headlights poured into the driveway. Teddy and Ben bolted from the patrol car as Cecil and Mitch flew out of Mitch's Cadillac. Close behind them came two more patrol cars with four deputies inside. The deputies came out of the cars with their guns drawn.

Jameson ran down the steps and waved them down. "It's ok," he shouted. "It's over, Ben. It's over now."

They holstered their weapons and surrounded Jameson in front of their cars.

"What's going on?" Ben asked. He shone his flashlight at Ruby and saw she had blood on her. "Ruby? Are you alright?"

"Pete Reynolds is dead," Jameson said. "He's over there by the tree. Opal Tyler's inside and she needs an ambulance. It's bad."

"Where's Maude?" Teddy asked.

"I'm fine," she answered from behind Ruby.

Teddy pushed past the other deputies and rushed to Maude. "Are you hurt? Did he hurt you?"

"I'm fine," she said. "Stop carrying on like that, you'll wake the kids upstairs."

Teddy hugged her tightly and looked at the blood on the porch. He took a deep breath and guided Maude to the rocking chair by the shattered door. He kissed her before joining Ben, the other deputies, Jameson, Mitch, and Cecil as they walked over to Pete. Ben radioed for an ambulance. He leaned down and tried to find a pulse. "He's gone."

"We don't need an ambulance," Mitch said. "He needs a hearse."

"Jameson said Opal Tyler's in there hurt pretty bad," Ben said.

"There's a lot of blood on the porch. That ambulance needs to hurry on up," Teddy yelled into his radio. "She's inside. She's in the bathroom," he said. "There's a trail of blood up the steps and into the house. The door's been busted wide open and there's glass everywhere."

"All this blood? What in the world happened here, Jameson?" Ben asked.

"I don't know," Jameson admitted. "I got here mere minutes before you did. I checked on Pete and he's gone. Ben, that's my shotgun over there."

Ben turned to look over his shoulder and saw the discarded shotgun and shovel. "Malcolm, get the photographs you need. Flip him over and see what you can find. Jameson, I'm going to have to catalog these two unless," his sentence dropped off.

"We have to do this by the book. I know what it looks like," Jameson sighed.

"We'll deal with that in a minute. Where's Opal? Was she shot?" Ben asked.

"I don't know. I haven't seen about Opal yet," Jameson replied.

"I'll be up there in a minute," Ben said.

"Let's go see," Teddy said. He followed Jameson back up to the porch and through the broken door frame. The trail of blood stopped at the bathroom door. There were bloody handprints on the door and on the door handle.

Jameson knocked gently on the door and called, "Opal? Opal, it's me Jameson. Can you come out?"

"I can't come out," Opal replied softly.

"Opal? It's Teddy. Let us in," Teddy said.

"I can't," Opal said again.

"Go get Ruby," Jameson told Teddy.

~Chapter Twenty-Two~

Teddy ran to the doorway and saw Maude and Ruby huddled together. "Are you sure you're alright?" he asked Maude again.

Maude nodded. "Yeah, I'm okay."

"Opal won't come out of the bathroom. We don't know how bad she's hurt. What happened? There's blood everywhere," Teddy asked her. "Can y'all get her to come out?"

Maude shook her head. "Pete tried to break into the house. He smashed through the door and the next thing I know, he had Opal by the throat and I was chasing him out trying to fight him off. It's all a blur. One minute we're all fighting. Then next there was gunshots and," her voice trailed off.

"Oh God. Okay, let me go talk to Ben and see when the ambulance is going to get here. Please try and get Opal to come out of the bathroom. You need to get checked out, too," he told her.

"I'm okay. I didn't get hurt," Maude said.

"Even still, you need to go to the hospital," Teddy said.

"I'm fine," Maude protested.

"Maude, I think Teddy's right. You need to go to the hospital with Opal," Ruby said gently. She patted Maude's arm. Maude looked at Teddy for a moment. Eventually, she relented and agreed to go get checked out.

"Thank you. Now y'all please try to get Opal out," he asked nicely.

"I can't, Ruby. All that blood," Maude said. She stared at the trail of blood on the porch.

"Ok, stay here," Ruby said gently.

Ruby found Jameson still trying to talk to Opal through the bathroom door. "Honey, she won't come out. We need to see how bad it is."

"Ambulance is on the way," Mitch said. He had walked inside the house to find Jameson.

"Ok. She won't come out. I can't find the darned key either," Jameson said. He swiped his hand across the top of the door frame to see if the key was hidden on top, but there was nothing but dust.

"Opal? This is Judge Abernathy. Can you come out and let the paramedics take a look at you please?" Mitch asked gently.

"I just need a few minutes," Opal said.

"That's a lot of blood, Mitch," Jameson whispered.

"I know," Mitch sighed. "Ruby, do you know where another key is?"

Ruby shook her head and looked at Jameson.

"Ruby, I'm going to make sure the kids are ok," Jameson said. "Try and get her out. Break the door if you have to."

Jameson rushed up the stairs and left Ruby and Mitch to try and coax Opal out.

"Maude! I need help. Please help me over here," Ruby called over to her.

Maude sighed heavily and walked over to the bathroom door. There was blood covering the door handle and a pool of blood puddled under the door.

"Opal? I'll have Maude kick this door down if you don't come out this instance," Ruby ordered.

"Open the door, Opal," Maude ordered. Her voice broke when she said Opal's name.

"Ok," Opal said quietly.

They heard her turn off the water and the light switch. The door handle slowly turned and Opal emerged from the bathroom. Her face had been wiped clean, but the gash across her cheek was still oozing blood. Her eye was swollen shut and her arm hung limp at her side.

Seeing Opal in the full light for the first time caught Maude off guard. She knew her friend had been hurt, but she wasn't expecting to see the level of pain in her friend's face. "That son of a bitch," Maude said.

The ambulance suddenly arrived in a whirl of red lights.

Ruby and Maude settled Opal into the rocking chair on the porch. Ruby walked back inside to the staircase to wait for Jameson. Mitch met Ben at the steps and shook his head. "She's hurt pretty bad, Ben. He really did a number on her."

"Y'all see to Opal first. She's over on the porch," Ben told the medics. They nodded and began to talk to Opal who was sitting in the rocking chair on the porch next to Maude.

"They're fine," Jameson said to Ruby. He had come back down the stairs after checking on the kids. "Mavis is asleep. Wilbur's awake, but I told him everyone will be leaving here soon. I told him we'd both be up there soon. Stay here with Opal and Maude while I talk to Ben."

"Teddy's got Maude to agree to be checked out. He's going to ride over with them. I think that's a good idea," Ruby nodded. She walked back over to Opal who was being helped to a stretcher.

"It looks pretty cut and dry, Jameson," Ben said. "Looks like Pete broke in and a scuffle ensued. Looks like Opal shot Pete in self defense with his pistol. Nadine said she heard the shots on the line. They're loading Opal up now to take over to Junction to the main hospital."

"Hold on. Her arm's in pieces," Mitch said. "There's no way Opal shot him. Did you see her? Not in the shape she's in. Ben, she couldn't have. She can hardly move."

Ben looked around at the deputies, lawyers, and the judge who were some of his closest friends.

"I don't know. This, this kind of thing doesn't happen here," he sighed. "This is grisly." To his knowledge, there had never been a crime scene with this much blood and debris in Rhinestone. At least not in his working memory. "Maude needs to sit down with Malcolm and write out a statement. Jameson, we're going to need to get Ruby's statement, too," Ben sighed. "Only people who know what happened are those three and Pete over there."

"Ben, you know as well as I do that the damned fool probably shot himself," Mitch interjected. "Good riddance! We're lucky he didn't shoot anyone else. He near about killed Opal as it is. She's going to need multiple surgeries on her arm. Did you see her face? He near about cut her eye out."

"She keeps saying she's been maimed for life," Malcolm interjected. "I got some quick pictures of her injuries, but she said she'd die if they ever got out to the public. Said something about her face being her money maker or something."

"Look, they've been through enough tonight. Maude's going in the ambulance, too. She ain't right. This has all been too much tonight. I think the shock has set in and she needs some rest," Teddy said. "I'm gonna ride over with them if you don't mind."

"That's fine," Ben said. "We've got procedures we have to follow still. We've got to work through it all or else the DA will be all over us."

"Let me worry about Joel. He and Pete's public defender, Michael, won't be surprised about any of this," Mitch said. "Trust me. They know how Pete is."

"Speaking of Pete, he's still lying under the tree!" Teddy said. "Bag him and send him on his way. These ladies need to go to the hospital. Ruby, too, Jameson."

"I've got all the shots I need. We didn't see any ballistics or any entry or exit wounds, but in this rain I can't see much," Malcolm admitted. "He's got some kind of wound on his head and scratches and cuts all over, but I can't definitively say what killed him."

Jameson looked over his shoulder at Ruby who was holding Opal's hand on the stretcher. She was still wearing the same outfit that was soaking wet with rain, mud, and various blood droplets. "Ruby says she's fine. There's no way she's going to leave those babies upstairs, not tonight. She just needs a good shower and a good night's sleep."

"Look, he had the gun right next to him," Mitch interrupted. "I'm willing to bet he's way over the limit, too. Pete broke in, Opal tried to fight him off, and he attacked her. For what Pete does to his own kids, for what he did to Opal, nobody's going to bat an eye about Pete Reynolds. Somehow he ended up shooting himself in the ruckus, either that or he fell and hit his head. Whatever it was, he's guilty of a laundry list of crimes that led up to this. Period. The end!"

Ben looked at Jameson who didn't say a word. He sighed and shook the water from his gray hair. "Coroner should be here any minute," Ben said. "In this weather, there's no way any forensics can be processed out here. We'll still need statements, but I reckon they can wait 'til the morning. Jameson, the boy's still welcome to stay here?"

"Always," Jameson replied.

"Then it's about time to put all this behind us I guess," Ben said. "At least for tonight. I'll need y'all all down at the station first thing tomorrow morning. The boy, too."

"What do we tell Wilbur?" Jameson asked.

"I don't know," Ben admitted. "Tell him he's safe now. The system won't fail him again. Not anymore."

The dim lights of the county coroner's van pulled into the driveway. Mortimer Raven exited the vehicle and walked past everyone to the ambulance. He saw Opal on the stretcher with Maude and Ruby next to her. "Opal, my dear. Are you alright?" he asked as he leaned down close to her face.

"Oh, Mortie don't look at me. My face looks awful!" she protested.

"Nonsense. You could never look awful," he told her.

"I guess you're here because they told you Pete's dead?" she asked him.

"Yes. Did he do this to you?" Mortie asked her.

Opal nodded slowly.

"He will do no more damage tonight. Or ever," he said.

Maude looked up and met his eye. He nodded solemnly and said, "I am overjoyed to see you are not deceased, Ms. Cooper." He stood up straight and nodded gravely while the paramedics loaded Opal into the ambulance, leaving Maude and Ruby to wonder at his last statement.

"What did that mean?" Maude asked. "I ain't dead."

Ruby shrugged and handed Maude her purse while the medic helped her inside the ambulance. Teddy climbed in after her. He put his arm around Maude and smiled back at Ruby.

"Get some sleep Ruby. You look like hell," Maude smiled meekly. Ruby returned her smile and watched as the ambulance turned on its lights and rushed out of the driveway. She walked back to the porch and sat down in the swing. She wanted nothing more than to run upstairs and hold Wilbur and Mavis, but she'd have to shower before she could explain anything. She didn't want to frighten them or let Wilbur see any part of his dead father. Pete may have been a vicious man and a neglectful, abusive father, but he was still the only kin Wilbur had left in the world. She had no idea what she was going to say to him. For now, she deemed it best to sit on the porch and wait for them to take Pete's body away and see what steps they needed to take next.

Mortimer walked over to Pete's body lying in the mud where Ben, Jameson, Cecil, and Mitch were standing.

"Looks like he's all yours, Mortimer," Ben said. He looked up at Mortimer. The corner of the undertaker's right eye was twitching in a way Ben had never seen before. Ben wouldn't have believed it possible, but the twitch made him twice as terrifying as before. A moment later, the twitch was gone and Mortimer was nodding to Ben in his familiar, yet solemn way.

"And will there be an investigation?" Mortimer asked. They were joined by Malcolm who was going to help him move the body.

"Malcolm's taken all the crime scene photographs and roped off the area. Seems to be a pretty open and shut case of self defense," Ben told him. "As the coroner and the funeral home director, it looks like you're going to be pretty busy on this one. We'll need a toxicology screen run and the autopsy results as soon as you know them. I'm not sure about his final wishes or whatever it is he'd want."

Mortimer nodded and continued to stare at Pete's body.

"Opal's going to be ok," Jameson told him directly.

"Good. Then I shall prepare his body. I know it was his desire to be cremated," Mortimer said.

"Cremated?" Ben asked. "How do you know?"

"They're all alike in death," Mortimer pulled on a pair of rubber gloves with a snap. "The saints and sinners."

Ben looked over at Malcolm who looked as spooked as he felt. They quickly helped Mortimer lift the body onto the stretcher. Mortimer zipped the black body bag and loaded the body into the hearse. He bid them good night and was gone just as quickly as he had come.

"That guy gets creepier and creepier," Ben said. "Excellent and efficient at his job, but there's something about him."

"He's not so bad," Jameson said. "Opal's crazy about him. For what it's worth, he's a very nice guy."

"They're a funny pair, aren't they," Ben remarked. "Anyway, get Ruby on inside and cleaned up. We'll send the techs over tomorrow morning to clean up around here. Call me when y'all plan on coming in. If you hear anything about Opal before I do, let me know."

Jameson shook Ben's hand and clapped Malcolm on the back. "I'll be in early tomorrow morning. We'll get this all sorted out." He thanked Cecil and Mitch for hurrying over as well. When Nadine's voice came over the radio alerting the need for police at 1162 Magnolia Way, Jameson had flown out of his chair and left his full hand face up on the table. He didn't wait for anything or anyone. Teddy and Ben jumped into Teddy's patrol car leaving Cecil to tag along with Mitch in Mitch's Cadillac. They left mere minutes after Jameson, but Jameson had left them in the dust.

"They're packing up now," Jameson said. He slid into the porch swing next to Ruby and held her hand. "We need to get you cleaned up before we talk to Wilbur. He can't come downstairs and see the bathroom either. Ben says they'll send some techs out tomorrow morning to clean it, but we're going to need to seal it so no one goes in there. The rain's washed most of the blood over by the tree, but the porch'll need to be scrubbed. I'm hoping they can get it done while we're down at the station tomorrow. I'm sure the news has spread by now, so

I need to call Mother before she tries to drive herself out here."

"The phone's been ringing off the hook," Ruby said. She watched as the police cars backed out of the driveway.

"I'll handle it," Jameson said. "What a night this has been."

Ruby laid her head on his shoulder and took a deep breath.

"One day we'll talk about what happened here, but right now let's get you showered. I'll sweep up the glass and board up the door after I talk to Wilbur. If I know him, he'll be waiting for us upstairs. I don't think it's a good idea for him to see you like this, so I'll get your clothes and shampoo and whatever else you need. Better get cleaned up in Mavis' bathroom and I'll talk to him," Jameson said.

"What are you going to say?" Ruby asked.

"I honestly don't know," Jameson said. He wiped his glasses on his handkerchief and then helped Ruby up the stairs.

Chapter Twenty-Three

"Can you open the blinds a little more?" Opal asked sweetly.

Maude jumped up and let in a flood of light in the hospital room.

"Perfect," Opal yawned.

There was a soft knock on the door and Ruby peeked her head inside. "Hello," she called softly.

"Ruby!" Opal sang. "Come in, come in!"

Ruby edged into the doorway and closed the heavy door behind her. "Oh Opal, how are you?"

"Fine as wine," Opal smiled.

Ruby caught her breath at the sight of Opal propped up in the hospital bed. Maude stood up from the other side of the bed and walked around the foot of the bed to hug Ruby. "And Maude, how are you?"

"I'm fine. Now that I know this monkey will be alright," Maude smiled.

Opal patted her casted arm and grimaced. "Takes more than a few broken bones to put me down."

"It was more than just a few broken bones," Maude interrupted.

"Doctor Wilson said I should only need one other surgery on it," she said proudly.

"He put enough rods and pins to set off every metal detector from here to Nepal," Maude said.

"I'm an expensive piece of art, what can I say?" Opal laughed.

"And your poor face," Ruby said.

"Oh, she's already had the plastic surgeon in here earlier. He's assured her that her stage career is far from over. I told her she would have the perfect face for radio, but she wouldn't go for that," Maude shrugged.

"I can't even bear to look in the mirror. But Maude says it's not paper bag worthy yet," Opal replied.

"This should cheer you up," Ruby said. She opened the bag at her feet and pulled out some glass bottles that had managed to survive Pete's attack.

"Oh Ruby!" Opal cried. "I didn't think any had made it out alive."

Maude quickly caught Ruby's eye, but neither made a comment. After Opal inventoried her bottles, she directed Maude to line them up on the windowsill next to ten different vases of various flowers and plants.

"I see that Eddie's been here," Ruby smiled.

"He sent half his damn shop," Maude grunted. "Speaking of plants, how is the magnolia?"

"It's pretty battered," Ruby sighed. "But I think it's going to come back just fine in the spring. We won't have to rename the Manor after all." She winked at Maude and Opal.

A stone faced nurse entered the room with a clipboard. "Ms. Tyler?"

"No, I'm Scarlett O'Hara," Opal replied stoically.

The nurse was not amused. "Are you Ms. Tyler?" she repeated.

"Nope, George Washington," Opal answered.

"Yes, this is Opal Tyler, born January 13th, 1939. Born on Friday the 13th," Maude said. "Lucky us."

"Thank you. It's time to change your bandage," she leaned over Opal and pulled the white bandage from the gash on her cheek and Ruby saw rows of stitches. The nurse made quick work of her duties and exited the room in a hurry.

"Why do you keep doing that?" Maude chastised.

"Because she's annoying. She never smiles. One of these times I'll get a smile out of her," Opal said.

"I wouldn't count on it," Maude said under her breath.

Ruby smiled at her two friends. It was refreshing to hear their usual back and forth grumbling.

"Well, let's go ahead and address the elephant in the room," Maude said.

"Maude, don't talk about yourself like that," Opal grinned.

Maude shook her head, but she let Opal's comment slide. "I meant, we need to talk about what happened the other night at the Manor," Maude said. "I know you said you didn't want to say much over the phone after your day yesterday, but Teddy did say they weren't going to press any charges."

"That's what Jameson said, too," Ruby agreed.

"Good," Maude said. "What happened after we left?"

The door to Opal's room flew open. "Looks like this'll have to wait," Ruby whispered.

Ricky waltzed into the room singing his own version of some Madonna song loudly. He brought with him two large canvas bags. He set them down on the bed and pulled out a flowing pink bathrobe, matching slippers, and a feathered hat. He also smuggled in some of Opal's favorite herbal soups. "You better eat these real quick. That mean old nurse out there was giving me the stink eye. All that frowning isn't good for the skin." He set the containers down on the table beside Opal's bed.

"Ooh, these are the best!" Opal squealed.

"Let me put your hat over here by the window. Oh goodness, look at all these flowers!" Ricky snorted.

"Eddie knows I love fresh flowers," Opal smiled.

"Who doesn't? He is a little much though," Ricky replied. He rolled his eyes quickly before turning his attention back to Opal.

Opal opened one of the soup containers and started to breathe in the steam.

"Dear God! That mess stinks to high heaven!" Maude said, covering her nose with her napkin.

"Maude, you really are so uncultured. One of these days you're going to realize how good these soups are," Opal told her. She unwrapped the spoon that Ricky had placed in the bag with her lunch.

"I'll stick to a hamburger," Maude grumbled. "Speaking of which, I'm starving. Want to walk with me down to the cafeteria, Ruby?"

"Of course," she smiled. She picked up her purse and they told Opal they'd be back soon so she could have some time with Ricky.

"It's been hard to get a word in edgewise," Maude told Ruby. "She's had a slew of visitors almost nonstop."

Ruby felt a pang of guilt in her stomach. "I wish I could have been here sooner. It's been one thing after another. We were at the police station and the courthouse all day yesterday. Wilbur and Mavis went back to school today. Jameson has painters at the Manor right now painting the bathroom and the kitchen. He was able to get a cleaning crew to come in and clean the rooms and the porch yesterday, but there are too many stains. The painters assured us that they can cover them up. They're going to repaint the porch tomorrow. We had to throw out the rocking chair and the swing, but Jameson ordered new ones from the hardware store this morning. We've got a new door coming this afternoon, too."

They went through the empty line and got their food and cups of water.

"I still can't believe it," Maude said. She sat down at the nearest table and sighed.

"I know what you mean. It feels like it happened to someone else, but then I see the blood stains on the porch and I remember," Ruby replied.

Maude nodded and sipped her water. "How's Wilbur?"

"Doing as well as can be expected. He hasn't said much, but he did ask to go back to school today, so we let him. I think he just wants some sort of normalcy again, not that he ever really had it to begin with," Ruby sighed.

After a few minutes of silence, Maude nodded and picked at the rest of her sandwich. "Reckon we ought to go save Opal from Ricky? He's probably redecorated half the room by now."

Ruby nodded and put the uneaten apple in her purse. They walked back to Opal's room silently and knocked once they found her door. There was a new vibrant green wreath hung on the outside of the door and they could hear voices on the other side.

"Hello?" Maude called.

"Come in," Opal said cheerfully.

Maude pushed open the door and was surprised to see Mortimer sitting on the edge of the bed. Ricky was sitting in the chair on the opposite side with his arms crossed. "All we need is Eddie to show up and it'll be a party," Maude whispered to Ruby.

"I was just leaving," Mortimer said in his usual tone of voice. "I came to make certain that Opal was being treated well. She assures me she is and that she will be home in no time. Good day Ms. Cooper, Mrs. Montgomery." He nodded at the two women and turned to Ricky, "Good day Richard."

Maude thought she felt a cold draft when Mortie mentioned Ricky's name.

"That man!" Ricky exclaimed. "If he'd just don a splash of color every now and again, he'd be so much happier."

"Maybe we can get him a pink Member's Only jacket for his birthday," Maude whispered to Ruby.

"Mortie is the jolliest man I know," Opal declared. She ignored the others. "He's just shy."

Ricky exchanged a look with Maude and Ruby who tried to stifle a smile.

"Any who, I must skedaddle, too. I have a fitting appointment this afternoon for some of the pageant girls. The sweetheart dance is coming up at the high school and I am booked every afternoon for the next two weeks!" Ricky exclaimed. He kissed Opal on both cheeks and waved goodbye to Maude and Ruby.

"I don't know how you do it," Maude said. "No, don't even answer that."

Opal patted the spot on the bed where Mortimer had been sitting. "Now spill it, I've been laying here asking questions, but Maude won't budge. She said we had to wait for you, Ruby."

Ruby sat down on the bed and Maude scooted the chair closer so they could talk quietly.

"I'll start," Ruby said. "I want to say I'm sorry."

"Ruby, stop. We ain't doing this," Maude interrupted.

"No, no, hear me out. I owe you both an apology for ever putting you in danger. It looks like Pete parked his truck in the woods and waited for Jameson to leave all weekend. And when he did leave, Pete pounced. I'm the one who told Jameson to go to the card game. He didn't want to. He even said he would move the poker game to the Manor, but I wouldn't listen," Ruby explained.

"You didn't know Pete was casing the place," Opal interjected. "You didn't know he was out there waiting."

Ruby shook her head. "But I knew he'd try something eventually. I was so ready to get back to normal that I put everyone in jeopardy."

"Pete made the decision to act like that. That's not on anybody else," Opal said. "It could have been so much worse."

"Opal," Maude started to say.

"I mean it," Opal interrupted. "Don't y'all feel sorry for me just because I got attacked. I'm fine. Nothing happened that can't be replaced or fixed or stitched. I'm alive. I wake up every single day and thank the Lord for allowing me to wake up. This morning was no different. Now, am I going to let y'all wait on me hand and foot? Yes. But am I going to let y'all wallow in pity or blame? No."

Maude and Ruby nodded. Satisfied, Opal continued. "Now, what happened after we left, Ruby? What happened yesterday?"

Ruby took a deep breath and launched into the story. "Right after y'all left, Mortimer picked up Pete. Jameson said that Mortimer already knew all about Pete's final wishes, but no one really asked how he knew. Then," Ruby was cut off.

"He's so understanding. He just knows certain things about people just by looking at them. That's what makes him so dreamy," Opal interjected.

"Dreamy?" Maude asked.

Ruby ignored Opal's pining and carried on with her story. "He said that Pete wanted to be cremated."

"How in the Sam Hill did he know Pete wanted to be cremated?" Maude huffed. She shivered at the thought of it.

"Hmm. I don't know. We don't normally discuss his jobs when we're on a date, but Mortie is good at his job. No one else could do what he does!" Opal smiled.

"You can say that again," Maude whispered under her breath.

"Well, after that, they all stood around and talked about what they think happened. I stayed on the porch and tried to stay out of it. When they left, I took a shower while Jameson talked to Wilbur. Poor boy was still wide awake. Through all the sirens and the storm and the yelling, I don't know how Mavis stayed asleep, but she did. Jameson left her in our bed and took Wilbur back to his room. When I got out of the shower and changed clothes, they were still talking. Wilbur didn't ask too many questions, but Jameson told him we would do our best to answer any that he did have," Ruby explained.

No one said anything for a few minutes. Maude looked like she wanted to ask a question, but she didn't know how to phrase it.

"I haven't told anyone what really happened," Ruby said. "I don't even know what really happened. It was so dark and the rain, I just. I don't know."

Maude nodded and looked over at Opal.

"Jameson said he doesn't want to know, even if I could tell him. He's just thankful we're all ok. He said doors can be replaced, but friends can't. He's right," Ruby continued.

"What's going to happen to Wilbur now that Pete's gone?" Opal asked.

"He's with us," Ruby replied. "We still have the temporary custody agreement in place. He said he wants to stay with us. I know Pete will always be his father, but I think the hurt runs so deep there. I'm sure there's things we'll never know about. He told Jameson when I ran upstairs and told him that everything was going to be ok, his first thought was relief. He feels guilty, Jameson says. Guilty because he felt relief that his father was gone. I never actually said Pete was passed on, but he knew. That's something he's going to have work through and we'll be here for him every step of the way. I know Wilbur loved his father, you know. That's the only parent he had for so long, but he also knows he's safe and loved and he will never want for anything ever again."

Maude and Opal nodded and listened intently.

"We're hoping to adopt him when the dust settles a little bit. Jameson is going to petition the court for a hearing once he goes back to work next week. It'll be up to Wilbur in the end," Ruby explained.

"Jameson is a good man, Ruby. I know there was a time I wanted to kick his tail when we were younger, but he's the best man for the job," Maude smiled.

"Yes. I don't know what in the world I would do without him taking care of everything. I got lucky with that man," Ruby admitted. "Really, everyone has been so kind during all of this. No one's asked too many questions. I did have to write a statement down at the station, but I didn't have much to say. They still want you both to write one, too."

"Just for the sake of tying up any loose ends," Maude said. "That's how Teddy explained it."

Ruby nodded.

"What did they rule Pete's death as?" Opal asked.

Ruby looked at Maude and then back to Opal. "Hasn't he told you?" Ruby asked.

"No. When I asked him about it, his eye started to twitch. He said 'Do not let your heart be troubled for Peter. He is transformed,' or maybe he said transfixed. I don't know. Ricky was humming and counting the flowers by the window and I couldn't hear everything he said," Opal answered.

"Mortimer ruled it an accident. He said that Pete fired the gun and shot himself. I think Jameson's exact words were 'self-inflicted, unintentional death.' Pete was cremated that night, so everyone took his word for it," Ruby explained.

"But," Opal started to interrupt.

"Opal, there was no way you could have hurt Pete. He near about killed you," Maude reminded her again.

"But his gun went off after he fell on me," Opal pondered. "Maybe when I was trying to push him off, I accidentally bumped it."

"Opal," Maude said confidently. "Let it go. There was no way you could have done a thing. You probably ended up saving all of our lives by doing what you did. You're lucky he didn't shoot you. You didn't hurt a single hair on his head. Let it go."

"Maude is right, Opal. He could have gotten all of us. You saved our lives, I know it," Ruby smiled.

"I'm just trying to connect the dots," Opal said.

"That's impossible to connect everything. It was so dark outside and in that storm, I don't even know. No one does. They said Jameson could have his shotgun and my garden shovel back soon. Jameson said he'd just pick me up a new one at the hardware store next week when he picks up the rocking chair and swing. What if it hadn't been nearby?" Ruby shivered at the thought. "Things could have been so different that night. I can't believe it happened to us."

"I know what you mean," Maude said. "Did Mortimer do any kind of test to see maybe what Pete was on?"

"Jameson said Mortimer did the autopsy and sent whatever off to the labs in Junction. The assumption is that Pete was over the limit for alcohol and God knows what else. His injuries were all over the place. Jameson saw the report in Ben's office. He said it was really inconclusive what wound or trauma killed him. Jameson said he could've had a heart attack or he fell at just the right angle. At the end of the day, only Mortimer knows for sure. Between the three of us, Jameson said no one cared enough to press it. So, Mortimer had him cremated and said he would see to it that Pete was buried somewhere nice," Ruby added.

"Someplace nice, my foot. He ought to be thrown in the landfill," Maude grumbled. She still hadn't gotten over how close she came to losing her best friend.

Ruby patted Maude's hand and smiled softly. "Mortimer will take care of it. It's over. Let's not speak ill of the dead. Pete can't hurt any of us anymore. But Opal, Maude said Mortie came yesterday and then today. I'm surprised he hasn't told you any of this."

"Before you two came back, all Mortie said was that Pete's death would bring new beginnings or life to something else. Something like that. I wasn't really listening," Opal said. She looked over at the vases and flower pots on the windowsill. "He did bring me the prettiest little snake plant and said all I had to do was keep the soil dry in between waterings. He said he already added some potash to the potting soil so I would be good to go."

Maude turned to Ruby with wide eyes. "You don't think," she started to say.

Ruby shook her head and said, "How nice." She swallowed hard. "Here's to um, new beginnings."

"Let's make a pact," Maude said. "None of this leaves this hospital room, agreed?"

"None of what?" Ruby asked.

"I agree with Maude. Any of this," Opal said.

"I think we all know what happened, so there's no need to speak of it again to anyone else. All three of us worked together, just like we always do, and we did what we had to do," Maude said.

Ruby and Opal both nodded in agreement.

Shall we seal it in blood?" Opal laughed.

"I think you've done enough bleeding for all of us," Ruby said. She took Opal and Maude's outstretched hands and they formed a small circle. "The Stone Sisters."

∽Chapter Twenty-Four∽

"I think this could have waited," Maude said. She had her lips pursed and the most uncomfortable look on her face. "Ow!"

"Trust me, it couldn't have waited. I don't think I've seen your hair this bad since the summer of '82," Opal sighed.

"What was so bad about my hair then?" Maude asked grumpily.

"Need I remind you about that time you gave yourself a permanent? Or should I say tried to," Opal said. "Do you remember that, Ruby? She looked like she stuck her finger in a light socket!"

"I remember," Ruby chuckled. "That was certainly an unforgettable look."

"Don't you start in on me, too," Maude huffed. She crossed her arms and slumped slightly in the chair. "And it wasn't that bad."

"Oh hush," Opal said. "Now sit up straight. I only have one arm."

"I told you this could wait. No one expects you to get back to work so quickly. It hasn't even been two weeks yet," Maude said.

"I'm bored! I can't sit in that house one day longer. Plus, I have things to do," Opal smiled. She glanced over at the wooden shelf by the register. Jameson had built her a strong shelf to house her latest items as a welcome home present.

"The new window looks beautiful," Ruby said. "It's so welcoming and elegant."

"Doesn't it!" Opal marveled. "Nadine worked all day yesterday to get the wording and pictures just right. That was so kind of her. She's coming here this afternoon to get her hair done. That's another reason I had to get back. All my customers have been patiently waiting for me to return."

"My day keeps getting better and better. Ow. Don't pull so hard" Maude grumbled.

"You're not still mad at her for telling everybody you were dead, are you?" Ruby asked.

"She damn near had my whole funeral planned!" Maude said.

"It wasn't like that, Maude. She was really concerned when she thought you were no longer with us," Ruby tried once again to add diplomacy into the conversation.

"Concerned enough to throw a party," Maude grumbled. She had fielded more gasps and questions in the last two weeks than she ever had before in her life. Since she brought Opal home from the hospital, every person in town who came to visit Opal had acted as though they were seeing a ghost when Maude walked through the door. The poor cashier at the Piggly Wiggly near about fainted when Maude went through the checkout line. Apparently, when Nadine heard that a hearse was needed at Magnolia Manor, she assumed the worst for poor Maude. Now, Maude couldn't walk down the street without encountering someone who thought she was risen from the dead.

"She didn't throw a party," Opal laughed. "She was very concerned. Who else could she continue to waste years worth of pranks on?"

What Maude failed to mention, and hated to admit, was that Nadine had been distraught beyond words thinking that her favorite nemesis had passed. Nadine had been the one who made sure their mail was checked daily and that someone was there to feed their pets. Despite the ongoing feud between them, Nadine clearly crossed the line into friendship which took a great deal of the fun out of it for Maude.

"Quit moving, Maude. One wrong move and you'll lose half your hair. Hey, Ruby, hand me that pink bottle," Opal directed. "The tall pink one there. And that round jar."

"What do you mean I'll lose half my hair?" Maude yelled. Opal ignored her.

Ruby found the correct bottle and handed it to Opal. "Thanks Ruby," Opal said. "Oh, could you open that one for me?"

Ruby opened the bottle and handed it back to Opal. "Perfect, this right here is going to take care of all of those wild hairs you got going on. Just smooth it down like this every morning and you'll look as good as new. Well, as good as possible anyway. You're such a rough sleeper, no wonder your hair looks so untamed every morning."

Maude rolled her eyes, but sat up straight and still. Ruby walked back over to the wooden shelf and looked at the various bottles and jars. "You've been busy, Opal. So many nice new products!" Ruby exclaimed. "Lotion, perfume, and toothpaste Wow! Shampoo, conditioner, styling paste, and, is that burn cream?"

"It sure is! Had to do something to occupy my mind. This one wouldn't let me do anything," Opal said, gesturing to Maude. She pulled the comb through Maude's much shorter hair and tugged once she got to a clump of paste.

"Ow! That's supposed to remain attached!" Maude grumbled.

"Alright Maude, voila!" She spun Maude's chair round so she could face the mirror. "What do you think?"

"Maude, that looks so nice!" Ruby exclaimed.

Maude ran her fingers through her new hair cut and sat up straighter. "Wow, Opal this is great."

"Always the tone of surprise!" Opal laughed. "Now scoot on up so I can get started with Ruby."

Maude and Ruby exchanged seats. Opal hummed to herself while she brushed Ruby's hair and shook the contents of the pink bottle onto the top of Ruby's head.

"What's that for?" Maude asked.

"This little beauty is going to make her hair even shinier," Opal explained. "It's my latest creation. I've got more orders than I can fill right now. This line has just taken off!"

"With a name like Color Me Crazy, it was bound to," Ruby grinned.

"There's so much more I want to explore with it. The options are limitless," Opal said.

"I can see that," Ruby said.

"You know, I had a great idea last night. It woke me up in the middle of the night! Wine!" Opal said.

"Wine?" Ruby and Maude asked.

"Yep, wine. Can you imagine how fun it would be to have a line of different wines?" Opal exclaimed.

"That's actually not a bad idea," Maude said.

"Glad you said that. Because I've already volunteered us for the next wine and cheese event over at the theatre," Opal smiled.

"Oh Lord," Maude sighed. "When is that?"

"It's not 'til March, so we have plenty of time, partner!" Opal said. "I've already started to look through Aunt Willie's recipes."

"Oh, Opal, speaking of recipes, I forgot to tell you, I'm going to need some of your favorite recipes," Ruby mentioned casually.

"My recipes? Sure, but what for? You finally going to take up herbal health?" Opal was thrilled.

"God, I hope not. Ruby's the best cook in town," Maude said.

"Not exactly. The Ladies Auxiliary is putting together a cookbook for the church fundraiser. The proceeds are going to the new fellowship hall,"

Ruby explained. "Maude, I'll need your best recipes, too."

"Oh, that's a great idea," Opal squealed. "Well, maybe not all of Maude's recipes." Opal turned to Maude and started to laugh.

"Am I missing something here?" Ruby asked.

"Oh, just saying you should probably omit that one Maude keeps at the very back of her cookbook," Opal howled.

"My popcorn stuffing recipe? What's wrong with that one?" Maude asked.

"You mean the one that blew the butt off the bird?" Ruby laughed. "I think Opal's right. We can leave that one out."

"Laugh if you will, but I've never served an undercooked bird. Once it sounds like the oven is about to explode, the bird is ready," Maude said with spirit. "Just because the fire department showed up a little bit later, didn't mean that dinner wasn't tasty."

"And we've been eating Thanksgiving dinner with Ruby ever since!" Opal laughed.

"Well, I doubt she wants your marshmallow disaster from last Thanksgiving either," Maude smiled.

"You sure seemed to like it," Opal reminded her.

"Before it tried to kill me," Maude said. "That wasn't pretty."

"Let's stick to ones that people would enjoy," Ruby said. "We want to sell as many as we can."

"Trust me, we'll help you make it the best cookbook this town has ever seen," Opal grinned.

"Ruby, are we dying your hair today or letting it be?"

"I think I'm going to stop fighting nature and let it be," Ruby said.

"Sounds good to me," Opal smiled. "You can totally pull it off."

"You just told me that I had to keep dying mine!" Maude said.

"Like I said, some people can pull it off," Opal repeated. "Let me trim these ends and you'll be good to go, Ruby. Natural gray is perfect for your age."

"Speaking of age, I still hate that we missed celebrating your birthday, Opal," Ruby said. "Let's make up for that soon. What would you like to do?"

"How about a late lunch at the new diner down the street? It opened three days ago," Opal said.

"Perfect," Ruby said. "I guess they did open after all."

"Forty-eight is already shaping up to be quite the year," Opal said. "I can't believe we'll be fifty in no time. Well, y'all will be old before me!"

"Don't remind me," Maude laughed.

"We need to make the most of it. Age is a privilege," Opal said.

"Well, we've already scoured the globe, been all over the Gulf beaches, and gotten kicked out of Graceland," Maude said. "Where could we possibly go that's grand enough for fifty?"

"New York City," Opal announced.

"We've already been to New York," Maude said. "Ruby bought half the durn gift shop."

"That doesn't count," Ruby said. "We only saw the airport. I agree with Opal. Let's go to New York City!"

"Do you know how much trouble we could get in up in New York City? It's like a whole other country up there," Maude argued.

"Maude, if we can handle crossing the globe, I think we can handle New York," Ruby smiled.

"Ok, I'll go, but only if Opal doesn't plan the itinerary," Maude laughed.

"Oh, I've already got a list of ideas," Opal smiled.

"Thank God we have almost two years before this trip," Maude whispered to Ruby.

"Alright Ruby, this looks great, if I do say so myself," Opal said. "I've got one more appointment before lunch and then we can go to lunch.

"Nadine?" Maude asked.

"Yes. You behave. She'll be here any minute," Opal said.

Maude waved Opal off and disappeared to the back room where she knew Opal kept a bag of M&Ms. The chimes above the door jingled and Opal turned her attention to the front door. "Hello Nadine! Right on time," Opal said.

"Oh Opal, how are you?" Nadine drawled. She sank down in the salon chair and continued, "It's so good to see you up and about."

"Glad to be back," Opal said. "Not much can keep me down."

"I can't imagine," Nadine replied. "It all sounds so awful."

"Thank you for your quick help," Ruby said. "You got the police and ambulance there so fast. We appreciate all that you do."

"Just doing my job," Nadine smiled. "I'm glad it turned out the way it did."

Maude walked out from behind the curtain that separated the lobby from the back room. "Well, hello Nadine."

"Hello Maude," Nadine smiled sheepishly.

"Alrighty, what are we doing today Nadine?" Opal asked.

"I think just a cut and color, like usual," Nadine said.

"I've got the perfect shade in that purple bottle. Maude, hand me that skinny one and open it on up," Opal directed.

Maude found the bottle and opened it for Opal. "I'm going to walk next door and see about getting some hot chocolate. Y'all want any?" Ruby, Opal, and Nadine nodded. "Be right back," Maude said.

"How are you doing, Ruby?" asked Nadine. "Sure was a shame that Pete had to go and shoot himself out there in your yard. I heard all those shots over the phone and I just knew something bad had happened. I told Sheriff Owens that's exactly what happened. Shooting himself and near about killing Opal, too." Nadine shivered at the memory.

Ruby nodded and smiled softly. "Thanks Nadine, you sure saved the day," she repeated.

Nadine smiled and straightened her shoulders. "How's Wilbur doing? I bet this has all been such a shock for him. He's so young and timid."

"He's doing well, really. We're thankful he's healthy and safe," Ruby said.

Ruby could tell that Nadine wanted to ask more questions, but she seemed to understand that few details were going to be given. She decided to move on and asked Opal about her upcoming product line.

"I was just telling them that I'm thinking about adding a new wine line. Just a few flavors to start out with. Depending on how the muscadines do this summer, I might be able to expand to a full winery," Opal said. "I don't want to stick to only grapes. I'm thinking muscadines, peaches, pears, maybe even blueberries. A nice blueberry pear wine sounds heavenly, doesn't it?"

"Well that does sound interesting," Nadine said.

Ruby wasn't sure she was ready to see Opal dancing around in a giant vat stomping grapes and various other fruits, but it would definitely be an adventure. She also knew that somehow she and Maude would probably get roped into helping.

Maude returned a few minutes later carrying a tray of hot chocolate that she passed out to everyone. "I didn't know if you wanted marshmallows on top or not, but I had them add them," she said to Nadine.

"Thanks," Nadine said.

Maude nodded and went to sit down by Ruby.

"Ok, we'll let this dry a bit and then I'll wash it out. These natural ingredients make the color take so much quicker than those chemically ones," Opal explained.

"Why's her hair purple?" Maude asked.

"You wouldn't understand the science behind it," Opal sighed. "You have to factor in the ph and natural undertones of each individual's hair structure. It's not all fun and games." She moved Nadine to the nearest dryer and set a timer for ten minutes.

"Go on and drink that before it gets too cold. Cold hot chocolate is the worst," Maude instructed.

Opal sat in the empty salon chair and sipped on warm chocolatey drink. "You know Maude, we can always try that color on you one day."

"Purple? I don't want purple hair!" Maude said.

"It won't be purple," Opal sighed. "I just told you that."

"Then what color will it be?" Maude asked.

"Blonde, of course," Opal rolled her eyes.

"I think I'll pass. I've never had any desire to be a blonde," Maude laughed.

"They say blondes have more fun," Opal shrugged.

When the timer went off, Opal washed the concoction out of Nadine's hair. Since her hair was so short, it took no time to dry it with a hairdryer. Opal used some of the same paste from the jar she had used on Maude and spun the chair around to let Nadine see the finished product.

"Opal, this looks wonderful. Even without your arm, you're still the best hair stylist in Rhinestone!" Nadine gushed.

"Thanks!" Opal beamed. She rang Nadine out at the register and put the purchased items in a fancy bag. "That paste every morning and that cream under your eyes will make a world of difference."

Nadine smiled big and hugged Opal before turning to Ruby. "I'm so glad you are ok," she said. She hugged Ruby and picked up her purse and shopping bag from the counter. She patted Maude gently on the arm before she walked out the front door.

"Let me sweep this all up and we can walk down to the diner," Opal said.

"I'll sweep, you one armed monkey," Maude said. She found the broom and tidied up Opal's workstation. "I hope they have a hamburger."

"I'm sure they have a hamburger," Ruby said. She wiped down the counter and put Opal's combs and brushes to soak in the disinfectant.

"I bet it's fancy," Opal said. "It sounds so majestic: The Starlight Cafe."

Acknowledgments

We would never have been able to finish this book so quickly without the love and support of our families and friends. To our loved ones, once again we hope we haven't embarrassed you too much with this next installment of the Magnolia Manor series. If we have, let us know so we can write another book!

To all of our family members who have inexplicably been mentioned in these pages, whether by name or not, we thank you for supplying us with laughter and stories for yet another book.

Finally we'd like to thank the ladies at Southern Willow Publishing. Jaimie, Jennifer, and Victoria continue to believe in us and support our adventurous tales. It is due to their professionalism and experiences that we have been able to publish three books already this year. We look forward to many more adventures ahead.

About the Authors

Wanda Jennings and Louise Turner have known each other since they were young(er). They began their writing careers later in life after retiring from their professional careers in civil service and social work.

When not writing the Magnolia Manor series, Louise and Wanda enjoy traveling, spending time with their families, and learning how to quilt.

Dear Reader,

We hope you enjoyed Color Me Crazy. We are truly blessed that you took the time (again) to spend a few hours with some of our favorite members of the Rhinestone gang. Rhinestone has a collection of true characters, that's for sure! It's hard to not fall in love with them over and over again.

We are currently working on the next book in the Magnolia Manor series that will be out in the spring of 2021. This next book takes place during the summer of 1980. The Stone Sisters decide to take a trip to get Ruby's mind off of her estranged daughter. It will finally be revealed why Opal has been banned from Graceland. If you enjoyed Dirty Laundry, Saints & Sinners, and Color Me Crazy, please make sure to join us on our next adventure in Double Trouble!

Thank you again for reading Color Me Crazy. We would really appreciate it if you could take a few minutes and leave us a positive review on Amazon.com and Goodreads.com. Your feedback is very important to us and it helps spread the word about our series. Join us on Facebook (@LouiseandWanda) to keep up with all of our adventures. We love to interact with our fans!

Thank you again for humoring two old ladies. We always wanted to share the Rhinestone gang with the world and we are so thankful that we found a way to do it. We look forward to a long line of books in this series

Love,
Louise & Wanda

Books in the Magnolia Manor Series

Dirty Laundry

Saints & Sinners

Color Me Crazy

Double Trouble (Due Spring 2021!)

The adventures will continue next spring. Join Opal, Maude, Ruby, and the whole Rhinestone gang in

Double

Trouble

Available Spring 2021!